The Lies We Bury

THE LIES WE BURY

Copyright © 2025 by Tracy Tripp

All rights reserved. No part of this book may be reproduced or transmitted in any form or by any means, electronic or mechanical, including photocopying, recording or by any information storage and retrieval system, without permission in writing from the author or publisher. This book was printed in the United States of America.

Published by Tracy Tripp Books

This is a work of fiction. Any characters, names and incidents appearing in this work are entirely fictitious. Any resemblance to real persons, living or dead, is purely coincidental.

Print ISBN: 978-1-7349409-8-5

The Lies We Bury

Tracy Tripp

"It is better to light a candle than to curse the darkness."
- Eleanor Roosevelt

PROLOGUE

Dylan Phillips

Derby, VT
July 2024

THE SIDE OF THE house bowed out like the hunched back of an older woman who had been through hell and stood, feebly, in defiance. Dylan gazed up toward the darkened window on the second floor, which was once her childhood bedroom. Inside, an old white curtain hung from a broken rod. How often had she sat on the floor of that room gazing out into a world that had terrified her?

Now, her two children, aged nine and seven, still far too young to understand her story, traipsed around the old, ghostly house, studying each decaying board as if they would get to know a side of their mother by doing so. But they couldn't. Not the secret parts of her she had refused to share with them or anyone, even those closest to her.

She rested her hand on the handrail of the cracked steps leading up to the front porch. The porch swing was still there, but only one side remained attached by a rusty chain. If she closed her eyes, she could still see her younger parents swaying side by side as they watched her play innocently in the yard.

Slowly, she set one foot on the bottom step and applied her weight. The boards moaned, warning her to tread carefully. *Don't awaken what's been put to bed.* She took another step and then another. When she reached the top, a held breath escaped her. The house still had the strength to hold her.

She turned and looked over the yard. The flower beds that used to be filled with peonies were now covered in weeds, but that didn't stop the memories from dancing around in her mind. She saw the two of them: her and her sister. They were so young and dressed in their Sunday best. Her mom was smiling, holding the camera, and asking them to sit for a moment. Dylan and Jessie settled in front of the large pink flowers. As always, giant black ants crawled among the delicate petals, forcing her and Jessie to keep some distance, so none of the creatures would race up an arm or leg. She shivered at the memory of the insects' quickness and determination. Jessie and she tried to obey her mother's wishes holding as still as possible as their mother smiled from behind the camera. When the pictures were complete, Dylan and Jessie would race from the bushes, screaming as young girls often do. Dylan should find those pictures of their cheerful, youthful faces. They still existed somewhere; she was sure.

"Can we come up?" Thomas asked from the bottom of the steps, panting after his run. She smiled at the sight of him, so different from her own appearance. His blond hair and blue eyes reminded her of their father, while his sister's dark hair and eyes resembled her own.

"Carefully," Dylan warned. "This house is ancient."

"How old is it?" Chrissy asked.

"It was built in the 1870s, believe it or not."

"Holy cow!" the children said together.

"That's older than Grandma," Chrissy added.

Dylan smiled at her daughter's innocence. "That is way older than Grandma."

"Did you really milk cows in that barn?" Thomas gazed back over his shoulder at the building behind him.

Dylan smiled. "Yes, we did." She looked out across the yard at the barn. Half of it had collapsed some winters ago after a heavy snowfall.

"Can we go in it?" Chrissy asked.

The gentle breeze played through Dylan's hair, stirring up memories she had long tried to suppress. The fields surrounding the old barn, once vibrant with towering cornstalks swaying in the fall sun, were now barren and lifeless, their golden ears harvested long ago. Yet, as the wind brushed across her cheeks, it carried with it echoes of the past—soft murmurings that felt like a ghost recounting its secrets, tales of laughter, hard work, and fleeting moments that lingered in the air like the scent of earth after rain. And with those memories were the ones that haunted her.

Thomas slipped his hand into hers. She had hoped the blood draining from her face was not evident, but her son had noticed. "What's wrong, Mommy?"

"Nothing." Dylan stared out at the empty cornfield. How much had those fields seen? Too much. Yet besides the whisper of the breeze, they remained silent.

"Can we go into the barn?" they asked again.

Dylan nodded. The kids skipped before her as Dylan's heart hammered in her ears. The large sliding barn door now existed only as broken pieces hanging from rusted metal. Half the roof had collapsed, letting in beams of sunlight illuminating all but the deepest corners.

Dylan stared down the barn past the area the cows long ago stood to be milked. Her gaze drifted to the spot the milking machines once hung from. Wonderful childhood memories mingled with her nightmares. Her gaze settled on the far back of the barn built to house the manure spreader. The gutter cleaner would push the manure around the barn, up the ramp, and drop it into the awaiting equipment. She closed her eyes, and a memory of uncovered bones flashed on her eyelids, which served as a movie screen. A chill shot up her spine. She should have never come back here.

When she opened her eyes, her children were halfway down the barn.

"Come on, Mom," they called.

With a deep breath, she took one step into the barn. She would take her children through as much of the property as possible. She would tell them how she and Jessie taught the calves to drink from the milk pails. She would explain how the calves' rough tongues tickled their fingers and how the suction was so strong fear sometimes hid in their giggles. Dylan would reminisce about watching the calves being born and how her children's grandfather had taught Dylan and Jessie to stick straws of hay in the newborns' nostrils to make them sneeze and begin breathing independently. She would tell them how Dylan and Jessie ran through the fields, finding wild strawberries and eating them no matter how close they grew to the cowpies. Dylan would tell them many things. But she wouldn't tell them everything. No one could ever know everything because still, after all this time had passed, some secrets are better left buried.

CHAPTER 1

Dylan Phillips
Present Day

THE CHILLY MORNING WIND blew through the cornfields, causing the leaves to cling together like sticky hands, grabbing Dylan's clothes like she was a fugitive on the run. She raced through the stalks as they bit at her cheeks. The scratches stung her skin, reminding her that, for better or for worse, she was still alive. The truth of the fact was more of a burden than a gift. Faster, she ran until she tripped on a root and fell to the ground, catching herself with both hands before face-planting into the dirt. She could never run fast enough or far enough away. She stood panting, hands on her knees. A tear dripped from her right eye. She watched the small part of her fall to the ground. The earth absorbed it as if it was nothing, as if her pain would never be noticed by anyone.

"Bandit," she called breathlessly. But only the wind spoke back. Despite the beagle's love of hunting and his training, he was not exceptionally skilled in the area. Perhaps that was why her father, Conner Phillips, stopped taking him out with him on the rare occasions he went. Now, Bandit entertained himself by running rabbit and deer while trying to avoid dog catchers.

Bandit generally kept to their farm but occasionally crossed the border into Canada. Their property spread out over four hundred and sixty acres, with the fields behind the barn backing up to the Canadian border. The land included fields of corn, now nearly eight feet tall and a month and half away from harvesting, fields for growing alfalfa and hay, pastures where the cows grazed, and wooded areas that generally went untouched except for hunting. She only searched the cornfield closest to her house, seldom venturing to the large one across the road and never to places far from the barn.

Dylan didn't spend as much time with her dog as she used to, but she didn't want to see him euthanized by a dog catcher who had grown intolerant of country dogs running wild and free. But it wasn't her fear of the dog catcher that forced her outside on this chilly morning. What fueled her was the dream she had woken to, the one that made her sit bolt upright, gasping for her next breath. She was holding flowers and staring at a headstone. Tears streamed down her cheeks, but as she wiped them away, flesh-colored liquid pooled in her hands. In her dream, she could see her face from outside her body. Her skin was melting, her eyes were drooping down her cheeks, and somewhere in the distance, a man was laughing.

In the middle of the cornfield, the dream still made her sob. At least out here, no one could hear her cry, and she didn't feel disappointed when no one tried to comfort her. She could pretend they weren't running to her side because they didn't know her pain.

"Bandit, where are you?" She paused to listen but could

only hear her own heavy breathing. Her warm breath hit the chilly air, forming a slight cloud that rose and dissipated as if it had never existed. What if Bandit was caught in a hunter's trap? Did she dare walk as far as the small beaver pond where the traps were located? Before deciding, she heard footsteps running toward her through the stalks.

"Bandit?" She peered through the corn and saw a figure, too large to be her small beagle, nearing her. Dylan's breath caught in her throat as her neighbor's bloodhound bounded through the corn, dropping an object from his mouth before approaching her. She knelt on the cold, hard ground to come eye to eye with his sad, droopy eyes.

"Hey, Sarge." She stroked his head, trying to avoid the slobber dripping from his oversized lips. "Have you seen your buddy out here?" Sarge stared at her in silence. "I'll take that as a no. Or are you pleading the fifth?" Dylan sat cross-legged, and Sarge settled beside her and rested his big head on her knee. His drool dripped onto her jeans, but sitting next to him, stroking his head, brought her too much comfort to mind. She enjoyed the many times Sarge crossed her path while she walked their property. Sarge didn't care that she was an outsider at school, disliked by many. He didn't care that her family was falling apart. He didn't care that she found talking to animals easier than people. Sitting hidden behind the cornstalks, the outside world didn't exist.

In the distance, she heard her neighbor, Tim Burrows, calling for Sarge. He was an older man, she guessed to be in his sixties. He walked with a slight hunch and generally wore a pinched expression.

"You better get home before your boss gets angry."

Dylan didn't mind their neighbor. Most of her memories of him and his late wife ranged from cordial to kind. But her father felt differently, and if he didn't care for someone, no one else dared to either. To her, Tim was the man who lived down the road—nothing more, nothing less. Years ago, her father made it clear they were not to bring her mom's homemade cookies to him anymore after her father had heard rumors about Mr. Burrows weighing in on a family matter, placing the blame on Conner Phillips. One rumor was all it took to form the wall between them.

The last time she heard the two men speak to each other was a few months before. Dylan had been riding in the hay wagon, stacking the hay the hired man tossed to her while her father drove the tractor. When her father saw Tim walking through the field with Sarge, he stopped the tractor and hopped off.

"What are you doing on my land again?" For a moment, the two men stared at each other. Dylan couldn't understand what the big deal was about walking in the field, but her father's deep-rooted resentment was still strong.

"Did you hear about the smuggling going on?" Tim asked.

Dylan's stomach twisted as it generally did when the subject arose.

"We're all aware. What does that have to do with your being on my property?"

"Just curious, I guess."

"Curious about what?" The tension was tangible. Her father seemed to dare him with his stare.

"Come on, Sarge. Let's get home," Tim Burrows said before turning his back to them.

Conner watched the old man and his dog walk back across the field. Her father didn't turn around until both of his neighbor's feet were off his land. Dylan remained silent, which proved to be her go-to reaction.

Now, as Dylan ran her hand down Sarge's back, she was grateful Sarge cared little about old fights or rules humans tried to enforce.

"Sarge!" Mr. Burrows called again.

"He's getting angry." They both rose from their sitting positions. "Don't forget your treasure."

Sarge turned away from her and sauntered back to whatever he had found.

"What do you have there, Sarge?" Dylan followed the bloodhound as he picked up the object. When he turned, whatever he held was mainly concealed by his mouth, but Dylan saw enough to drain the color from her face. "Sarge, let me see what you have." Dylan's heart pounded in her chest. She stepped closer as Tim called for Sarge again. The authoritative tone in his voice made the dog's ears perk up. Dylan took another step toward the canine. "Drop it," she said, her voice trembling. But Sarge bolted into the field and toward his home. Dylan chased after him, struggling to keep up. By the time she reached the edge of the cornfield bordering Tim's lawn, Sarge had dropped the treasure at Tim's feet. Tim was already off his porch and leaning over the object, inspecting it. The old man's mouth was agape and his skin ashen. Dylan slipped into the cornfield and raced through the stalks, fleeing from the nightmares from which she could never wake.

CHAPTER 2

Conner Phillips
Present Day

CONNER PHILLIPS SQUATTED NEXT to an old Holstein. Her udder overflowed with milk, making the white liquid squirt onto the filthy floor. He washed each teat with a paper towel and rushed to get the milker in place before he lost any more of his livelihood to the gutter. His daughter, Dylan, was across the barn working along the other row of cows. Silence settled between them like hardening concrete.

"Dylan, the milker on Betsy needs to be adjusted before it falls off." He barked the words but didn't mean to. The tone had become a habit too addictive to give up. Dylan finished with the milker she was using and, without a word, went to Betsy with time to spare. His daughter could do these chores in her sleep, but she had been distracted the last couple weeks and, if possible, acting even more standoffish and strange than usual. Jittery almost.

Sirens sounded outside, and she nearly tipped over the bucket filled with cleaning solution. Derby was a quiet town, and sirens seldom pierced through the air, but this was the second time in two weeks. Last time, the police stopped at the neighbor's house. What possible reason could the meddler have to call the police? For a moment, Conner thought maybe he had been injured, but the ambulance never came, and he saw him driving by the farm days later. He was left to assume the issue wasn't serious, at least, and better yet, it didn't involve him since he heard nothing more about it.

Conner observed his daughter. Her face shone with sweat despite the morning chill. "Were you running around the cornfields again?" She seemed to be out there every morning of late, despite his reprimands.

She avoided his gaze. "I was looking for Bandit."

"That dog will find his way home on his own. You don't need to knock down my cornstalks looking for him."

"I was careful."

Conner shook his head and turned back to his chores. The squawking of machines filled the silence between them. Nearly half an hour passed without them speaking. Conner moved the milkers down the line of cows, mindlessly going through the motions. He bent down next to an old Holstein and massaged her udders, pushing out the last drops of warm milk. As Conner pushed his stiff legs up to stand, her tail swatted him in the face, covering his neck with manure. As he uttered expletives, a man cleared his throat.

"Mr. Phillips." The authoritative voice startled him. Rarely did uninvited guests enter the barn, but as his gaze settled on the two uniformed men standing before him, his surprise transformed into frustration. This visit had to be related to the incident at the neighbor's house. What was Tim going to blame on him now?

He looked up and down the barn for anything to help his

mind make sense of the scenario, but only saw Dylan slipping between two cows. She disappeared too quickly to make eye contact, but God help him, that child was impossible to read anyway.

Steeling his facial expression, Conner turned toward the men. "Can I help you, officers?"

"We hope so."

Conner's throat tightened with dryness. He turned his back to the officers and picked up his cold, forgotten coffee from the rolling cart. Carrying the milking machine, Dylan walked out from between two cows. Conner swallowed the bitter beverage as he watched his daughter slip between the following two cows and plug in the machine. She was listening to every word. How he knew, he could not be sure. But how could she not? She kept her eyes down as if it could prevent the officers from knowing she was there.

The older officer glanced at Dylan. "I think it would be best to step outside the barn."

"If you think it's necessary."

"I do, sir."

Conner waved his hand toward the barn door to encourage them to lead the way, which they did. The three men emerged from the dark barn into the bright sunlight. The morning was still cool, yet a line of sweat dripped down Conner's T-shirt collar.

The officer in charge cleared his throat, preparing to speak while the other scanned the cornfield to the left of the barn.

"I'm Detective Baker," he said, pausing before continuing. Conner guessed him to be in his late twenties or early thirties, the age where one's arrogance was surface level, while inside, one shook with fear and doubt. The officer's stomach protruded as if he spent more time in the bars than the gym, but his strong jawline and thick head of hair gave him a look of authority.

"Okay." Conner glanced back at the barn full of cows waiting to be milked, and his impatience grew.

Detective Baker shifted his weight and cleared his throat again. Conner was unsure whether the throat clearing was due to the barn smells or nerves.

"We have a few questions about a young man who used to work here."

"We've had quite the characters, that's for sure. I don't have the luxury of being picky. The job doesn't pay well, and let's face it, it's not for everyone."

Detective Baker glanced at the row of manure-covered tails. "No. I suppose it's not."

"So, which character is in question?"

"David Miller."

Conner nodded, attempting to hide his distaste for the man. "I'm not surprised. But to be honest, he wasn't the worst employee I've ever had. People warned me not to hire him, but he showed up and did his work. I was pleasantly surprised." Not every part of what he said was a lie.

"Can't say the positive review doesn't surprise me. We've gotten to know him pretty well down at the station."

"Like I said, I've heard the rumors about him."

"David doesn't go very long before he gets himself in some sort of trouble, but the funny thing is, we haven't heard a thing about him in months. Last we heard, he was working for you."

"He was until about six months ago."

"Can you tell us how his employment here ended?"

"He didn't show up one day. This stuff happens all the time with hired men. Here one day, gone the next."

Conner stared at the other officer as he jotted notes down on a pad. "And you are?"

"My apologies," Detective Baker answered for him. "This is my partner, Detective Randolph." Randolph was thinner than his counterpart and had red hair. His sparse stubble only accentuated his youth.

Randolph nodded to Conner.

"The kid was a drifter. What else can I say?" Conner glanced back into the barn. He needed to get back to his chores and away from these men.

"That he was."

The officers both watched Conner. The intensity of their stares made him shift from leg to leg. Would they just get to the point? What did they learn recently to bring them to his doorstep?

"Why is David going missing coming up now?"

"There's been a development that's..."

"A development?" Conner's tone hinged between curiosity and annoyance.

The officers glanced at each other before regaining eye contact with Conner. "Your neighbor's dog just uncovered his jawbone."

Conner stared at the officers for a long moment. His Adam's apple rose and fell with a dry swallow. Did they notice? "How do you know it was David's jawbone?"

"DNA." They let their words settle like dead weight. "There's no denying the fact the bone is David's."

"But it wasn't found on my property."

"Your neighbor owns under an acre of land surrounded by hundreds of yours."

Conner glanced over his property, confirming to himself the point they were making.

Conner nodded, which was all he could bring himself to do. He couldn't deny their need to speak with his last employer. Would they be combing his house, the barn, his shed? Conner glanced up and down the barn for his daughter, but she must have run into the milk room. The present hired man leaned against a pole, watching their every reaction. At least he couldn't hear anything.

"No one on this farm saw David after he left our house with that friend of his, Jeremey, I think his name is. Ask him. He's the one that had to drive him to work every day after he lost his license. He'll tell you."

The officer stared at him through dark sunglasses. "Is that the story you want to stick with?"

Conner struggled to hide the nagging fear creeping into his thoughts. "That's the only story there is. So, yes, I'm sticking to it." He struggled with his expression, knowing he was being studied. Suddenly, he had no idea how to appear innocent.

CHAPTER 3

Jeremy Biggs
Present Day

FIGHTING A HANGOVER BROUGHT on by a drinking binge enjoyed solely between himself and a twelve-pack of Miller, Jeremy drifted in and out of sleep. Sometime in the night, after Jeremy had passed out during an episode of CSI, his father, who had been throwing them back at the pub with his local losers, had stumbled into the trailer, knocked into the coffee table, and spilled the last of Jeremy's beer onto the dingy rug. Once his father had closed his bedroom door, Jeremy waited, listening for the creaking of his bed. When enough time had passed, making him confident his father would not rise until morning, Jeremy stumbled down the hallway to his room and fell into bed wearing only his underwear.

A persistent knocking on the trailer's rusted metal door brought him to full consciousness. Rolling from the bed, he fumbled for a dirty pair of jeans that lay crumpled on the floor. "I'm coming," he yelled. When he passed his father's bedroom, he heard the familiar deep snore that used to alert him that his father had been on a drinking binge. Now, it was a nightly occurrence.

As Jeremy approached the front door, his tired mind had not considered who might be so eager to speak to one of them. In fact, moments passed before the uniformed officers waiting outside registered as a part of reality. Now, as he gazed at them through the screen, his naked chest exposed to them, reality slapped him awake.

"Can I help you?" Jeremy asked. His heart raced as he tried to look past them to view his father's truck. Had there been an accident? It would not be his dad's first DUI.

"We have a few questions for you, Jeremy." The officer with the dark hair and protruding belly spoke first.

Jeremy glanced back at the coffee table lined with empty beer cans. His father's raucous snore echoed down the hallway. Jeremy pushed open the screen door and stepped onto the small porch where the three men now stood with only a couple of feet between them.

"What's this about?"

"I'm Detective Baker, and this is Detective Randolph. We need to ask you a few questions about a friend of yours: David Miller."

Jeremy's breath stopped, and last night's beer swirled in his belly. "What about him?"

"When did you last see him?" Baker asked.

"The day I dropped him off at work at the Phillips farm." What had David done now? At least Jeremy might finally get some of the answers he'd been looking for as well.

"Do you know what day that was?"

"Not off hand. Maybe sometime in April. I'll have to think about the exact date."

"We're going to need you to do that."

"Okay, yeah, sure."

"When you dropped him off, did you notice anything strange?"

"No."

"Conner Phillips said you generally pick him up as well."

"I do, but he wasn't there when I went to pick him up."

"Did you talk to any members of the Phillips family when you were there?"

"No. I never do, or at least, not much at all. I waited in the driveway, texted David, and waited a bit longer. Then I left."

"He never texted back?"

"No."

"And you never saw him after that day?"

"Like I said, I haven't seen David since I dropped him off. If he's gotten himself in trouble again, I'm not a part of it. It's been months since I've seen him."

"Are you two close?" the officer asked.

"You could say that." Bile rose in the back of Jeremy's throat. Were they close? Jeremy wondered that himself.

"If I hear you correctly, you dropped your friend off at the farm, and he wasn't there when you went to pick him up later that day. You left, never heard from him, and never contacted anyone about it?"

"Yeah, that's about it." He knew how crazy it sounded, but the truth would land him in handcuffs.

"I'm having a hard time getting my brain around that."

"It's what David would do sometimes. Here one day, gone the next. I've gotten used to it through the years."

Squirrels bounced around the old metal furniture his

father had purchased when he thought he could class up the joint. Now Jeremy looked over the weedy and sparse lawn, the old mattress thrown against the tree, the beer cans, and the crap furniture, knowing what the officers thought of him. He was trouble, just like his friend David.

"Can I ask what he did this time?" Jeremy asked, fearing the answer.

The officers looked from Jeremy to each other. A silent communication took place before Baker spoke. "I'm sorry to say, but it appears your friend has gotten himself killed."

Jeremy's breath caught in his throat; before he could breathe again, he was retching over the side of the porch. The sound of the police officers backing down the porch slipped in between the heaving. When the urge to vomit paused, Jeremy rested his forearms on the splintery wood and readied himself to face them again.

"What... Where did you find him? What happened?"

"A bone was discovered by Conner Phillips's neighbor."

"Are you sure it's David's?"

"The DNA test proves it. We're talking to his friends and family to figure out the timeline of events leading to his death."

The list wasn't long. David had one friend and one family member, his mother, Bethany.

"Oh, my God. I can't believe... How?"

"Do you know of any bad blood between Conner Phillips and David?"

Jeremy chose his words carefully. He wasn't ready for these questions. He needed time to think. "No. I mean, who loves their boss?"

"So, David didn't express any concerns."

"No." Jeremy's voice came out high-pitched.

"Do you know anyone who would have wanted to hurt David?"

"Not that I can think of." The urge to vomit again was strong. Everyone wanted to hurt David.

The officers both stared intently at Jeremy. Could they see the lies on his face?

"We all know David's been in his share of trouble. Are you sure you don't know of anything that was going on with him before he went missing?"

"No, man, I can't think of anything."

Baker nodded in a way that accepted Jeremy wouldn't give anything up that easily.

"How about you stick around town in case we have more questions? You work at Little Italy, don't you?"

Jeremy didn't like that they knew anything about him, but it was a small town.

"Yes, sir, I do."

"I guess we know where to find you then."

"Yeah, sure. Ask me anything."

"Oh, we will," Baker said, handing Jeremy his card and then turning away.

Jeremy stayed frozen on the porch until the police car was no longer visible, then heaved over the side of the porch until every part of him felt empty.

CHAPTER 4

Dylan Phillips
Present Day

DYLAN'S LONG, DARK HAIR dangled in front of her eyes. She liked it that way. It made her feel as if she was watching the world from afar. On summer days, the heat forced her to pull the strands back into a ponytail, but today, as the barn refused to warm up despite all the cattle lined up one by one in their stanchions, her mane warmed her face.

She watched the men: her father standing with a hand on his hip, his weight on one foot; the one detective with pad and pen ready; and the second speaking and staring at her father through his dark glasses.

Her dad's ghastly pale face surprised her. He was afraid, but she couldn't be sure of what. Did he recall his argument with David the day before he went missing? The moment remained fresh in her mind, as she was sure it did in her sister Jessie's.

Dylan was a year and a half older than Jessie. They were both young, but Dylan's fourteen years had been difficult. Life had forced her to mature before nature intended. She understood more of life's cruelty than most of her classmates would ever know. One such cruelty was that David was an evil man, and the world busted at its seams with men like him.

She watched her father speaking to the officers but could not hear their words. She adjusted her milkers and then ran to the milk house hoping to get within earshot. A word here and there drifted through the air. They were asking her father about the day he went missing. She remembered the morning well. She had watched for David through the milk house window. Her father was sleeping in, as he often did on Saturdays. It was his one day when both of his girls were home in the mornings to take turns doing chores. Ideally, whoever was the hired man at the time showed up for work. Conner gave the hired men Sundays off, not necessarily by choice.

That fateful morning, Dylan had prepared the pipes as usual by realigning their paths into the bulk tank. They were, as always, left in the washing position until the next milking. All was quiet. David should have arrived thirty minutes ago. A piece of her had wished he would never show. She could handle the work, even if it took her until the evening milking to finish the morning chores. Moments passed as she stood stuck in the past until the officer's words jolted her back to the present. Their neighbor found a jawbone. Even though she expected this, the words made her dizzy.

Her father caught her eavesdropping. Too many emotions filled his expression; she wasn't sure which one would win: anger or fear. Conner watched the officers as they backed down the dirt driveway and turned left to head back to town. When he reentered the barn, his head was down, hiding the secrets Dylan might read from his expression.

He walked past her. "Get back to work. You leave that machine on Seventeen any longer, and she'll have mastitis."

Seventeen was an old cow named before Jessie and Dylan took over the job. Now, the numbers used as names were relics of a time before they offered ones they deemed more fitting for living beings, including Bessie, Gert, April, and many others. Five years had passed since Dylan and Jessie'd gotten their way, and since then, no incoming cow suffered with a number for its name.

Dylan rushed over and removed the machine, eyeing her father as she stood. He was squatting between two cows, one a young heifer prone to kicking. The milking machines' pumping noises filled the barn, easing the silence she had grown accustomed to between her and her father. Her dad didn't speak much besides giving orders that she followed without question. But this type of silence disturbed her, making her stomach twist to the point of nausea.

"Why were the police officers here?" Her voice shook.

Conner's face was turned toward the cow he knelt beside. "If I wanted you to know I would have told you. It's nothing for you to worry about."

"But..."

"You heard me."

Dylan busied herself with the machine, watching her hands shake as she placed the mouthpiece over each teat. Once adjusted, she called to her father. "I need to use the bathroom."

"Don't take all day. I'm not watching your milkers and mine."

Dylan raced across the yard and up the steps to their old

farmhouse. She wanted to keep going, far away from this family, this barn, and the haunting cornfields. But even if her legs could carry her a million miles away, it wouldn't be far enough to make her forget all she had witnessed.

CHAPTER 5

Conner Phillips
Present Day

W HETHER DUE TO THE jawbone or not, within a few days of the discovery hitting the press, Conner Phillips's hired man politely resigned, leaving Conner to struggle through chores alone or with a family member forced to play hooky for the day. The local paper headlines finally had pertinent information to announce in bold front-page news. *Dental Records Prove Jawbone Belonged to David Miller.* The article explained that David Miller had gone missing nearly six months before, after he was last seen on the Phillips farm. Shortly after the papers had been tossed onto every driveway across town, cars began driving by the farm slower than usual as the inhabitants of the vehicles scanned the property. What were they expecting to see? Busybodies, that's what they all were. Desperate for a morsel of gossip to flavor their conversation at The Coffee Shop.

If history predicted the future, Tim Burrows would be the one leading the talk. Years had passed since Conner or his wife Claire had entered the shop hoping to catch up with the townsfolk. On their last visit, the hushed tones made the casual sharing of pleasantries impossible. When they left the building for the last time, they envisioned the conversations that burst forth as soon as their departure freed the townspeople. Maybe all the conversations weren't judgmental, but even pity had the power to separate friends.

David Miller's associates ranged from low-lifes to criminals. Why weren't the investigators looking more closely at Jeremy Biggs? He claimed to be the last person to see David. The man's lame story about thinking his best friend had up and run off sounded suspect even to Conner, and he had never served in law enforcement. At this point, the bone was never seen on the Phillips farm, even though its proximity was suspect.

Tim Burrows must be loving this latest turn of events. In Conner's opinion, Tim needed some hobbies. The widower had too much time on his hands, forcing him to worry about other people's lives. Conner had seen Tim walking around his property more times than he could count. Conner'd overlooked it more times than he called him out on it, but not anymore. That man most likely pointed his finger right at Conner the minute the bone showed up, overlooking the fact that the Canadian border lined the back of his field, and everyone was up in arms about some organized crime family smuggling drugs across the border.

Conner needed someone to flip past the first page of the paper and see his help-wanted ad. Running a farm was not a one-man show. Conner had placed the advertisement in the paper a week ago and had yet to receive a response. Thanks to the jawbone being found, no one wanted to work on the farm, which was thought to be a burial ground for a no-good slug.

The slow response to the ad wasn't completely unheard of. In fact, the Phillips family had once gone three weeks without help. Even Claire had to contribute to the morning milkings during that period. This time, the girls took turns skipping school to help with chores. If they minded, they didn't say, but then their complaints would have fallen on deaf ears anyway. From what Conner knew, their grades weren't excellent, but they weren't failing either. He dealt little with those affairs. The farm had to come first. Without that, the family had nothing.

Conner tinkered with the tractor's power take-off (PTO) shaft, which refused to spin again. Just another piece of equipment that should be replaced, but the budget wouldn't allow for it. He laughed to himself when he considered the budget. There wasn't one. They were sinking fast, and no one, not even his wife, knew how bad their finances had become. Claire knew they were struggling to the point of poverty, but she was unaware that each month, Conner wondered if it would be their last one with a roof over their heads.

A few times, the family was forced to apply for government aid to put food on the table. Claire drove to the next town to buy groceries with a pocketbook full of food stamps. He had failed her, and it killed him inside. But why did Conner feel so angry with her and his girls about his shortcomings? Conner worked every day without vacations or sick days and still had to ask for government help. The system sucked, but to whom could he complain? Afterall, he had chosen this profession.

Once a week, due to the empty bank account, Conner

straddled the PTO shaft that connected the tractor to the manure spreader, knowing that at any moment whatever had caused it to stick could give way, grab his clothing, and wrap him around the shaft, making sure Conner knew, once again, that the farm had won.

After one final tightening of a screw, the PTO shaft spun slowly at first and then at a speed that could rip off a limb. He stood, hand on his hip, watching his accomplishment. For the moment, the problem was solved. He climbed up onto the tractor and killed the motor. As he did, a black F150 pulled an old camper into the driveway. A man in his early thirties climbed out of the cab.

What now? Conner assessed the stranger as he approached. He had brown hair and a short beard that was probably three days from a shave. He wore jeans and a Carhartt jacket that looked fresh off the rack.

"Can I help you?" Conner asked.

"I hope," the man said while extending his hand. "My name's Eli Simmons. I saw your ad in the paper. You're looking for a hired man?"

Conner met Eli's hand with his and gave a tentative shake. What load of trouble would this guy have to add to the equation? But Conner was desperate, so he'd hire him no matter what.

"Yeah, I'm shorthanded now. You ever worked on a farm before?"

"That's what I do. Every farm is different, but I'm a quick learner."

Conner pointed to the truck and the camper. "What's with all that?"

"Well, if you don't mind, I generally park my camper in a field. Keeps me close to my work."

"Tells me you don't plan on staying."

"I stay until I'm not needed. I never leave unexpectedly."

Conner eyed him suspiciously.

"I have references."

The hammer would fall eventually, but what could be worse than having the police search his property for body parts?

Conner sighed and rubbed his forehead. "When can you start?"

"When do you want me?"

"I'll show you where you can park that thing. Get settled and come back to the barn by four."

"Do you want to see my references?"

Conner laughed. "Sure. You can bring them back with you this evening." Short of being a serial killer, the man had the job. And who knew, maybe Conner'd hired a couple of those in his day as well. "See the pasture on the other side of that cornfield across the road?"

"Yeah."

"Find a spot in the back of that field. Make sure you always keep the gate shut. The cows will be in the pasture with you sometimes. Do you have a problem with that?"

"Not at all, sir. I rather like seeing them roam around."

Conner shook his head. "To each their own."

"I'll have it set up in no time and be ready for work at four."

"Get to it then."

Eli nodded and headed toward his truck. Conner watched the man back down the driveway. Something about him unsettled Conner, but the strangest part about it all was that something about the stranger also gave him hope.

32

CHAPTER 6

Eli Simmons
Present Day

A T THREE-FORTY-FIVE, ELI WALKED up the gravel driveway of yet another beginning. His new boss, Mr. Phillips, stood near the barn talking with a teenage girl Eli assumed to be his daughter. They shared the same dark hair and stood with a similar stance. Phillips turned his attention to Eli, his eyes narrowed as if annoyed by Eli's interruption. The daughter's long bangs hid her expression, but the way she stared downward spoke volumes. Conner's gaze drifted back to his daughter before he waved her off like a pesky bug. Her shoulders slumped as she headed to the milk room.

Conner watched her until she was out of sight, not immediately giving Eli his attention. He finally sighed and said, "The cows need their grain."

Conner spoke curtly. Eli had worked for many types of bosses, but never one so cold. Perhaps the vibe came from a fight with his daughter, but Eli sensed it was more than that. "Follow me. I'll show you the granary."

Conner walked him to the area within the hayloft where the granary was located. "I've got to go fix something in the milk house that my daughter managed to break again. We start the evening milking in an hour. The quicker you get the cows grained, the better. I'll send Dylan out here to get you started." Conner turned on his heel and headed toward a small room off the haymow. A rusty spring pulled the door shut with a bang.

"Thanks for the warm welcome," Eli said into the air.

He glanced around the hayloft piled nearly to the top with hay bales. The last of the day's light snuck in the cracks of the old barn walls, making hay dust dance in the sunbeams. The effect left Eli spellbound until he sensed someone's gaze on him.

Eli faced the girl he had seen earlier in the driveway. Her previous submissive demeanor now hid behind her hostility.

"You okay?" Her voice dripped with teenage sarcasm.

"Absolutely," Eli said with a forced smile. "Just trying to acclimate myself. I'm Eli, the new help."

"Whatever."

"And you are?"

"Dylan."

"Nice to meet you."

She rolled her eyes before grabbing a piece of cardboard roughly the size of a sheet of notebook paper. "Here's the list."

"The list?"

"It tells you how much grain each cow needs." Again, her tone dripped with annoyance.

"Thank you. Cardboard?"

"You work in a barn. What did you expect?'

He looked at the scribbles with a mixture of politeness and confusion: April-¼, 17-1, Betty-¾. "It's a bit hard to follow."

With a shaky finger, she pointed toward the numbers. "April is the first cow. I'll show you where she stands in a minute." Her eyes stayed downcast, and her shoulders slumped. How many years had passed since he was that teenager, lost and alone? He knew the posture well because he too once walked with hunched shoulders afraid to look up and see the nothingness around him. What was her story? What made her hide behind those bangs? Eli inhaled deeply, searching for the patience he needed.

"The list goes in order. The more milk the cow produces, the more grain the cow gets. The scoop is there." Dylan pointed in the grain mill. "Fill the wheelbarrow and walk it down both mangers following the list."

Eli picked up the shovel and began filling the wheelbarrow. He stopped when the grain reached the top. The girl watched quietly from a distance. He was torn between wanting her to go away and wanting her to stay.

"You need to fill it until it's heaping."

Eli added more and glanced her way.

"More." But this time, anger filled her voice.

"I've worked on many farms, so I know how to fill a wheelbarrow."

"Then you should know to fill it higher."

Eli added more, and she nodded. Her expression eased.

"I'll show you where to go."

Eli got behind the wheelbarrow and lifted. At first, he struggled to find the balance. The girl walked ahead of him, so she could not have noticed.

She reached the manger and pointed. "That's April. Start there. She only gets a quarter of a scoop because she's dry."

Someone had written a big D in waxy crayon on April's side. This meant the cow had been given a medicine to make her dry until she gave birth. The milker could not go on her without contaminating the entire tank of milk. He had made that mistake once when he was much younger and promised himself and his former employer it would never happen again.

Eli pushed the wheelbarrow to the first cow, scooped and poured, checked the list, and then scooped and poured the second and third. Then he lifted the wheelbarrow and tried to move forward. Using its head, one of the cows scraped off the top of the load. He glanced back at the girl, who was nervously looking at the milk house door.

"You have to move faster." Dylan rushed to the pile and began scooping it back into the wheelbarrow. "Let me show you," she said in almost a whisper.

The girl lifted the wheelbarrow Eli had found heavy, pushed it about five cows ahead, and scooped out the various amounts without glancing at the list. Eli stared at the fifty hungry heads lining the barn's manger. On the other side of the barn, another fifty cows awaited. She picked up the handles again and hurried to her next spot—scoop, scoop. She had the row done in no time.

She set the wheelbarrow legs back onto the concrete and looked at him directly. "You need to be faster than that, or you'll lose all the grain."

He tried to hide his annoyance with her teenage tone. "I'm only seeing the list for the first time. Be a bit patient with me."

She rolled her eyes. "Memorize the amounts, but always

check. My dad changes them all the time. They won't all change at once, though."

Eli looked down at the list in his hand and nodded. "I'll do that. Tonight." Then he glanced back up at the girl. "Thanks for your help. The last farm I worked at had wider mangers. It wasn't such an issue." This was a small lie, one he felt was innocent enough.

She nodded but didn't make eye contact.

"I appreciate your help, Dylan."

The girl was quiet for a moment. Then, in a nearly inaudible voice, she uttered, "Whatever" Her anger went beyond normal teenage angst, but why?

Dylan disappeared into the milk house, leaving Eli alone with his chores. Maybe he should hook his truck to his camper tonight and head out to the next town, but that wasn't his character. Eli wouldn't bail without warning. Other jobs had started rough, and he always managed to leave in good standing. He'd figure something out. But something was unsettling about this place. Dark energy swirled around him, clouding his thoughts. Like an animal before a storm, he decided the best way to survive whatever was approaching was to stand firm against it.

CHAPTER 7

Dylan Phillips
Present Day

DYLAN LEFT ELI TO finish feeding the cows and headed to her favorite spot in the barn. She opened the chicken coop and stepped inside. With the pitchfork, Dylan began cleaning all the soiled hay from the ground.

Of all the areas in the barn, this was the only one where she heard the ghosts of happy times, the giggling sounds that no longer existed. It was strange to her that despite all her happy memories of the farm, these were the only ones she still found pleasure in. The others had been drowned out through the years, but not the ones in the chicken coop. The memories formed within these walls, for some reason, remained untouched.

When the coop was again clean, Dylan picked up one of the chickens and sat on the upside-down pail she had placed there months before. The chicken quickly settled on her lap. Dylan closed her eyes and rested her head on the wall behind her as she slid her hand over the soft feathers of one of the only animals that she could call her own. She still couldn't believe her father had allowed her to get the chickens. Tears filled her closed eyes until they overflowed down her cheeks.

The Phillips family had been so close to feeling whole again when her world was ripped apart for the second time.

Her mind drifted to her school day, and a sour pit formed inside her stomach. Dylan was now in the fall of her eighth-grade year, but a fresh new school year could not erase the past. She had lived through heaven and hell, yet somehow, she'd ended up right back in the same spot. Only now, terrible secrets tormented her mind.

On the outside, she appeared to her classmates and teachers precisely as she did a year ago, a loner who stared out the window not speaking and not being spoken to. Besides the times she caught people looking at her and then sharing whispers followed by laughter, she wondered if she existed at all. But their sneers burned deeper now because she had tasted something better.

On rare occasions, her mom, when she wasn't too busy or too self-absorbed, would try to get Dylan to reach out to her friends again. What friends?

"Dylan, why don't you hang out with so-and-so anymore?"

Dylan would glare at her through her bangs until her mother turned back to what she was doing. How did her mom not understand that those girls weren't her friends? They never were. The reality was that her mother didn't want to know the hard truth about her daughter. She didn't want to believe her daughter was a misfit who struggled to converse with kids her own age.

The chicken purred in her lap, a sound that calmed Dylan, but couldn't stop her tears. At school that day, she'd gazed back at the classroom, at the backs of the heads belonging to all the kids who ignored her daily. She told herself that she hated them. But she didn't. If she did, it wouldn't hurt so much when they laughed together at the cafeteria table, had sleepovers, passed notes in class, and didn't include her.

They blamed her. Even if the police never proved a thing.

CHAPTER 8

Dylan
The Past

*I*T WAS JANUARY OF *her seventh-grade year when a glimmer of hope entered Dylan's life. Marybeth moved into town. People were drawn to Marybeth, unlike Dylan who had an energy that pushed people away. Marybeth was new and shiny in their little town where nothing seemed to ever change.*

In the cafeteria, Dylan occasionally glanced around at the would-be friends, but mainly the world outside the window served as her abyss. Sitting close to the window made the panic inside her subside just enough.

On Marybeth's first day, she sat alone at a cafeteria table on the other side of the room. Christina and Olivia rushed over and invited her to their table, where they laughed at their private jokes. Perhaps snickered better described the sound. Marybeth laughed, too, but not as sincerely. Dylan noticed how her shoulders sloped, and her hand nervously brushed her long red bangs from her eyes. These actions mirrored her own, making her drawn to the new girl as well. They were the mannerisms of an insecure person who fought desperately to fit in with people who were always ready to push aside the outcast.

Once, when Dylan glanced back over to the center table, her gaze locked with Marybeth's, and for the first time in her memory, Dylan sensed a kindred spirit. The sensation shocked her, and her gaze darted back to the gray world outside the window. She didn't glance Marybeth's way again.

Dylan shared a few classes with Marybeth. One was PE, the most horrific period of the day. She was forced to strip down to her underwear, gray and dingy at that, and reveal her pale legs covered with bruises from completing chores. Brutal comments passed from one student to the next through looks, if not words. The looks would bounce around from girl to girl before snickers followed. She hated PE. She hated it so much.

She and Marybeth were also in the same math class, as were Christina and Olivia. For the most part, Dylan remained invisible to them. She spent most of her time staring out the window at the school parking lot.

The third class they shared was science. Science was okay until they broke off into groups, and she had to witness the dread in her classmates' eyes when their teacher paired them with her. Again, the ones lucky enough to escape being her partner giggled while the unlucky ones stared dumbfounded at the teacher or at the floor, depending on their personality.

"She smells like cow manure," she had heard one whisper. Even when Dylan thought they had broken her as much as possible, a comment could cut her down even further. The only part of her life that kept her going was knowing she had to be strong for Jessie.

Jessie stepped onto the bus at the end of each day, avoiding eye contact with her sister. Without words, Jessie would let her know her day had been the same sort of hell as Dylan's. Dylan would lift her chin in defiance of all the injustice in the world and wave to her sister until she had settled into the seat next to her.

Someday, somehow, Dylan would make it better for them both. Even if their parents were lost to them forever, or at least, that's how it felt. Her parents were nothing more than walking corpses, lost to the same terrible incident. As a result, each day, all energy and hope drained from Dylan as well.

And then, one day, something changed. Ms. Bates called out partners and announced that Dylan would be partnered with Marybeth. At first, Dylan's heart raced with fear. This girl, with whom she had shared only one glance free of distaste, picked up her books and headed toward Dylan's desk. Dylan prepared herself for the tiny light in her memory to be diminished, but instead, she was met with a smile. Without knowing it was possible, Dylan smiled back.

Their assignment was to devise five science experiments and list each of them in an if-then hypothesis. One of the experiments would be an ongoing project.

"Do you have any ideas?" Marybeth asked, staring at Dylan with her crystal blue eyes.

"No."

Dylan's voice sounded strange to herself. She had uttered so few words in the confines of this building.

"I heard you live on a dairy farm."

Dylan's heart sank. Here it comes. Dylan worked hard to get the smell of manure off her skin, but each time she got nervous, it seeped out in her sweat. The scent kept her captive to the farm no matter where she went.

"Yeah, I live on a dairy farm. So what?" She hadn't intended her tone to be so abrasive.

"I didn't mean to insult you. I love animals. I was thinking we could write experiments about animals. Do you have chickens? We could do experiments with eggs." Marybeth's eyes lit up, and her words filled with excitement. "Have you ever hatched eggs in an incubator? The babies are so cute."

"Why would we use an incubator if we had chickens to sit on the eggs?"

"That was kind of silly of me." She laughed, and her blue eyes danced with light. Her laugh was magical. "So, does that mean you have chickens?"

"No." Marybeth's smile faded. "But I can ask my dad. Maybe he would let me buy one. We used to have some, so we have the space for them."

"That would be awesome. Could I come to see your cows? I love animals." She laughed again. "I think I already said that."

"Yeah, you did, but that's okay." Dylan swallowed hard, scared of the pressure her following promise would create. "I'll ask my dad tonight. I'll get him to say yes."

"I'm so excited." Marybeth grabbed her paper and pencil. "So, the first hypothesis is that if a hen sits on her egg, it will hatch faster than an egg kept in an incubator."

Dylan didn't want to tell her that if the egg wasn't fertilized, a tiny new life would never chip away at the shell until it was freed from its confining space. The experiment would also involve getting a rooster, which made the possibility of her dad saying yes shrink to nearly zero. Instead of voicing her concerns, Dylan smiled. This day would be one to cherish. How many times could Dylan expect the miracle of friendship to enter her life?

Over dinner, Dylan cleared her throat nervously and spat out the question. Her father raised an untrimmed eyebrow.

"Don't you have enough things to care for around here?"

"Chickens are easy, and we'll have fresh eggs every morning."

He picked up the paper and started reading. Dylan, with a crushed heart, stood to clear her plate.

"How many do you want? And if I get them, I'm not doing a damned thing with them. You'll have to work off the cost of them."

"Two or three?" Dylan's heart raced. "And could we get a rooster?"

"A rooster!" Conner bellowed. "Why the hell do you want a rooster? Then you'll be raising baby chickens and listening to their horrific sound every morning." He set the paper down and rested his folded hands on it. "Let me think about it. It might not be a bad idea to raise some chickens to eat anyway."

Happy tears burned in Dylan's eyes, and her heart whispered old forgotten feelings toward her father. He had no understanding of her need for these baby chickens. With them, there was hope of friendship and acceptance. Two things Dylan was starving for.

"Thank you." Dylan took a step to hug her father, but he raised the paper higher and dismissed her with a wave.

CHAPTER 9

Jeremy Biggs
Present Day

JEREMY DIDN'T TAKE THE day off work despite his raging headache and the pit in his gut refusing to go away. The cops had come by again last night asking more questions, which led to another night of binge drinking. He stood in the kitchen where the smells of frying garlic, basil, and simmering tomato sauce threatened to bring the dry heaves back with a vengeance. One of the chefs chopped vegetables nearby. The sound of the sharp knife hitting the cutting board reverberated through his aching head. Jeremy folded napkins and filled parmesan cheese shakers to put them on the tables while trying to listen in on his boss interviewing a man slightly younger than himself. If Jeremy remembered correctly, he had graduated from the local high school a few years behind him. Still, Jeremy wasn't one to pay attention to the freshmen or sophomores, or anyone for that matter. He was a loner, except for his friend, David Miller.

The kid being interviewed slid his references across the table to Carlo, a burly Italian man wearing a white dress shirt and a tie wrapped too tightly around his thick neck. His boss scanned the resume, but Jeremy knew the kid named Allen would be working at the restaurant with him no matter what the paper stated. They needed someone with contacts and a lack of morals. If Jeremy remembered correctly, this kid was the perfect fit.

Carlo glanced over his readers at Allen, who shifted uncomfortably under the weight of the man's stare.

Carlo flicked the paper with a meaty finger. "If I call these numbers, someone will vouch for you?"

"They sure will," Allen said with a nod.

Carlo set the paper down and stared a moment more. "When can you start?"

"I can start now if you need me."

Carlo cleared his throat before calling over his shoulder. "Jeremy."

Jeremy stepped out of the kitchen. "Yeah?" His voice was nearly inaudible.

"Show this guy around." Carlo locked back at Allen. "Well, go on. We'll deal with the paperwork later."

Allen climbed out of the booth and followed Jeremy to the back.

"You'll want to wear this," Jeremy said, holding out a large rubber apron. "You'll end up soaked with greasy water if you don't."

The kid slid the apron over his head.

"Jeremy, I'm heading out for a bit. You can leave when the dishes are done and someone from the dinner shift shows up," Carlo called.

"Got it." A doorbell chimed, signaling Carlo had left, and Jeremy exhaled in relief.

"How's he to work for?" Allen asked.

"Fine. I guess." Then he showed Allen where to find the supplies and put the clean pots and pans. "I think I recognize you from high school."

"I graduated a couple years behind you. I passed you in the halls, I'm sure."

Jeremy nodded. "It's a small school. I'm sure you did. I haven't seen you around town."

"My parents had me stay with my uncle and aunt for a while. That plan ran its course, so I'm back home to save up before getting my own place. What's your deal now?"

"About the same as yours, but a few years ahead of you on the savings thing." This wouldn't be a lie if his dad hadn't drained Jeremy's account to pay property taxes. That was the story anyway, and it may be true since no one had kicked them out of the trailer yet.

A silence followed. The kid wouldn't bring up his arrest, but why would he? Jeremy wasn't about to talk about his with him either. Allen's proved more embarrassing yet less detrimental. The police showed up at the school with their drug dogs. Allen was handcuffed and bent over the roof of his car in front of the school. All over one measly joint, from what Jeremy recalled. Allen had gotten off easy that time. Rumor was his uncle worked on the force nearby, which explained the wrist slap. If Jeremy remembered correctly, Allen got suspended and was back in class laughing off the scene within days. Allen was popular enough that his peers laughed with him. The next time Jeremy heard Allen ran into some trouble, Allen disappeared. That must have been when he was sent off to the uncle's house a few towns over.

Jeremy didn't have connections. When he and David

were caught with a similar amount of weed, it meant hours of community service. His dad had little money, and nothing saved for Jeremy's college. Jeremy and David occasionally hung out with some other kids, but the two of them were already bad news. As if criminal records were contagious, people kept their distance. His father let him know what he thought of the two of them. *Losers going nowhere, that's all you are. You'll be lucky if I visit you in jail.* What was the difference between the joint he got caught with and his dad's nightly whiskey?

After Jeremy and Allen washed and dried the last pan, the bell on the front door chimed. A young girl called out, "Where is everybody?"

Jeremy rolled his eyes as he hung up his heavy rubber apron and reached for Allen's. "That's Amber," Jeremy said. "Good chance she'll try to sleep with you before the week's out. Don't be too flattered. It seems to be a perk of working at Little Italy, but I'd stay as far away from her as possible."

"Did you have a run-in with her?"

"I've never been stupid enough. I can tell when someone is fishing for gossip just to take you down. I never took the bait."

Amber rounded the corner. Her T-shirt had been cut so short, Jeremy could almost see the bottom of her bra; that's assuming she wore one, which was doubtful.

"Where's Carlo..." When her gaze fell on Allen, her words seemed to stick in her throat. "Well, hello. Who's the new guy?" The question was aimed at Jeremy, but her eyes never left Allen.

"This is Allen. He's married."

Allen's gaze shot toward Jeremy in question. Amber

stretched her arm toward the kid, exposing a complete sleeve tattoo. He shook her hand while she scanned him up and down, smiling the entire time. "What are you, like twenty?"

"Twenty-one, actually."

Amber eyed him up and down with a scoff.

"It happens," Jeremy said.

"I don't see a ring."

"He doesn't wear it while washing dishes," Jeremy replied.

"Damn shame," Amber said over her shoulder as she left the kitchen.

Jeremy watched until she was out of earshot. "Trust me, I just saved you. Stay far away from that one."

"Noted."

"And trust me, if she knows something, then everyone in town will know it too unless she can blackmail you with her information."

"Well, I can't blame a girl for trying to make a buck."

"We'll see if you still feel that way in six months."

A smirk lingered on Allen's face. The smile reminded Jeremy of the one he wore when he returned to school after his suspension. Did this kid believe he was untouchable? Jeremy detested him, and yet something about him, the cockiness perhaps, reminded him of David. Maybe Allen should be reminded of where David's self-assurance had landed him.

Jeremy headed toward the door. "I'll see you back here tomorrow," he called over his shoulder. When Allen didn't respond, Jeremy looked back. Allen was heading into the kitchen, his eyes set on Amber.

CHAPTER 10

Eli Simmons
Present Day

Eli's phone alarm blasted through a dream, forcing it to slither into the recesses of his mind. Five o'clock. To complete the morning chores, such as feeding, he needed to be in the barn by six. He hit the snooze button and drifted back into a deep sleep until the alarm sounded again. He had stayed up too late setting up his camper and memorizing a picture of the list the girl had given him. There were too many details to remember in one night, but he had made headway. Eli sat up on the side of the bed and rubbed the sleepiness from his face before slipping on his jeans, old T-shirt, and jacket.

Eli stepped outside his camper into the chilly morning air. The end of summer brought with it unpredictable temperature drops as the earth let go of one season and embraced the next. Large maple trees surrounded the pasture. In the coming weeks, they would transform into brilliant colors. So much beauty surrounded him, yet the family across the street threatened to suck all of it into an abyss of sadness. He gave thanks for the cornfields blocking his view of the family while he sat in his camper, one with nature. More cornfields on the other side of the road served as a wall between them and their nearest neighbor. They could stay hidden, all of them, and the secrets they seemed to share.

He walked up the driveway. A light in the kitchen window shone in the darkness. He had beaten Conner to the barn, which should make his new employer happy. The squeak of the main door's hinge, followed by the slamming of the screen door, rang through the brisk air. Conner strutted across the yard and into the barn, not even looking up at Eli. The disregard unsettled him, but he had survived worse. Eli glanced at the sky; the stars twinkled on the dark backdrop. He took a deep breath, allowing the air to sting his lungs. As Eli exhaled, his breath created another cloud in the chilly morning air. He liked the sensation. He liked how he connected with the world and how the cold air changed when it reacted with his body. The idea grounded him.

Eli strolled into the barn, where the frozen air was thick with scents of hay and manure. The cows stood with their heads in their stanchions, tails swatting at imagined flies. The cool morning air made the insects slumber as though winter had already set in. Soon, the pesty bugs would go somewhere in the ground and wouldn't wake again until the spring sunshine welcomed them back. Conner had kept the cows in last night due to a frost warning. Eli suspected it also made the first full day with his newly hired help easier.

He went directly to the granary and filled the wheelbarrow. He needed to be speedy this time. The routines were necessary for the cows to drop their milk. Milking immediately followed their grain meal. With a deep breath, Eli lifted the heaping wheelbarrow and found his balance. The balance was the tricky part. He could handle the weight but throw in a hundred heads working against him, and the task bordered on impossible. Walking quicker helped, and he did just that. He set the wheelbarrow down in a spot near April and scooped out each specific amount—scoop, scoop, scoop. His actions were faster, and the cows had little time to work against him. He had this.

The milk house door thudded shut. Out of the corner of Eli's eye, he saw Conner walk behind him with the milkers. He needed to be faster—scoop, scoop, scoop. The wheelbarrow emptied, and Eli turned to refill it. Conner stood in the path between the manger and the milk house.

"Do you know how much I pay for grain?" His voice was shy of a shout. "The price of grain is more than the price of milk. Look at the damn list, and give them the amount I've written there, or I'll deduct your pay."

Eli stared blankly at his boss as he bit back his frustration. "Sorry, Mr. Phillips." Eli grabbed the list he had tucked between the metal and the grain. "I'll..." But when he looked up, Conner had moved on.

While Eli finished, Conner scraped the manure from under the cows and into the gutter behind them. The ripe smell of the sloshy feces filled the barn. Eli couldn't get used to the odor, especially in the months when the cows stayed inside more often. Tomorrow, he would eat plain toast before work. Maybe a banana.

After finishing his chore, Eli joined Conner and grabbed a stiff brown paper towel. He dipped it into a mixture of water and a blue cleansing agent and then stepped between the first two cows. Milk was already spraying out of the feces-covered teats. Eli struggled to hide his fear as he scrubbed away the dried-on remnants, and the cow kicked his hand. He adjusted his arm in a position that would protect him from another unexpected kick. Eli finished the task, then put the milker on the other cows, noting there were no marks telling him the milk was contaminated with medicines. In time, he would know which cows would kick and which would not, but he needed to be cautious with them for a while.

Conner spoke when necessary. Despite Eli's quiet nature, angry silences made him uncomfortable. The attention demanded by overseeing three milking machines while Conner watched three of his own took his mind off his boss's odd behavior.

As Eli stood, a wet, sloppy tail swatted him across the face. He fought the urge to vomit as he rushed to the pail and wiped his face with the stiff towel he'd dipped in the cleaner. The blue water had already faded to a gray and had debris floating on the top.

When he looked up, two young police officers stood at the end of the barn.

Eli cleared his throat, and when Conner looked his way, he pointed to the doorway.

His boss stood from between two cows and glanced down the barn. He mumbled, "Son of a bitch," before strolling toward them. "Watch my milkers." Conner grunted the words over his shoulder.

A young heifer kicked her milker off just as another

milker began to squawk, drawing his attention away from Conner. He darted from one milker to another, and when he next looked up, Conner was back, even more agitated.

"Piece of trash gets himself killed near my property, and I'm going to hear about it for years."

Eli swallowed hard. "Someone died?"

Conner glared at Eli under his unclipped eyebrows. "I wasn't talking to you."

"Sorry, sir, but..."

"I said I wasn't talking to you." Phillips grabbed a towel to wash another cow. "You might see some police dogs running around the fields today. That's all the liberties the authorities get to take on my property. Not that I have a choice," he mumbled. "But I'm not harvesting my damn corn before it's ready just so they can search the fields easier."

Conner slid between two cows, and other than the sound of pumping machines, the hours drifted by silently. When the chores were complete, Conner headed toward the door and then paused.

"Claire has lunch ready."

"Claire?"

"Yeah, my wife. Are you coming?"

"Yes." Eli stammered. "Thank you."

"Tell her that. I didn't make it."

Eli followed Conner into the house. He was curious whether the older man's mood would soften in the presence of his wife, but the tension grew as Conner pulled out a chair and sat in front of a plate left on the table.

Conner motioned to the other chair. "That's yours."

"Grilled cheese and tomato soup. A personal favorite."

Conner stuffed a quarter of the sandwich into his mouth. A small clock ticked the moments away uncomfortably.

"Will I be able to thank the hostess?"

Chewing slowly, Conner wiped his mouth with his napkin. He sat back, swallowed, and called to his wife. "Claire. Come meet..." Conner paused and looked at Eli as though he scrambled to recall his name.

"Eli. Eli Simmons."

"Come meet Eli."

The sound of shuffling feet, as if the woman wore slippers, came from the next room. Claire appeared in the doorframe, and as he predicted, she wore giant fluffy slippers and a tattered housecoat.

"Claire had a rough night, it seems. Hasn't managed the whole shower thing yet."

Claire edged closer and lifted a timid hand. "It's nice to meet you, Eli. I hope you like grilled cheese."

Eli shook her hand and let his hands drift back to his lap. "I love grilled cheese. And you cooked it to the perfect golden brown."

"It's a pretty easy meal." She shrugged off the compliment, refusing to make eye contact.

"It's still much appreciated. I'm happy to bring my lunch, though. I don't want to trouble you any."

"The hired men are always offered lunch and dinner when working. It's up to you if you want to eat with us or not," Claire said. "Not all the hired men choose to eat in here."

"Well, if you don't mind, I think I will take you up on your offer."

She nodded and began to turn away before stopping. "I saw a police car in the driveway."

Conner grunted. "We'll probably see more of them before this is over."

"Did they have any new information?"

"Not that they shared. They're just gonna run their dogs all over my corn until they dig something up."

The quiet that seeped in between their words petrified Eli. What secrets were they not discussing due to his presence? He wanted to hook up his camper and disappear from this place, but something held him back from deserting the Phillips family.

"Do I need to be afraid?" The words surprised everyone, especially Eli.

"What the hell do you have to be afraid of? Some druggy kid got himself murdered near my property. He ran with the wrong crowd, did some stupid shit, and turned my farm upside down. There ain't nothing to be afraid of here."

Claire wrung her hands as she stood beside the table.

"You can go back to whatever you were doing, Claire." Conner didn't look at his wife as he spoke.

"Nice to meet you again, Eli."

Conner stood, and Eli followed suit, lifting his plate as he did so.

"Leave it. Claire will take care of it."

Claire's body stiffened. If Eli weren't present, where would this scene end?

"I'll be late again tonight." Claire set her jaw as the words pierced the air.

"And why is that? The girls..."

"No, the girls don't need me. I'm meeting with my study group again."

Conner studied his wife. She stood with her back against the counter, not losing eye contact. "The same study group you were with last night?"

"Yes, it's always the same one."

Each minor sound echoed through the house in the silence. The heater kicked on and dry hot air rose from the floor vent. The clock ticked, and the house somehow creaked without the help of human movement. Eli looked from one to the other, and set his plate back on the table. Finally, Conner turned for the door and Eli followed closely behind. The screen door slammed shut behind them.

"You have a couple of hours before afternoon chores. Be back here at four."

Conner continued toward the barn.

"You sure you don't need any help?"

Conner kept walking. A crisp fall wind pushed against Eli's back and across the cornfields surrounding the farm. The corn swayed, opening and closing doors into the planted rows. A chill ran up Eli's spine. How did a hired man end up a corpse in the fields around the barn?

CHAPTER 11

Claire Phillips
Present Day

ER HUSBAND, SHE FEARED, could read her mind--or, worse yet, see into her heart. After Conner left the kitchen with their hired help, Claire's thoughts drifted back to the night before when Claire had sipped a glass of wine at the local pub. The women surrounding her were years younger, their skin still taut with an overabundance of collagen. They never glanced at their watches to check the time or appeared to wonder who was pacing the floors at home waiting for them. Their off hours were not eaten up by teenagers' bizarre and complex personalities, needing them and pushing them away simultaneously.

Claire had given up her life to raise children who wouldn't speak to her. Her husband barely spoke, either. He only barked out orders at their daughters or her. She woke, cooked, and cleaned, then cooked some more, cleaned some more, and finally went to bed to do it all over again the next day.

A year and a half ago, something inside her snapped. Claire didn't tell anyone about the epiphany until she knew she could follow through, and then, what she waited for arrived in the mail.

"I'm starting nursing school." She announced this fact after eating fried chicken and corn on the cob. The girls froze. Conner chewed his bite, swallowed, and slowly set down the half-eaten chicken leg.

"The hell you are."

"I *am* going to nursing school. I've applied and today, I received my acceptance letter."

Conner sat back in his chair, crossed his arms, and spoke through gritted teeth. "Have you not heard anything I've been telling you about our situation?"

"Oh, Conner, I've heard about our situation my entire married life. Nothing ever changes—until now. I'm changing things."

"And where are you getting the money for nursing school?"

"Financial aid."

"It's all covered?"

"Not all, but some. A good amount."

"We don't have a dime extra." Conner picked up his fork and stuffed a piece of chicken in his mouth. "You can't go to school now. That's final."

Claire straightened herself before replying. "Conner, I am going. If you can't find it within yourself to support me financially and emotionally, then I will pack my bags and leave." The words left her lips before she had considered what they would do to her girls. She pushed the guilt down. Something had to change, and if it meant walking away from them to come back stronger, then that's what she would do.

The room fell silent. The girls eyed each other over the table. The clock seconds ticked louder than Claire had thought possible.

Finally, she stood and began clearing away dishes. The meal was over whether everyone had finished or not.

"Come on, girls, we've got milking to do."

The girls stood and put on their boots. Claire's back remained to them as she scrubbed the dishes piled in the sink. She fought back the tears until the screen door slammed shut and then broke down in heaving sobs.

"Are you okay, Mom?" Dylan's presence startled her. She quickly grabbed a tissue from her apron pocket and wiped her tears, never turning to face her daughter.

"I am now. Go help your father. Everything's going to be okay." Dylan walked out the door, leaving her alone.

Now, a year and a half later, she still believed in her decision. It had been so long since everything was okay with their family Claire feared her girls had forgotten what normal looked like. She had to fix it, but first, she had to fix the broken parts inside herself. Claire had nothing to give to anyone, just as Conner had nothing to give to her. Her state of being wasn't what she would call depressed, more like adrift. Her mind was always somewhere else and nowhere at the same time. She didn't linger on the past often because it was too painful. Claire survived by not actually living at all. She was numb.

Sometimes, during dinner, when she heard the scraping of forks on plates and the sounds of chewing undercooked vegetables, she inwardly screamed at herself to wake up if only for her girls. They looked gothic, lost behind their hair, and shared somber glances with each other. Where had the sound of their laughter gone? She didn't need to ask. She knew.

Years had passed since the light in their family's life had been extinguished. Since then, things at home spiraled even more than Claire would have imagined possible. The worst part about it all was that Claire didn't care anymore. They were all adrift in an ocean of nothingness, waiting to be engulfed by it.

But she had finally found something to cling to, and she'd be damned if she let go of it to save people who weren't attempting to save themselves. How did she become this person? She would have walked through fire for her family before, but now, when it came down to survival, she had nothing left for anyone but herself.

As she stood in the bar last night, a small piece of her remembered how to breathe. She'd glanced around the bar at the young women, all of them carefree and laughing. She wanted nothing more than to be one of them. To forget about the farm, the bills, and the children who drifted in and out of the house like ghosts with attitudes. She wanted a fresh start, a chance to be someone else entirely.

But it wasn't only the friends and classes making her feel alive. Standing in her slippers in the cold kitchen, her face flushed as she revisited the forbidden memories that she both savored and feared. Claire had been laughing at something one of her newfound friends had said when he bumped her arm and said, "What's so funny?" Nolan Dempsey was the only male nursing student in their class and a good ten years younger than she was. Throughout the year and a half, he'd been in several classes. The first time she noticed him, he triggered an old feeling of longing that her body had become unaccustomed to. At first, she didn't associate the feeling with him as much a rekindled sensation associated with her younger self. But as the semester went on, she began looking for him in the crowds, hoping he could trigger that feeling of life and desire again. She allowed the feelings to grow thinking them harmless, maybe even helpful, but she had lost control of the feelings and as she stood in the bar last night, they were powerful enough to ruin everything.

Her heart skipped a beat, and she stumbled with finding words clever enough to sound relaxed when she was anything but. The adrenaline rush that overtook her threatened her family and her reputation. She was vulnerable, and the feeling was intoxicating.

She'd glanced up into his smiling blue eyes. "I'm not sure I can share our secret jokes with you." In truth, she couldn't have shared the joke because when the women were speaking, she had been lost in a different world. Her laughter was merely a mimicked expression.

"Be that way." He glanced at her glass. "Almost empty. Chardonnay?"

"I shouldn't have another."

Nolan had already caught the female bartender's attention with the slightest lift of his hand.

"She'll have another glass of whatever she's drinking."

The waitress nodded, and Claire downed the final sip.

"Thanks, I guess. You might be getting me in trouble."

"How's that? You deserve a night out now and then. What are you missing back home anyway?"

Claire envisioned her family and their nine o'clock routine. The chores would have ended about an hour ago. They would have showered and maybe had another bite of the crockpot meal she had left. Conner would be reclined in his chair watching some sport she didn't care about, and the girls would hide in their rooms pretending to do schoolwork.

"Nothing."

"Exactly. Drink up."

Melony shot Claire a look that said, *You go, girl*, in the childish, single-woman mindset she had. Melony didn't live by the rules. Her motto seemed to be *If it's fun, do it*. Since she had never met Conner, Dylan, or Jessie, they didn't exist. Nolan's wavy dark hair, dimpled cheeks, and tight backside were free to take in Melony's world. On the other hand, Claire had made vows. But when she'd spoken those promises on her wedding day, how was she to know all the horrid experiences life would throw at her and Conner and how those things would change them into two unrecognizable people?

All she knew was she wanted out. Last night, she'd stared at the young man vying for her attention and glimpsed light shining through a cracked door. Claire's lips parted into a smile as she clinked her glass to Nolan's bottle. He then raised his drink to his lips. She'd studied the movement of his Adam's apple as it rose and fell, letting the liquid pass into his system.

Nolan then set the bottle on the bar and took her hand. "What do you say we dance?"

CHAPTER 12

Conner Phillips
Present Day

CONNER TOSSED STRAW UNDER the cows lining one side of the barn. They could go outside tonight; it wouldn't be overly cold, but chores were easier if they stayed in a bit more while Eli settled into the job. Jessie finished washing the milkers and headed inside, and Eli finished bedding the cows on the other side of the barn.

"Can I help you finish your side?" Eli asked.

"You head on back to your camper. I'll finish up on my own." His voice, usually laced with anger, was surprisingly calm. Conner, who had grown accustomed to his own harsh tone, found the change just as surprising as anyone else would. Somehow, Eli's tranquil qualities soothed the turmoil Conner sensed within himself. A piece of him wanted to fight this feeling off, but he was too exhausted.

"You have a nice night, Mr. Phillips. I'll see you bright and early tomorrow morning."

"See you tomorrow, Eli."

Eli stopped before stepping out into the night.

"Mr. Phillips..."

"You can call me Conner."

"Very well, Conner. Do you mind if I say something?"

Conner's insides clenched. What now? Couldn't he have one moment of quiet in his mind?

"I understand your fear of change, having your wife go off and start a career, but she's probably scared of the change, too."

"Eli, I'm going to say this once, my marriage is not your business."

"My apologies. It's just that maybe if you asked about..."

"Goodnight, Eli."

"Goodnight, Conner."

As Eli drifted into the darkness, Conner plunged the pitchfork into the last hay bale.

What Claire and Eli didn't know when she served Eli his first lunch in their cold kitchen was Conner was seething inside from the night before when he had tried to reach out. After another long, hard day, Conner had stretched out on his old recliner. The material had worn so thin Claire had found a somewhat matching throw blanket to lay over what was weeks away from becoming an outright hole.

He flipped through the channels while intermittently checking the clock. Claire should have been home hours before. Ever since the night she announced she was going to nursing school, the tiny connection she had left to their family disappeared. She was somewhere else—a stranger. He could hardly blame her. For each small fortune made, five misfortunes followed. Grain bills were skyrocketing, but the cost of milk remained the same, or at least his portion of the profits did. Machinery broke, cows gave birth to bulls sold off instead of turning into investments, and the weather mocked him during planting and harvesting time. The weight of his isolation pressed down on him, suffocating his spirit.

Music blared from the girls' bedroom as if warning him not to come near. Part of him wanted them to keep their doors closed, to not step out of their secretive worlds until chores or school demanded they do so. He couldn't stand the look of disappointment in their eyes. He had failed them. Moments that might otherwise have been memorable sat in the path of their family's life like debris on the road. Could he change a memory? No. He could only move forward. Tomorrow, the cows would need milking, the bills would need paying, and everyone in his family needed to do their part. How could Claire be so selfish? How could she walk away from a commitment? No. Not a commitment. A vow. His frustration boiled over, threatening to consume him.

Conner slammed down the remote and grabbed his keys and jacket off the hooks Claire had created back when she cared. The girls would never know he had left. He slid behind the wheel and headed into the town six miles away. There were only a few places Claire could be at this hour in their small town; one was the local pub, The Watering Hole. Anger welled inside of him. His hands held the steering wheel so tightly they were turning white. This mood would not work. He needed to calm himself. He sucked in a deep breath.

The old telephone poles lined the dark road, and he scanned the roadside for deer. In the distance, he spotted four or five sets of glowing eyes. They stood still, watching him as intently as he watched them.

What would he say to his wife, who felt like a stranger to him, if he found her in the pub? As a few deep breaths calmed his frustration, he knew what to do. He would go to the bar, order her a drink, and send it to her table, where she would be sitting laughing with the other nursing students. She would look up, expecting an angry husband, but not tonight. He would smile and toast her in the air with his own drink. She would smile at him like she used to forever ago and walk up to him at the bar. If he did everything just right, maybe she would remember the old them, too.

Conner parked his car in front of The Watering Hole. The sound of an acoustic guitar and a male voice singing a slow country song spilled from inside. As he pushed open the door, a surge of hope and anticipation washed over him. He scanned the bar, his eyes landing on a corner table where several young women were engaged in lively conversation. Empty glasses littered the table, but Claire was not among the women. He continued his search, his heart sinking with each empty table. Perhaps he had come to the wrong place. He walked further in, his arm resting on the bar, his gaze sweeping the room.

"Can I get you something?" A young female bartender wiped her hands on a bar towel.

"I'm looking for..." and that's when he saw his wife. She was wrapped in a young man's embrace as they slowly spun in circles on the dance floor, her ear pressed against his chest, her eyes closed, and her lips tilted into a smile Conner did not recognize anymore. The scene starkly contrasted with the image he had painted in his mind, a painful realization of the distance between them. His disappointment was palpable, a heavy weight on his heart.

"Sir, can I..."

"No. You can't," Conner snapped before turning to the door. Did Claire hear the squeal of his tires as he sped away? Did she care?

CHAPTER 13

Eli Simmons
Present Day

Eli crossed the country road and walked to his camper in the back of the pasture, which was not visible from the house. The privacy worked for him, but he suspected Conner also appreciated the separation. On his way through the field, he picked up sticks and then tossed them into the firepit he'd made of a circle of stones. Conner had given a "Whatever" approval of his fire. Eli wasn't sure his boss had even heard his request, but Eli had done his part by asking.

He opened the door to the 1979 Komfort nineteen-foot trailer, which had been his home for over a decade. Small areas of rust had started to eat away at the exterior, but overall, the camper had held up well. Eli took pride in the upkeep, especially since he had promised Mr. Burkett, his former employer, he would take excellent care of it. A framed picture of Mr. and Mrs. Burkett hung on the wall by his kitchen nook. Their picture and an old sign that read, "All that wander are not lost," were the only wall decorations he had added to the camper decor. He liked having the Burketts watching over him as he traveled from family to family, never planting roots. They grounded him without ever making him stay still.

How many years had passed since Mr. Burkett's death? A few years later, Mrs. Burkett died in a nursing home. Eli had to think about his age and the passing years since no one consistently celebrated them with him, and he wasn't much about keeping calendars.

His first birthday memory was one with his favorite foster family. They didn't have other children, or at least they hadn't when they took him in, but he suspected the pregnancy was what ended their need to foster him any longer. At least in front of him, they were always happy and acted in love. The mom had made him a cake that looked like a yellow smiley face and tasted of lemon, served with heaps of vanilla ice cream on top. He could still see his foster parents smiling as they sang "Happy Birthday" to him. He was eight. He remembered other birthdays since that one. Still, they did not compare, maybe because discovering for the first time that such a thing as a birthday celebration existed was the most intriguing aspect of the experience. He didn't crave attention and, in fact, found that part of it uncomfortable. He was thirty-two now, and the only way he knew his age was because his license reminded him.

Eli sat on the camper's metal step and untied his shoes. The cows were in a different pasture today, so he couldn't entertain himself by watching them through the camper's small windows. He had other things to do, anyway.

He stepped up into the kitchen area, listening to the familiar creaking sounds of the camper. Above the tiny kitchen sink was a window. Eli carefully tugged the weathered, floral curtains together, closing out the world. Above the window was a cross left over from when the Burketts used the camper for family vacations. With his hands curled around the sink edge, he bowed his head. "Lord, you have been with me in very dark times and places of my life. I am once again in a place where I don't feel you. I only feel darkness, but I know you are here. Let me know if I should run from here or if, in some way, I am needed. I'm unsettled around these people, but if this is your will, give me strength to fulfill my purpose in the place you have sent me."

Eli breathed in deeply and let the air slowly escape his lungs. He repeated this exercise many times before some of the weight inside of him lifted. How was he to sleep tonight knowing that a body was decaying somewhere in the cornfields surrounding his temporary home? And who had killed the man they referred to as David Miller? He thought about how Claire tensed around her husband, and fear started to creep back into his emotions. Eli looked back up at the cross. He had prayed, and now he would wait and listen.

He went to the kitchen cupboard, pulled out a blue-speckled coffee cup, and started the coffee maker, hoping the hot beverage would chase away the chill in his body. Eli headed to the bathroom while the machine prepared to spit out its hot, dark liquid. He needed to shower, despite having to return to the barn within the next few hours. He seldom resented his tiny shower with its small water tank and limited generator, but today, he fought to find the positive in his life. It was rare, this feeling of disquiet.

He stripped off his clothes, threw on a towel, and tossed his filthy clothes in a bin kept outside the camper door. On

Sunday, he would go into town and use the laundromat. He didn't need much, but his home needed to be tidy, no matter how old and run down. The task didn't prove too difficult since he owned so few items.

He slid into the shower stall only when the steam filled the room. The smell of manure increased as the water loosened the filth from his skin. Finally, the water won the battle, and he scrubbed until his skin became raw. Eventually, he began to feel clean and fresh.

After slipping on clean jeans, a T-shirt, and his jacket, he returned to the kitchen and poured his coffee. With his fingers curled around the steamy cup, he walked outside and sat on his metal stoop again. Eli pulled out his phone. He didn't have a strong signal, which generally didn't bother him much, but today, he wanted to research what had happened on the Phillips farm before his arrival. Finding an article about the neighbor's dog and a jawbone didn't take long. The warmth the coffee had created within him dissipated. He put his phone down and focused on the nature surrounding him.

At first, the land seemed quiet, but the world came alive when he surrendered to his senses. Birds, invisible to him before, flitted from branch to branch, chirping out a language he wished he could understand. Squirrels chased each other up tree trunks and along the limbs. Clouds floated across the late afternoon sun. He swallowed his coffee and embraced the warm sensation as it traveled down his throat and into his stomach. He took another deep breath and allowed himself to embrace the settled feeling despite the voices wanting to torture him with doubt and fear. All was well, or at least, it would be.

~~*~~

When Eli walked up the driveway for afternoon chores, the younger daughter strolled toward the barn. She wore dark blue sweatpants and an old green jacket. Her shoulders slumped, and her boots shuffled along the gravel.

Eli began whistling one of his favorite tunes to get her attention. He had yet to be introduced to her and thought now would be a good time. She disappeared into the barn without looking back. His mood darkened to meet her coldness. Her energy could so easily rub off on him, but then he remembered the transference could go both ways. With a deep breath, he recentered, imaging the birds and squirrels. He wouldn't let the Phillips family change him.

For the nighttime chores, Conner often joined in late with the milking since one of his daughters would be there to help. He tooled away in a shed off to the side of the barn or worked on farm equipment demanding attention. Eli needed to take this opportunity to get to know Jessie. Instead of going right to the job of graining, he followed the sounds of metal clinking together in the milk house. When Eli gently swung the door open, Jessie spun around to face him. Her eyes bulged, and her face paled. For a moment, Eli froze, not knowing how to proceed. Why was she so on edge?

"Um, I wanted to introduce myself."

She stared at him without uttering a word.

"I'm Eli Simmons."

Still nothing.

"I believe your name is Jessie."

She nodded.

"Well, it's nice to meet you, Jessie." Eli smiled a smile

he considered charming and disarming. "I guess I'll go start graining the cows." He turned toward the haymow, which held the granary.

As the door was about to close, he heard her voice. An almost inaudible whisper. "Okay." He would not consider her one-word response a success story, but he would take it.

A half-hour later, the milkers were on the cows, and he and Jessie worked awkwardly side by side.

"Hey, do you mind if I run to my camper? I'll be back in under five minutes. I just put the milkers on the cows so they..."

"Go if you want to."

Another success. Sort of.

He returned with a speaker. "What do you listen to?'

Jessie paused, a dripping cloth in one hand, her brown eyes staring through her thick, long bangs.

"I like the Lumineers."

"Me too." Eli scrolled the playlist, hit a few buttons, and the lyrics chased the creepy atmosphere from the barn. "Good taste."

"My sister likes them, too."

Wow. These were Jessie's first words that went beyond an expected response.

"I'll have to play some of their music tomorrow if it's her turn to do the chores."

Jessie nodded and bent to wash off the next cow.

"What do you do when it's your night off?" Eli asked.

"Homework. Clean the house."

"You two will leave here with a good work ethic, that's for sure."

"What do you mean?"

"Work ethic. You'll know how to work hard. That gets you far in life."

"You must not have had a good work ethic."

Eli was stunned into laughter.

"I wasn't kidding. No one with good ethics becomes a hired man."

A million questions raced through Eli's mind. "Well, first of all, whatever job you end up doing, you should do it with good work ethics, and secondly, sometimes it's not only your ethics keeping you from becoming a neurosurgeon."

"So, you're not bright?"

"I'm content with my IQ." Anger began to gurgle inside of him, but negative emotion would get him nowhere, and after all, he was the adult. "Sometimes, life throws a person some curve balls. It has a way of taking you exactly where you're supposed to be."

Jessie switched the cow's milker and went to the pail for a new cloth. For a moment, Eli feared the conversation had ended.

"This is your life goal, then?"

"I'm happy."

Jessie looked at him through slanted eyes. "Then you're crazy, just like the rest of them." The words were hissed rather than spoken.

Something about the way she spoke sent a shiver down his spine.

"Are the hired men that bad?"

"The dead ones are the best ones."

Eli froze. How the hell was he supposed to respond to

that statement? Was she referring to the guy whose jawbone was found on the property or some other nightmarish hired help? Conner's voice split through the air before he could speak.

"Jessie," he called. "Go feed the calves and then take the night off. Don't you have a test to study for or something?"

"Fine with me," she mumbled. She slithered off toward the calf barn to grab the pails. What had happened? Why didn't Conner want her to finish that admittedly odd conversation?

As Eli tended to the milking machines, he watched her walk back and forth from the small barn to the milk house where they stored the formulated milk. On one of her last trips, their gazes locked. What he saw behind her eyes was sadness, begging him to be different, demanding he stay and rescue her from something. But what could that something be? He was sure of only one thing, and that was he was not giving up on this family.

CHAPTER 14

Jessie Phillips
Present Day

JESSIE RACED THROUGH THE bitterly cold air and into the house that stood silent. Tears formed in the corners of her eyes. Why was everything so messed up? It hadn't always been this way. Not before. Before all the stuff that no one talked about. It's like her whole family died that day. She raced into the bathroom and slammed the door shut, locking out people who would never bother to come to check on her anyway. She stripped down and stepped into the scalding hot water, watching her skin turn pink. Her loofah sponge hung on one of the three hooks. She grabbed it and began scrubbing away the pain, the secrets, the betrayals. But she couldn't. She was incapable of performing miracles, and bringing her family back to life would be nothing short of one.

Once finished, she toweled off and slipped into her flannel pajamas, which had once been Dylan's. Most of her clothes were once her older sister's. They were close, sort of. However, since that day, Dylan had been transforming into a parent rather than a sibling. They used to run through the fields giggling and making forts. They would race their

Matchbox cars down ramps their father built. He would even join them and hoot and holler when his car won. Their mother would smile and very occasionally join in. They were poor but happy, and since Jessie wasn't aware of finances back then, she hadn't worried about money and bankruptcy; she only knew their life was good.

Outside, on the dark autumn night, fall leaves drifted to the ground. Instead of triggering memories of piles of leaves, carved pumpkins, and ghost stories told by their father next to his makeshift fire pit, Jessie only envisioned real ghosts and death. Death was everywhere, even in the living. She curled up in bed with her novel, leaving studies for another day, and tried to forget them, to forget everything. After a short time, her eyes struggled to stay open, and her mind drifted from her story into strange dreams. Her book crashed to the floor, waking her.

Male voices drifted up toward her window. She crept toward the sound and parted the curtains. Down below, the usually dormant fire pit was aglow once more. Her father and the hired man sat in chairs on either side. This interaction was strange and new. Her father never invited the help for a drink by the fire. Did he sense something different about Eli as well? A welcome reprieve from the line of hoodlums who had passed through their barn doors. Could there be hope despite the canines traipsing their fields looking for body parts that refused to surface?

Dylan entered the room and eased up beside Jessie as if knowing her thoughts. Dylan peeked through the window momentarily and backed away, turning Jessie to face her.

"Don't trust him, Jessie. They're all bad, and we're on our

own to protect each other." Jessie couldn't help but freeze under her stare. "You believe me, don't you?"

Jessie nodded and swallowed hard.

"Dylan, do you think…"

"Don't even say it, Jessie."

"But he was really mad. I've never seen him so mad."

"David Miller was trash, and whatever happened to him, he deserved." Dylan took a deep breath, calming herself. "Jessie, people are capable of anything when pushed too far, but no, I don't think Dad killed him."

Jessie stared back at her sister through teary eyes.

"Everything is going to be okay. I promise. Go back to bed, and things will seem better in the morning." Dylan's tone was one of a strict-but-caring parent Jessie craved. Jessie watched her sister pull her bedroom door shut, and then gazed back out the window. As she did, her father got up and left, and Eli's attention turned toward her window. His curious stare startled her, and she let the curtain fall back in place. What if Dylan was wrong? What if this man had been sent to their family for a reason?

CHAPTER 15

Eli Simmons
Present Day

T HE NIGHT AIR BIT through Eli's clothes as he
grabbed one last haybale to be used to bed the cows.
Another day was over, but the Phillips farm still felt as off
as the previous day. Conner kept the cows in again for the
night. As the nights grew colder, this practice became more
common, and the chore of pitching the bedding under the
animals was a nightly occurrence. Eli dragged the hay to
the barn floor and cut the strings. Using his pitchfork, he
fluffed the golden straws. The comforting aroma wrapped
around him. The cows he cared for were clean and well-fed.
He would sleep well knowing he had offered them comfort
as they stood until they surrendered to sleep in the tiny part
of the barn.

When he walked by one of the cows known as Twenty-
Three, he patted her on the head. "See you in the morning,
old girl." He paused, and his hand lingered on the tuft of
hair where small horns would be if the farmers allowed
them to grow. He looked the animal in the eyes. Her
soft, oversized eyes stared back at him. He didn't see the
manure-covered mammal that enjoyed torturing him by

tipping wheelbarrows. Instead, he saw a creature strapped in a stanchion. Once winter was in full force, her moments outside would be limited until spring allowed her to be released back into the pastures. Eli again patted the tuft of hair on her bony head.

"You'll get through this, old lady. We always do."

"You want a drink?"

The words came out of nowhere. Eli spun around to face Conner. How long had his boss been watching him?

"A drink would be great." Eli seldom drank, but the opportunity to get to know his mysterious boss was too valuable to pass up.

Conner turned toward the door. Eli's hand slid away from the old Holstein, and he followed Conner outside. In the backyard, a fire blazed in a makeshift fire pit, and two lawn chairs sat on either side.

"You drink bourbon?" Conner asked, already pouring some into a foggy water glass.

"On occasion. What's the make?" The make mattered little to Eli. Bourbon would remain a putrid liquid no matter the label on the bottle.

"It's cheap shit. You got a problem with it?"

"It's the only kind I drink." Eli took the glass from Conner and settled into one of the lawn chairs. One broken strap hung beneath the seat, making him a bit more uncomfortable than this quiet moment with Conner already was.

Conner settled into his chair and let out a long sigh. "This business isn't for the faint of heart. But you've lasted more than a day. Thought we should toast it at least."

"Here's to me sticking it out." Eli raised his glass.

The fire crackled between them.

"So, Eli, what brought you to Derby?"

"I can't say, to be honest. Sometimes, it just happens to be where my truck leads me. I like autumn in the north, where the leaves are more colorful. Maybe that's what drew me here."

Conner eyed him through the smoke. "You aimlessly travel around with your truck and camper? Don't you have family?"

"I was raised in the foster system. I have no recollection of my father and possibly a hazy one of my mother. I'm not sure if the memory is of her or a foster mom. Doesn't matter, I suppose."

Conner gulped his drink but didn't respond for a bit. After a few moments, he said, "Well, I guess you've seen your own bit of trouble in your days then."

"I'm sure we all have."

Conner nodded. "Yes, we have." They watched the flame snap and spit ashes into the air. "What makes you want to work on a farm?"

"It's what got me out of foster care. I ran into a farmer who had a room for me to stay in and work for me, too. Farming is the only work I've ever done. It's been good to me: farm life, the animals, the physical work, being outdoors. It keeps me busy and pays the few bills I have."

"Maybe you're not as dumb as I thought."

Eli swallowed his rebuttal. He couldn't allow his pride to wreck the moment.

Conner took another swig and set the glass on the arm of

his lawn chair while he studied Eli. "You asked about David Miller."

"I can't help but be a bit curious, but forgive me if I've overstepped my bounds."

"You didn't, but I would rather not discuss the whole situation. We've had enough hoodlums at this farm for a lifetime."

"I'm not a hoodlum, Conner. I can promise you that." Eli paused and dared to jump into the waters, knowing he could drown. "Was David as bad as everyone says? Your daughters seem to hate all hired men."

"My daughters are reaching the years when they hate everyone." He paused and took a sip. "The hired men, they've all had their issues, David included, but I don't know what happened to that kid. I wish I did. But his death didn't really surprise anyone. David Miller's ending was written a long time ago. I only wish it didn't involve my family. I've got cops crawling all over me, pushing me to harvest the corn immediately. I'm not wrecking my crop over some punk who got himself killed. I harvest in a couple of weeks anyway. They can wait."

Eli glanced around at the cornfields on either side of them. "What happened with the canine unit?"

"They couldn't find a damn thing." Conner glanced out at the swaying stalks. "I suppose if a guy's jawbone is in one of my fields, there's a good chance the rest of his body is nearby. But the guy's dead, and he's probably been dead since the day he went missing. Waiting a couple of weeks from discovering the first bone won't change a damn thing, and the cops know it. At least their threats to shut down my whole damn farm have subsided. They're a bunch of country boys that understand that cows need to be milked and manure needs to be spread even if it may happen on a crime scene."

"Can't say I disagree with you. Bit creepy, though. Having someone's body out there waiting to be discovered."

"This place has felt like death for so many years. The fact there has actually been one doesn't surprise me." He took his last swallow and poured another glass, filling his three-quarters of the way. "You ready for more?"

"I should stick with one."

"Suit yourself." Conner's tone carried more disdain than his words. "You go to the bars often?"

"I'm not much of a drinker, and I'm pretty wiped out by the time I finish the chores."

Conner nodded and appeared to contemplate his following words. "I was pretty short with you the other night when you brought up Claire."

"As I said, sometimes I overstep my bounds. I apologize."

"You did overstep." He watched the flames dance upon the logs. "I tried, you know, to reach out to her. But things fell apart."

"How so?"

"Claire's hanging out in bars at night. Can you believe that?"

"What makes you think that? Eli studied Conner's expression. Did he fear his wife was being unfaithful? His boss's eyes had a hint of anger, but even more than that, Eli saw his sadness in the way his shoulders drooped. Eli was sure of one thing; Conner loved his wife. "Maybe she just needs some time with friends."

"She tells me she's with her study group." The tone dripped with sadness. "If she is, they're doing anything but studying. My wife, the mother of my children, is off drinking with her nursing friends right now." Then the anger returned. He took another swig from his glass. "And nurses aren't all chicks anymore."

Elli nodded, confirming more to himself than to Conner that his boss questioned his fidelity.

Conner leaned forward and stoked the fire with a stick. The fire hissed before letting off a loud pop and shooting a flame in their direction. "The problems keep piling up, one after another. I guess she's so sick of dealing with them she's decided to become one of them."

"Sorry, Conner. I'm not quite sure what to say."

"Not much you can say, I guess. But if you ever find yourself at The Watering Hole, I'd appreciate you telling me what you see."

So, this is what the friendly drink by the fire was about. Conner wanted Eli to spy on his wife.

"I can do that for you." Eli's words surprised even him.

Conner threw the remnants of his drink on the fire, and the air between them lit up. When it died down again, Conner was standing.

"Throw some water on that before you leave, will you?" Then he turned and walked into the house.

A feeling washed over Eli. Someone was watching him. When he looked at the upstairs window, Jessie was staring back at him. Did the girls, like Conner, suspect their mother was being unfaithful? If he discovered Claire had secrets, could he share them with Conner and destroy the girls even more? The curtain fell back in place, and the hint of Jessie's shadow disappeared into the room's depth.

CHAPTER 16

Dylan Phillips
Past

*D*YLAN'S FATHER NOT ONLY *caved easily to her request to get chickens, but he responded quickly as well. The day after she had asked him, she stepped into the barn and heard the subtle clucking of hens. She ran to the coop that had stood empty for years. Three red chickens and a rooster pecked at the straw thrown across the coop floor. She turned excitedly to find her dad, but she didn't have to run far. He stood behind her with something resembling a smile on his face.*

"Don't forget, these things are your responsibility."

"I know," she called over her shoulder as she raced to the house. "Mom, can I have a friend over?"

Her mother froze, holding a dish towel, and stared at her daughter as if she were a stranger. "You want a friend to come here?"

"Yes, please."

"Of course. I'd love that. Will your friend be staying for dinner?" Dylan ignored the slight expression of panic on her mom's face as she looked at the bland hamburger meat on the counter. Her mother would make meatloaf despite knowing no one would be happy about it.

"Mom, how would I know? I haven't even asked her yet." Dylan's fingers punched in the numbers on their family phone. Her parents had refused cell phones, which Dylan figured had more to do with cost than anything else.

An hour later, Marybeth stood beside Dylan inside the coop. They named their new friends Gertrude, Beatrice, and Lady Bella. They named the rooster Buck. The hens all looked quite similar except for the little bits of white on their back feathers.

"I can't believe you get to be around all of these animals every day." Marybeth's arms shot up in exclamation.

"You know, it's not all fun and games. I work hard after school, on weekends, and all summer. You might not like it as much if you had to do the milkings and feedings, plus clean up after them."

"Oh, boohoo. This is my heaven. I'd rather hang out with the animals than hang out with most people, present company excluded, of course."

"Of course." Her heart fluttered in excitement despite the voice in her head warning her feelings this good never last.

"Show me everything," Marybeth exclaimed. "Can I help milk the cows?"

Dylan laughed. "You're crazy, but yes, I guess you can. It's Jessie's turn tonight, so we can do what we want and then leave."

"Perfect."

The girls walked out into the main barn. "The cows are getting their grain now. Then we all eat dinner before the cows get milked."

As if on cue, David Miller rounded the corner, pushing a

heaping wheelbarrow full of grain. He wore jeans that hung low on his hips, with the inseam dropping ten inches down his leg. Dylan assumed that beneath the sagging pants were dingy briefs, though they were thankfully concealed by a dark green T-shirt with a stretched-out collar. Her expression tightened at the sight of him.

David set the wheelbarrow down and stared at Marybeth. "Whoa! What's this? One of you nerds actually has a friend."

"Just because I don't bring people out to the barn doesn't mean I don't have friends."

"And it doesn't mean you do, does it?"

"You're an ass."

Marybeth laughed out loud, clearly shocked at Dylan's boldness.

"Oh my. You had better hope your daddy doesn't hear you talk like that, Dylan. And listen, don't take it personally. I never much cared for the kids in school either." He picked up the wheelbarrow and headed down the manger.

"Don't mind him. He's just the latest piece of crap we had to hire."

"He doesn't seem that bad. Maybe he was connecting with you, not picking on you."

Dylan glanced down the manger as David scooped out the grain, stopped, yelled at a cow, and continued his chore. Was it possible? She hadn't really given him much of a chance. David then swatted the cow in the head, reaffirming her distaste.

After the tour, Dylan and Marybeth went inside to help set the table for dinner. Fitting six people around their small kitchen table was a tight squeeze, but Dylan would have sat on the floor just to have her friend stay. David didn't always join them for meals; he was a recluse, and Dylan recognized that he was probably being honest about not having friends in school. Aside from the one who dropped him off and picked him up, Dylan had never heard David mention anyone else. Even now, years after graduating from high school, David remained a loner.

The kitchen was filled with energy. Dylan was excited about meatloaf, boxed mashed potatoes, and green beans from a can, which she generally only tolerated. The aromas made her house feel like a home, and her mother danced around the kitchen like a weight had been lifted from her shoulders. Dylan knew what had weighed her down. But for once, Claire's oldest daughter portrayed a normal teenager that fit in with her peers.

Meals at the house were often quiet. They ate, then cleaned up while whoever had barn chores drifted out the door. But tonight, there was chatter. Even David spoke, asking Marybeth where she was from and where she lived; small talk, but Dylan sensed he was also interested.

Marybeth's presence lit a fire in her family, illuminating parts of each of them Dylan had not seen in forever. When Marybeth praised the meatloaf, Claire nearly blushed before adding that her secret ingredient was sausage.

"Sausage makes everything better," she announced with a smile.

Conner smiled with pride at his wife. "Well, aren't you creative?"

Her parents locked eyes momentarily before Claire looked down to adjust her napkin. Had her mother actually placed her napkin on her lap? She glanced over at Marybeth, whose napkin was not visible beneath the table. Dylan grabbed the wad she had tossed by her plate, placed it on her lap, and smoothed it out.

Her father set his fork beside his plate. "Marybeth, why was the basketball court all wet?"

"Excuse me?" she asked.

Dylan studied her father. "Dad, please don't tell me you're telling a dad joke." But that's not what she was thinking, not at all. Inside, Dylan beamed, and across the table, Jessie watched her father in amazement.

"I don't know. Why was the court all wet." Marybeth's eyes danced with amusement.

"Because the basketball players dribbled all over it."

Her laugh danced around them, and soon they were all laughing. Even David pointed his fork at Conner and announced with a mouth full of food, "Not too bad for a dad joke."

The sound of his voice failed to wreck Dylan's magical moment. She had a friend, a friend who laughed with her family, loved the farm, and even accepted the unpleasant hired man. And her family, all of them, seemed to love her back.

After cleaning up after dinner, Dylan taught Marybeth how to milk a cow. They even squirted the milk across the barn at Jessie until their father reprimanded them. But even his reprimand was softened by the smile tugging at his lips. Dylan didn't wonder why she and Jessie weren't enough to cut through the gloom. She knew why. They were a part of it, and together, they were lost in the darkness. As a seventh grader, she understood divorce. She even understood why her parents might want one after the tragedy. But Marybeth made them forget all of that.

When Marybeth's parents came to pick her up, Dylan stood and waved goodbye, a smile beaming on her face. School didn't seem scary knowing Marybeth would be there. If Christina and Olivia teased, she would have a friend by her side. Even the farm and her family didn't seem as dismal. And when Dylan headed back into her house, she believed life was about to change, that somehow, Marybeth's friendship could bring happiness to all of them.

CHAPTER 17

Jessie Phillips
Present Day

T HE ROOSTER CROWED OUT in the barn, waking Jessie just as her sister opened her door.

"You up?" Dylan asked.

"Yeah," she answered with a yawn.

Jessie's schoolbooks lay sprawled across the floor.

"Did you finish your math?"

"Sort of," Jessie answered, swinging her bare feet over the bed.

"Sort of? Jessie, you're about to fail that class."

"I know, but I can't do it. It doesn't make any sense."

"Show me one of your problems."

The two of them sat cross-legged on the floor next to the textbook. Dylan studied the page, tracing her finger across the question. "I hate word problems," she said.

"Me, too."

Dylan read the question out loud as if it would make more sense that way. Then she stared at the words while Jessie yawned and rubbed her eyes. Dylan looked up from the book. "Are you even going to try?"

"I tried all night, Dylan. I just don't understand it."

Dylan's reprimands made her stomach clench. She didn't need her sister to add to her stress. She already knew failing the class was a real possibility, and the idea of repeating a class, let alone a grade, terrified her.

"What time did mom get home?" Dylan asked.

"I don't know. I was asleep." She didn't tell Dylan she fought to stay awake, fearing where their mother was in the middle of the night. The idea of her studying so late into the night wasn't believable, and if she weren't studying, then what was their mother doing, and why was their father allowing it?

"Let's get ready. Maybe it'll make more sense when we're more awake."

"Doubt it."

The girls walked down the creaky stairs. Their father would wake soon, but their mom's hours had become less predictable. The house had one bathroom, so while Dylan washed her face, Jessie stood on the register, letting the warm air from the old kerosene heater attempt to warm her body. But no matter how much warm air surrounded her, it couldn't rid her of a deep chill growing inside of her.

"Do you think Mom has a boyfriend?" The question slipped from Jessie's lips.

"Jessie, what are you talking about? Of course, she doesn't."

"How do you know that? Parents have affairs all the time."

"It happens, but not all the time." Dylan sighed. "Jessie, Mom is not that young. Think of how long you spent on your math and still didn't finish it. She probably needs a lot of help with her classes which keeps her out late."

"But who's helping her?"

"Stop. We're going to miss the bus if we don't get going."

Dylan brushed her teeth while watching Jessie in the mirror. "If mom leaves Dad, who would we live with?" Jessie asked.

"Jessie, I said stop."

"Seriously, just answer me."

"If Mom leaves Dad, I think she'll be leaving all of us, but she's not leaving us, Jessie."

Jessie stared down at the register, watching the air blow on her sweatpants and hiding the tears that formed in her eyes. Dylan's hand rested on her shoulder. "Jessie, everything is going to be fine."

"No, it's not, and you know it."

"Jessie, get ready. I'll look at your homework again."

But Jessie held no hope of Dylan completing her math, as math had tortured her sister since elementary school as well. On the way out the door, Dylan slipped some change into Jessie's hand. "For ice cream," she added.

"You stole from the change drawer again."

"We deserve it occasionally," her sister said with a half-smile. "Let's go, I hear the bus."

The sound of the air brakes sliced through the morning air as the bus stopped at the end of the driveway. Dylan and Jessie boarded, taking a seat toward the back. Jessie took the window seat, and Dylan sat by the aisle. When Jessie looked toward the barn, Eli, the mysterious hired man, was standing there. He waved, but Jessie didn't wave back, even though some part of her wanted to. She dreaded sitting in a classroom all day but didn't want to stay home either. There wasn't a place in the world Jessie imagined would make her happy. What she longed for was not a place but a time. If only they could be transported back in time and make different decisions. Her stomach clenched as it always did when she thought about it all.

Across the aisle, two boys, Jake and Kyle, spoke in hushed voices. They glared at the girls before continuing their secret conversation.

Years ago, the boys had come to her sixth birthday party when her father allowed them to have goats. Jessie and her schoolmates were petting them and laughing until her mom brought out cupcakes, and the attention shifted to the sweets, leaving the baby goats to jump and kick around the hay bales. They all laughed with frosting-smeared lips as the babies entertained without meaning to. They were almost friends once. How different the world was now. There were no birthday parties, no frosting-smeared giggles. No friends.

Jessie turned her face to the window and didn't look away until the bus pulled into the school driveway. Jessie thought of Eli, watching them from the barn with his knowing eyes. But how much did he know?

CHAPTER 18

Eli Simmons
Present Day

F ROM THE OPEN BARN door, Eli watched as a yellow school bus squeaked to a halt in front of the farmhouse. Dylan walked five feet ahead of Jessie. Both girls stared toward the ground; both wore baggy, dark clothes. They stepped onto the bus, and the doors shut, swallowing them into a world he suspected that they dreaded. They were teenagers, or nearly teenagers, after all, being forced to learn information that they had yet to understand the value of alongside a bunch of other kids who felt the same.

Jessie settled by a window toward the back of the bus. As the vehicle started pulling away, she glanced up at Eli. He waved nonchalantly. Jessie only looked back at him, her eyes never releasing their hold until the bus's motion forced the break.

A heavy sadness weighed on his heart for the young lost child. Why didn't her parents notice? Why didn't they care?

When the yellow bus disappeared down the country road, Eli returned to his chores. Conner walked out of the house and approached.

"Morning," Conner said as he passed by. His voice was

gruff but not grumpy. Eli thought back to his fireside chat with his boss. Some of the tension had lifted between them, but would the openness last?

After the morning milking, Eli let the cows out into the pasture. Conner said he needed to run to town for a part and would return by lunch. The quiet barn had a ghostlike atmosphere. He walked to the back of the building and hit the switch, bringing the gutter cleaner to life. He grabbed the hoe and began scraping the filth left over from the morning milking into the gutter. The chore started at the area farthest from the spreader so the gutter cleaner would carry it around the building before climbing up the conveyor belt, and the thick, heavy liquid slopped into the manure spreader. After about half an hour, the inside was as clean as possible, and the manure spreader was filled nearly to the brim.

He climbed up onto the tractor and pulled forward. Despite his attempt to be careful, the tractor still lurched with enough force to spill some of the contents over the side. He would need to clean the area before Conner saw the mistake. Once Eli got out into the field, the fetid odors were drawn downwind, and he could almost smell the crisp fall air filled with all the aromas the season offered. And then the wind shifted, and he was back to the stench swirling around him.

In the field, he reached down and hit the switch, activating the spreader. Manure whipped out of the machine and spread throughout the area to fertilize next year's crop. Eli scanned the property as he drove. The spreader was nearly empty when he noticed a man and his dog walking in the field near the edge of the property. The two trespassers watched with bored interest as Eli approached. When he got close enough, he shut off the tractor and climbed down.

"That a bloodhound?" Eli asked.

"Sure is," the stranger replied.

"Mind if I say hi? I've always been partial to bloodhounds."

"Suit yourself. Ol' Sarge won't bite."

"Come here, boy," Eli called.

Sarge barreled toward him with such intensity, Eli took a step back toward the tractor. When the dog reached Eli, he sat, tongue out, waiting for his next direction. Eli faced the back of his hand toward the bloodhound's nose, allowing Sarge to smell him before petting his head.

"Eli Simmons." Eli reached out his hand to the man, who tentatively took hold of it.

"Tim Burrows. I live in that house there."

"Nice to meet you. I'm new in town and haven't got out much to meet anyone."

Tim didn't offer a response.

"You live here long?" Eli asked. He needed this man to open up and offer information that might help him understand the Phillips family, but he couldn't appear too desperate.

"Too many years to count."

"I obviously work on the Phillips's farm." Eli nodded toward the barn. Tim looked over Eli's shoulder at the property with a look of distaste.

"I'd appreciate you not mentioning seeing me out here."

"I can't see why Mr. Phillips would mind a man walking his dog in his field. It's not like you're hunting the land or anything."

"Sometimes people surprise us."

"They sure can."

Tim looked down at Sarge with parental affection. "Sarge needs to wander." Agitation tainted his words. "I would love to say I could keep him off this property, but…"

"Your secret's safe with me, but I can't say the investigators would be happy with a dog running through their crime scene."

Tim huffed. "Maybe that's exactly what this case needs. Sarge would solve it faster than a bunch of small-town cops. They need some outside help."

"That they do." Eli shifted on his foot as an awkward silence passed between them. He needed to tread carefully. "Was it your dog that found the bone?"

Tim studied Eli before speaking. "It was."

"How do you know for sure it was found in the cornfield? Or on the Phillips's property for that matter?"

"Nothing is for sure, but I own one acre that has been searched thoroughly. Conner, he owns hundreds of acres, and it's going to take some time to search all that land. Sarge likes to run, but he never goes beyond these fields, and those cornfields make the most sense."

"Did the investigators look in the other fields?"

"They sure did. They searched the pastures, the cornfields, the hayfields. Once they get this corn harvested, they'll uncover something. I'd bet my house on it."

Eli gazed out over the abundance of swaying corn stalks. "It would be easy to overlook something in all those rows."

"It sure would be." Tim motioned toward the barn. "Are you feeling nervous working there?"

"Not really," Eli lied. "I'm curious about what happened to David Miller, though."

"I think a lot of people in town are." Tim lowered his voice. "That family, well, they haven't been normal in the past many years."

"Why do you say that?"

"They were nice enough at first. The mom used to bring home-baked cookies to us now and again. She would stand on my porch, kids clinging to her legs, with a plate of warm kitchen sink cookies. They were good, too." Tim shook his head. "Those girls, sweet little things, always dressed like tomboys but had colorful ribbons holding their hair up in ponytails. They possessed what a mom and dad would want in their daughters. Now those girls can't lift their heads up to greet you, let alone smile or wave."

"They are a bit hard to get to know."

"I'd say so. I told my grandkids to keep a distance, but they were doing that on their own."

Eli's jaw tightened at the neighbor's remark, but he bit back the harsh words he wanted to say, words meant to defend behavior he knew didn't justify defending. He settled himself before speaking. "The behavior is typical of kids their age, don't you think?"

"Typical? No." He glanced back at the barn. "And if you think getting to know them is going to change a thing, you're going to be disappointed. No one is going to change."

"Why's that?'

"I think Conner blames himself."

"For David Miller?"

"No. Not David Miller. Not to my knowledge anyway." The neighbor studied Eli. "You don't know?"

A truck rumbled up the driveway, far enough away the sound of tires against gravel almost didn't catch Eli's attention. The truck door slammed, and the distant figure of Conner walked across the lawn and into the house.

"I better get home before he sees me out here," Tim said, "and you'd best be getting back to work."

"You're probably right."

Tim turned to go. As Eli climbed back onto the tractor, Tim called out to him.

"All that stuff I was going to say. Well, it's all public information. I suggest you do a little investigating. To be fair, I'd probably be a different person if I went through what he went through."

"Thanks for the heads-up."

"Good luck to you..." The man tapped his head, trying to recall.

"Eli. Eli Simmons."

As Tim turned away, Eli heard the quiet words, "And be safe."

Conner was waiting in the yard when Eli emerged from the barn after returning the tractor and spreader. He walked side by side with Eli into the quiet house. Conner didn't speak, leaving Eli to wonder if it was his boss's way of telling him he'd seen him with the neighbor or just an awkward bonding attempt.

Lunch of grilled cheese and tomato soup awaited them again, but Claire was nowhere to be seen. Conner attempted small talk, only surface-level topics.

When Eli headed back across the road to his camper for his afternoon break, Conner yelled to him, "Hold up."

Eli froze, not knowing what to expect.

"You remember what we discussed the other night?"

"Yeah?"

"Are you still good with the plan?"

"Yes, sir." Eli hadn't realized there was an official plan, but Conner's intentions by the fire were becoming evident.

"This Friday, I suspect Claire will be at The Watering Hole. I'll let you go early so you don't miss her." Not waiting for a response, Conner walked away.

As soon as Eli was curled up in his camper bed that night, he opened his phone. The neighbor said the Phillips's story was public record, but what exactly was he searching for? He typed their names and scrolled the headlines that appeared. Most of them referred to David Miller and the discovery of his jawbone. Eli's eyelids grew heavy, and his unconscious mind began to run practice dreams, mixing reality with fiction. Just as he was about to give up, a headline made him bolt up in bed, no longer sleepy.

Hayden Phillips Dies at Age Five.

CHAPTER 19

Jeremy Biggs
Present Day

L ITTLE ITALY SAT ON the corner of two busy streets, with windows lining the two exterior walls. The small town's comings and goings revealed themselves as a quiet film refusing to get to the heart of its story. Across the street from the restaurant, The Coffee Shop was the gossip center. The locals caught up on the daily news, shared their hardships and successes, and made or lost friends depending on how the conversations were handled. However, not all gossip was terrible. Many of the exchanges brought out the warmth of the townsfolk, displayed by the organizing of home-cooked meals for the sick, sharing of hand-me-downs given to those in need, and small chores completed for those unable. The people of Derby Line were, at the heart of it all, good. But even good friends sometimes proved disloyal when someone threw a juicy bit of news into the mix.

Jeremy watched from the windows of Little Italy as the women, talking like chatterboxes, walked out of the shop, holding their steaming cups of coffee. The men often sat inside by the window, reading the paper and enjoying a freshly baked Danish, pretending not to care about the women's chatter but always with ears perked up and ready.

His father would have never set foot in the place; it's hard for the townsfolk to gossip about someone when he's seated beside them, and it's harder for the person of interest to sit in awkward silence.

His mind wandered to David's mother, another person who would also avoid The Coffee Shop. Bethany Miller observed the world from her front porch, never trying to fit in. According to David, she only attended one party in high school, where she got pregnant by some loser who left town the next day. Bethany insisted the young man never learned he had a son because they had never bothered to learn each others' names in the heat of the moment. An angry grandmother mainly raised David while his mother worked two jobs until her weight became such an issue that she was able to collect disability. David's mother demanded one thing of him: to earn his high school diploma, something she never accomplished herself. Somehow, David managed to earn his degree but denied her the joy of watching him walk across the stage to receive his diploma. Instead, he was out getting drunk, and Jeremy knew this because he was with him.

Whenever Jeremy visited David's home, Bethany rarely interacted with them. She wasn't one to yell or give orders; she rocked on the porch, seemingly lost in depression and defeat, or at least that's what Jeremy believed. Her presence filled him with a wave of guilt as if he should be helping to change her son for the better, even though Bethany likely didn't see him as capable of the task. How was she coping with David's death? He considered reaching out to her but feared the guilt that might come with that encounter. No, he decided, it was best to leave her be.

"What are you looking at, nerd?" The voice startled him back to reality. Amber had slithered up beside him.

"None of your business. Believe it or not, not everything is."

"I only care about the interesting stuff. I'm no different than anyone else."

"Oh, you are very different, Amber." Amber was fueled by other people's problems. Listening to her work the customers for gossip made Jeremy irate, and although he had never become a direct victim of her ways, he had watched too many others' misfortunes used to energize her days. Standing next to her made his jaw clench which was why he avoided her as much as possible.

Jeremy headed back to the kitchen to avoid further conversation.

"I'll take that as a compliment," she called to him.

Taking a hit from his vape, Allen leaned against the large metal sink. "Who's getting their fill of morning gossip today?" he asked, blowing smoke into the air.

"Bunch of people I don't know." Jeremy tried to sound nonchalant.

"We all know what they're talking about today."

"Do we?"

"Yeah, the creepy cornfield." Allen spoke in an eerie voice, making fun of the news.

Jeremy busied himself putting the dishes back in their appropriate places.

"Hey, dude. Weren't you that David guy's friend? You know, the jawbone..."

Jeremy dropped the metal pan in the sink and spun to face Allen.

"Woah. Don't get all worked up."

"You're talking about a person. A person I knew. You don't just spit out shit about his jawbone like it's nothing."

Allen raised his hands in surrender. "My bad, dude. It just hit me, that's all. Didn't mean to be callous."

"But you were." Jeremy turned back around. He had a right to be mad, but not this mad. His heart raced in his chest. Ever since the police questioned him, he had been on edge. Not just because he could be a suspect, but now he knew David had not run off. Someone had killed him, and that person could want Jeremy dead as well.

Allen was silent for a moment. "I can't say I knew him. I only knew of him."

"Not many people knew him. They only liked to judge him."

"He gave people some reasons."

Jeremy stopped putting away the dishes and faced Allen again. "Do you want me to kick your ass?"

Allen laughed. "No. Of course not." He took another vape hit, keeping his eyes focused on Jeremy. "Not to mention, I'm pretty sure you wouldn't stand a chance of taking me down."

"Guys like you think the world owes you. You can get away with anything and laugh while the rest of us burn."

"Oh yes. The world has blessed me by giving me this job, scrubbing filthy pans next to a lowlife that can't even succeed at that." Allen laughed. "How many times have you been assigned highway cleanup?"

"I would shut my mouth if I were you." His fist clenched.

"My bad." Allen blew smoke into the air as his lips curled into a sneer.

Amber walked in from the dining area. "I'm heading out on my break before you two go to blows." She tossed her apron onto the counter and headed to the front door.

Jeremy had only received community service twice during high school. Even for him, the punishment had been humiliating, walking along the roads in town, poking trash and stuffing it into garbage cans. Other high schoolers, probably Allen included, would honk and yell comments out their windows as they sped past. Sometimes, they even tossed beer cans in the ditches, which Jeremy would be forced to pick up.

Moments after Amber left, the bell jingled again. Carlo strutted in the front door, his expression hardened as he eyed Jeremy and Allen who were visible through the large opening exposing the kitchen, a feature Jeremy despised. Carlo walked directly to a booth and called for Allen. Jeremy attempted to make eye contact, but Allen looked away. He slid across the plastic booth seat on the opposite side of the table to their boss. The conversation was intense and not intended to be overheard.

Jeremy ran the water until it was hot enough to melt the grease without scalding his hands. Since they had finished the dishwashing chore, he picked up a clean dish and pretended to rewash it. Jeremy watched Carlo and Allen through the opening between the kitchen and dining area. He shut the water off and slowly dried the dish, straining to hear their conversation. Jeremy walked to the employee bathroom, opened the door, and let it shut loudly without entering. He then snuck back to the doorway leading into the dining area. Their words were muffled, but with effort, they were discernable. He filled in the gaps with a bit of imagination.

"You told us you'd get us the information. The pick-up must be this week, and it's your job to ensure it's all clear." Carlo's words came through clenched teeth. "We do not want them waiting."

"It's just that…"

Allen's cockiness had vanished.

"It's nothing."

"I'm being watched. I can feel it."

"You can feel it?" Carlo spat. "Now you're crazy. No one is watching you."

"My uncle…"

"Your uncle has been more than compensated. He has the connections. Tell him to use them."

"We have to be careful."

"Listen, kid, I don't think your uncle wants your blood on his hands. He has his connections with border patrol. He can tell us when they will be out there and where. He's retired. No one is watching him. He tells us when it's safe to do the pick-ups and his nephew stays alive and out of jail. It's not that difficult."

"His informant with border patrol, well, their relationship isn't what it used to be. My uncle's afraid he could turn on him."

"If I were you, I would be more afraid of what happened

to David than some informant turning on you. If the guy working for border patrol gave your uncle a tip in the past, his ass could go to jail as well. He'll keep his mouth shut."

"So, the mafia did kill him." Allen's voice trembled. A trickle of sweat dripped down Jeremy's neck. The mafia's involvement was an obvious possibility, but hearing the words spoken terrified Jeremy.

"Hell, I don't know what happened to that kid. You think they share that shit with me? All I know is he wanted to back out, and now his body is fertilizing next year's crop. That's what you need to be afraid of. These small-town cops are no competition for the mafia. As you know, the cops would sooner take a little under the table than to go head-to-head with organized crime."

Silence followed as Allen contemplated his options. "I'll talk to my uncle today."

"And you best make friends with Jeremy. He'll be with you out there. From what I gather, the air between the two of you is hostile. You better learn how to get along before you get each other killed."

Silence filled the restaurant. Jeremy couldn't see the two men. Had they sensed him there? Were they walking toward him?

"I want an answer today." Carlo's words were firm and unwavering.

"Yeah, yeah."

"Yeah, yeah, nothing. Go now. I need answers."

Allen's shoes squeaked across the floor with each step. The bell jingled as he opened the door, but before he could leave, Carlo called to him.

"Allen, you don't need one more enemy."

Allen didn't respond. Jeremy heard the door close behind him, and the room fell quiet once again. There were questions Jeremy would never have answered: Was Allen's interview just a formality? Was he explicitly hired to replace David due to his connections? What had transpired behind the scenes with Allen's uncle and the hidden ties? Jeremy didn't want to know. He already understood enough. One undeniable fact was that he was doing business with some evil men, and another crucial point was that Allen was involved in matters far more complex than either Jeremy or David had ever encountered.

Jeremy slipped to the back and opened and closed the bathroom door. After counting slowly to five, he walked toward the entrance. Carlo's full attention was drawn to a spreadsheet on the table.

"I finished the dishes. You need me for anything else?"

Carlo sat back, pulled his readers off his head.

"Take the new kid to the pub. You're going to need each other soon."

Jeremy swallowed hard. Things had been quiet since the dog discovered David's jawbone and the investigators started crawling all over those fields, but he'd known the silence would not last.

Carlo's readers covered his eyes again, and his attention fell to the debits and credits of a struggling business. "Turn the sign to closed on your way out." Jeremy nodded to no one and did as he was told, leaving Carlo to the numbers that drove him, numbers that controlled so much. They could corrupt good men and turn bad men into pure evil. Would there ever be enough for some people, and was there anything some people wouldn't do for the love of those dollar signs?

The Watering Hole sat on the adjacent corner. It would be open for lunch, but what Jeremy cared about was the sign offering 'Buy One, Get One Free' during happy hour. He scrolled his phone to find Allen's number. He'd been given it in case of illnesses and shift coverages. After typing and deleting several messages, he settled on one and hit send.

Man, you looked like you were getting your ass chewed about something. Drinks on me tonight.

The phone remained silent. Allen wasn't dumb. They both knew what initiated the text, Carlo's demands. He drove home, glancing at the screen every now and then. Nothing, not even the bubbles representing an attempted response. Jeremy gave up and jumped into the shower. His phone beeped as he reached for his towel, and Allen's name appeared.

Sure, see you in 30.

~~*~~

When Jeremy entered The Watering Hole, Allen was seated at the bar with a half-finished beer. The happy hour crowd had yet to show in full force so most of the tables remained empty. The one-man band was in his corner adjusting and tuning his equipment, looking less than thrilled to be there.

Allen lifted his drink in greeting, and Jeremy nodded in his direction. Behind the counter, the bartender served a young woman who leaned over the bar farther than necessary, drawing focus to her chest. The bartender, Jeremy knew, was in his early forties, but not one part of him showed his age. He smiled politely at the young patron, giving her the perfect amount of attention. This establishment was where the likes of Jeremy and his father went for their gossip, even if their evening tended to make them a part of it.

"Can I get another beer over here?" Allen called.

The bartender excused himself and made his way to them.

"What'll you have?"

"Something light," Jeremy said.

Within moments, a mug of frosty beer sat on the counter in front of Jeremy. He raised his glass to Allen. "Here's to working together."

His colleague took a long swallow, never losing eye contact.

"You busy tonight?" Allen asked.

"You're looking at me being busy. Why?"

"What do you say to a little adventure?"

Jeremy's heart raced. Apparently, the all-clear had been given.

"Sure."

With a wave, Allen smiled and got the bartender's attention again.

"We'll take two whiskey shots." Allen's gaze held Jeremy's, and his smile turned into a sneer. "It looks like you've got yourself a new partner."

CHAPTER 20

Eli Simmons
Present Day

ELI HADN'T SLEPT AFTER reading the heart-wrenching article about Hayden Phillips, the five-year-old who had been taken too early. How could life be so cruel? He thought about Conner and Claire. The silence between them wasn't filled with hatred; it was filled with pain. Even if the girls didn't realize it, their gothic clothing served as a sign of mourning, indicating to the outside world that they didn't want to be touched or seen by anyone until they had healed. Unfortunately, there had been no treatment for their wounds, allowing their pain to transform into despair. Their mourning attire had morphed into something darker—a wall that kept out healing thoughts while letting in those that aimed to destroy. Their condition was slowly killing all of them.

The article told how Hayden had sustained a minor injury after jumping from a beam in the haymow with his two older sisters. A piece of straw, they believe, scraped his skin, drawing a small amount of blood that was easily treated at home. The cut did not cause alarm until it became hot and red. The family attempted more treatment at home until the hot, red wound began to grow at a dramatic rate. Once at the hospital, the boy was diagnosed with a resistant, flesh-eating bacterial infection called Necrotizing Faciitis. Doctors immediately started administrating antibiotics, but the infection had had too much time to settle and grow within the young boy's tiny body. Hayden died within days of the initial injury.

The article went on to describe Necrotizing Faciitis and give statistics. According to WebMD, in the United States alone, between 700 and 1150 people per year were diagnosed with this condition. It estimated that between one and five cases led to the death of the victim. The article warned readers that whenever in doubt, they should seek medical treatment right away for infected wounds. Early detection was critical to survival when dealing with flesh-eating bacterium.

Would Hayden have survived if Conner and Claire had sought medical care instead of trying to treat the wound at home? How many times a day did they still ask themselves that question? The girls were with their little brother when he jumped from the beam. Did they blame themselves?

Eli had only worked with the Phillips family for a short time, and he had twice now suspected that Conner was drinking throughout the day. He would disappear for a few minutes, and when he returned, Eli detected the smell of whiskey on his breath. Now, he understood that his boss had been trying to drown his memories, not realizing that he needed to make new ones instead. The mourning phase was intended to be just that: a phase. The family had hidden away from each other and the world too long, and like quicksand, they had been pulled in too deep. They had grabbed the wrong lifelines to pull themselves out of their despair. Why had they not sought professional help? But Eli knew the answer without having to be told it. Conner was a proud man who would not admit he needed help. Not to mention, they did not have the financial means to pay someone.

Being more aware now of the family's struggles, Eli's fear of them lifted. He watched them closer, trying to see them as they once were. Were they once happy? The neighbor spoke of the mom bringing cookies and the girls wearing bows in their hair. Yes, they had aged. Yes, preteens and teenagers often drifted from their parents; they became quieter, curling into their private cocoons until they transformed into more mature versions of themselves before becoming present again. In some ways, the girls' behavior was a natural progression. Still, Dylan and Jessie were left to transform without the proper influences or guidance. What would they transform into if left to figure it all out alone?

He knew for himself one was not meant to go it alone. He'd been lucky. The necessary people entered his life, not exactly when he wanted them to, but, in hindsight, they entered his life at the perfect times. If it weren't for the Burkett's, where would he be? The Burkett's saved him in many ways. And maybe now, he could be that person for this family.

Throughout the week, whenever he addressed one of them, he was met with coldness. Coldness was an understatement when it came to Dylan. She was downright rude. He wanted to retaliate often, but he bit back his words. He would never be able to help her if she didn't learn to trust him.

After dinner, Claire offered to throw some clothes in the wash for him.

"That's kind of you, but I'll run them into town. I use the laundromat on the corner. The machines are so big, I only have to do one load for barn clothes and one for my others."

"You have others?" Dylan's voice was full of condemnation.

"Of course, I have others. You just don't see me off the farm."

"You live in a run-down camper sitting in our field. Obviously, you don't have much going on outside of here."

"Dylan, you're being rude." Claire's cheeks flushed in embarrassment.

"It's okay," Eli said to Claire. Then he turned his attention to Dylan. "I'm pretty new here. You're right. I don't have too much going on, and although your farm keeps me busy enough, I probably should expand my horizons a bit. Can you suggest something for me to do on my day off?"

Dylan rolled her eyes. "Like I would know what a creepy drifter wants to do on his day off. Maybe you could go stalk someone in the nursing home."

"Dylan, go to your room right now," Claire said.

"Fine with me."

She pushed back hard from the table and stood.

"Clean your plate up before you go."

"What is it you want me to do, Mom? Go to my room or clean my plate?"

Conner slammed his fork down on the table. "You know exactly what your mother means, and you best do it without another word. You hear me?"

"Yes." Dylan's voice quieted in resignation.

The following Friday, Eli had about six cows left to milk before he could begin bedding the animals. Conner glanced at the large clock hung in the manger above the cows' heads.

"Eli, why don't you head on out early today? Dylan and I can finish the chores."

Dylan eyed the two men suspiciously. Although Conner's behavior was out of character, Eli, unlike Dylan, knew the reason.

"Much appreciated. I'll take you up on that." He dropped his rag back into the bucket. "I'll see you in the morning." They gave each other a knowing nod, and Eli returned to his camper to shower and change.

An hour later, he pulled up to the bar wearing jeans, a long-sleeved blue T-shirt, a Carhartt jacket, and hiking boots, which had never seen the inside of a barn. He was clean-shaven and smelled of cheap aftershave. He strode to the bar door as two young men stumbled onto the walk. One was obviously intoxicated, bumping into him as he passed by him. Eli asked them if they were okay and was given a small assurance they were. The smell of alcohol fumes radiated from the guy. The sober man, or at least Eli hoped he was sober, spilled his drunk friend into the passenger side of a car and then headed to the driver's side. The car rounded the corner, and Eli stepped into the warm, lively bar, which nearly erased the unsettling feeling the encounter had caused.

"What can I get you?" The bartender wiped his hands on a bar towel and tossed it on the counter. His face showed frustration.

"Tough night?"

"It was, but the latest problem just left."

"Tales of a bartender," Eli said with a smile.

"Never a dull moment, as they say."

"I'll take a light beer; hold the drama."

The bartender turned to retrieve his beer, giving Eli time to scan the bar. He spotted Claire sitting at a circular table blocked in by several young women sharing a laugh. But she wasn't laughing. Her lips tilted to a smile, but her eyes were empty and sad.

Claire's gaze lingered on someone on the dance floor. Five or six couples were swaying to the mellow country music. Whether the person who stole Claire's attention from the group knew it or not, he was breaking her heart.

Eli had a seat and took a long swallow of his ice-cold beer. It tasted good, much better than the stuff Conner had served him. *Patience*, he told himself. Claire had to notice him in her own time, otherwise his appearance would seem too planned. The song ended, and another began. People hooted like they had waited all night for that song. The young women jumped from their seats and ran to the dance floor. Eli watched Claire in the mirror behind the bar. She slid from the bench, eyed the dance floor again, and headed to the bar. She stood only a few feet from him but didn't notice him. Her mind seemed far away. She ordered a vodka tonic, and when the bartender turned to fill her request, she saw Eli. He gave a slight raise of his beer mug.

"Eli, what are you doing here?" Panic filled her voice.

"I needed a little time away from the pasture." The corners of his lips tilted up in a smile. "It's great to run into someone I know since just about everyone in this town is a stranger to me."

"We finished studying a little bit ago." The song ended, and involuntarily, he was sure, her gaze darted back to the dance floor. Her flushed cheeks exposed her guilt. "We thought we would grab a quick drink."

"Can't blame you for that." Eli took a swig of beer. "Are you enjoying nursing school?"

"Yeah. It's hard work, but it's always been a dream of mine, and, well, as you can see, I'm not getting any younger."

"You're plenty young enough to keep chasing your dream."

A small smile hinted at her lips, but her eyes held tears that didn't shed. She shook them away and straightened herself.

"So, how do you like working on our farm?"

"I like farm work. What can I say? I'm a rare breed these days." The bartender set Claire's drink in front of her. "The work sure makes the beer taste good."

"I don't work in the barn often enough to know if that's true. I'd like to never step foot out there again."

"Oh, it's not so bad. Sure, the work comes with its share of filth, but the animals are amazing if you take a moment to look them in the eye like they're not just property. And hard labor feels good sometimes."

"You have some valid points."

"But I think it's great you're chasing your dream. I think we've been given dreams for a reason."

Claire studied him, no longer afraid, it seemed, of staring straight at him. "And what would your dream be?"

Eli looked toward the man singing in the corner. "A

Nashville star, playing the guitar, belting out country tunes to adoring fans every weekend." He smiled. "Wouldn't be a bad life, would it?"

"You play the guitar?"

"Not a lick. And some might even call me tone deaf if they heard me sing."

Claire laughed, and Eli watched the tension dissipate from her shoulders.

"Not to be a pessimist, but you might have missed that Nashville boat."

"I would consider you a realist, not a pessimist."

"For real, what's your story?" Claire asked, her eyes full of genuine interest.

"That's a story for another day." He needed the conversation to be about her, and sharing his story in one sitting would require way too many drinks.

"Come on, give me something."

"Foster care, drifter, cowhand. Is that enough of a story?'

"It's a start. I'm sorry about Dylan. She's going through so much."

"Well, she was right about me being a drifter, but she had the tone wrong. My life is one adventure after another. It's not sad or depressing to me."

Eli motioned to the bar stool next to him. "Have a seat. I want to hear about Claire's story, or am I keeping you from your friends?" He wanted to ask a million questions about the girls, the bone discovered on their property, and especially Hayden, but this was a time to listen.

Claire laughed, but this time, sadness hid behind the sound.

A new song started, and the Claire's classmates continued to dance in a circle. "I don't think they'll miss me for a song or two." Claire sipped her drink. "They live in a different world than me. I can go to the same classes and drink at the same bar, but the differences are..." She shook her head and looked at the dance floor. One man was dancing in the middle of Claire's friends. "The differences are undeniable."

"Who's the guy?"

Claire's attention snapped back to Eli. "What guy?"

"The guy dancing with your friends."

Her hand shook as she brought the glass to her lips. "Oh, he's one of the nursing students. His name's Nolan. He's, well, maybe a bit of a player, I'm afraid."

"There is nothing to be afraid of unless you let him play you, and I have a feeling you are way too smart to let that happen."

"I would never..." The red welt rose from her chest and crawled up her neck. "I'm...I'm old and married."

Her discomfort was contagious. Eli lifted his hand as if it were a white flag. "Forgive me if I offended you." Eli scrambled to undo the damage. "I'm pretty good at putting my foot in my mouth sometimes."

Claire sighed and took another drink. "It's okay."

"Should we start over?"

A quiet moment passed between them. Eli's heart rate quickened. Had he wrecked the rare bonding moment?

"How is it working for my husband?"

Eli considered his words carefully knowing they could lead to trouble. "I'm grateful for my job."

Her laugh sounded more like a huff.

"Feel free to be truthful. Damn, hearing someone be truthful to me, to tell me real feelings, would be very refreshing."

"You sound a bit frustrated."

"Isn't it obvious every time you see me and Conner together? I don't even know that man anymore. I haven't had a conversation with him that lasted over two minutes since… hell, I don't even know when. He's always out in the barn or in his shed that he keeps locked, telling me not to disturb him." Eli listened closely. He had noticed Conner walking into the small shed. Eli assumed it was a storage for tools. "He's been growing more distant every year, and now David Miller's bones…" She emptied her glass. "Never mind. I don't know what I'm saying, just that I feel…" Claire took a deep breath. "I need to go."

"You okay to drive? I can give you a ride."

"I can handle two drinks and a quiet country road," she said. "But I appreciate the offer." She waved down the bartender and paid her bill. "Maybe I'll catch up with you another night. I come here most Fridays. If you figure out who the man that I married is, let me know. Believe it or not, we used to like each other."

CHAPTER 21

Jeremy Biggs
Present Day

HAPPY HOUR TOOK ON a new meaning as Allen threw in shot after shot between beers. The uncomfortable small talk shifted to a few memories of school they shared, teachers they couldn't stand, and where some classmates ended up that surprised them. They found the only common ground they could stand on together and began afresh.

Jeremy had avoided a second shot of alcohol, knowing he would be driving. On the other hand, Allen didn't seem to care about those details. By Allen's third shot and fourth beer, he relaxed. By the sixth beer in under two hours, the conversation turned, and Allen's secrets threatened to spew from his lips.

"Sometimes, you're damned if you do and damned if you don't, wouldn't you say, Jeremy?"

"I suppose that's true." Jeremy sipped his second beer and tried to make eye contact with his new colleague. Allen stared back, his eyes too thickly glazed for any connection. Reading through the drunkenness would be difficult. "So, what was Carlo chewing you out for earlier?" Was Allen drunk enough to mention his uncle's involvement?

Allen threw his head back and laughed sarcastically, catching the attention of a couple seated at the bar beside them. He noticed their whispered reactions.

"You got a problem?" Allen said to them.

"It's not me with the problem." The man turned to face Allen and blocked his date simultaneously. "You've bumped my chair one too many times. Maybe you should throw in a water."

"And maybe you should mind your own damned business." Allen staggered in his attempt to square up with the guy.

The bartender nodded to the bouncer, who was conversing with a young blonde who had entered with a group a short time ago. Jeremy only noted them because he was quite certain Mrs. Phillips was among them. He kept his head down when she passed, even though she probably had no idea who he was or that he had ever been at their farm. He always tried to be discrete when he met David there.

The burly man, obviously hired for his size, stepped between the two men, but allowed them a moment to make amends.

Jeremy turned his attention to the offended patron. "Sorry, my buddy's having a bad day. Let me get the next round for you and your date." Jeremy turned to the bartender. "Put their next drinks on my tab." Turning back to the man, he said, "Give me a little patience, and I'll get my friend out of here. Deal?"

The man eyed Allen over Jeremy's shoulder. "Whatever. Just get him out of here."

"Will do."

The bouncer stood at attention, watching for everyone's next move. "Once they order, close my tab out. This is for you." Jeremy slapped a generous tip on the counter.

The bouncer then motioned to the door. "I'll see you two out."

Jeremy and Allen grabbed their jackets and walked in front of the bartender. "You owe me, man. That's my day's wages."

"Good thing we have a side gig." Allen laughed, but the cockiness had dissipated.

Jeremy had always been David's driver, staying far from the danger and receiving less compensation. His low-profile duties let him believe he was less guilty of the crime, but he just wanted out now. The question was how to make that happen without ending up like David.

"Get moving." The bartender was losing his patience.

Allen swayed a bit as he leaned in toward Jeremy's ear. "Let's get out of here before we piss off someone else. The adventure awaits."

Jeremy wiped away the spit that had smacked his cheek with the pronunciation of each s. "Just don't get me killed."

Allen laughed again and put a finger up to Jeremy's face. "You're the one that gets to hide in the car. How about I try not to get myself killed?"

Allen staggered onto the moonlit street, bumping into a patron walking into the bar. The man looked to be in his early thirties and was wearing jeans and a Carhartt.

"Watch out, buddy," Allen scolded the man. The guy responded only with a look of concern.

"Sorry, man," Jeremy offered.

"You two okay?" the stranger asked.

"I've got him," Jeremy responded.

"Where's your car?" Allen scanned the cars.

Jeremy pointed to his rusty, blue sedan a few parking spots down.

"Pole position. Nice." Allen slurred each word.

He sensed the stranger watching them as he spilled Allen into the passenger seat.

Jeremy climbed into the driver's side and cranked on the heat while Allen rubbed his hands together to find warmth.

"Where to?" Jeremy asked, hoping it wasn't where he expected it to be.

"You drive. I'll tell you where to turn."

"You can't share where we're going?" Even in the cold air, Jeremy felt the heat traveling up his neck. Carlo had to know better than to send them back to the same place, didn't he?

"Don't worry about it. You'll be fine, but first, I need food. Go through the drive-thru up here."

"Sure. I could use something myself." Jeremy's stomach swirled with nerves and beer. He wasn't sure if the food would help or hurt. Still, as he sat in the parking lot watching Allen inhale a giant burger, fries, and drink, he knew it was exactly what the guy needed to sober up enough to get through their so-called adventure. Jeremy picked at his meal until Allen finished, threw his wrappers in the bag, crinkled it, and tossed it into the back seat.

"It's time."

"Are you going to tell me where we're going now?"

"You'll see soon enough. Just drive."

Jeremy shook his head in annoyance and pulled

out of the parking spot. Allen spoke little besides giving directions, to take a left or a right. The food had done its job. Allen appeared more sober and serious. Too serious. The mood in the car made Jeremy tense as he listened and responded to each command. Allen's directions led them to the dreaded country road lined with farmland and cornfields, just as Jeremy had feared. The pick-up spot remained the same one that he and David had used. He was right back at the Phillips's farm, the very place his friend had gone missing.

"Drive slowly. There's a tractor path hidden between two of these cornfields coming up."

"I know." How could they send them back out here with so much going on?

"You've been here, then?"

"Too many times."

"Turn here." Allen pointed to the right, but Jeremy had already slowed in preparation.

Jeremy turned onto the dirt road that was hardly more than a wide path and killed the headlights. The full moon illuminated the tall cornstalks that blocked off his view. Every part of his body was on high alert.

He drove deeper into the field.

"I should stop here."

"Just a bit farther. It'll be fine."

"This road is one way. I need to back out. The further in we get, the harder it is to get out. Trust me, I know. This is the same place I would drive David at night."

Jeremy felt Allen's gaze on him.

"Fine, stop here." Jeremy killed the engine, and the world

went silent. "So, this is part of the Phillips's farm?" Allen asked.

"How do you not know that?"

"I haven't lived in this town for years, and even if I had, I don't know everyone here."

"You haven't done a drive-by like everyone else in town?"

"Can't say that I have."

They both stared at the path before them, leading into the darkness.

"You sure you know what you're doing?" Jeremy asked.

"Sure, yeah." Allen looked around. "They found the bone on this farm?" He appeared pale in the moonlight as he connected the facts.

"The bone? That jawbone belonged to my friend."

"Sorry, man. Not trying to be insensitive again." The moonlight lit the interior of the car. Allen rested his shaky hand on the car door handle. "I'll be back in under fifteen minutes. If I'm not back in thirty, you can leave."

"You want me to sit in the dark in a freezing cornfield for thirty minutes? David was never over fifteen minutes."

"It shouldn't be that long." Allen cracked the door open. "You'll be fine." He stepped out of the car, and within moments, was swallowed by the darkness.

Ten minutes had passed when something moved near the side of the path. Jeremy only saw it out of the corner of his eye. He focused on the spot ahead of him, but whatever it was had disappeared. The silence in the car pounded against his ears. The thought of David's bones hiding somewhere under the stalks sent a chill through his body. He had known the minute he headed down the road where they would end up. They had passed the barn, dark now that chores were done, and the farmer had gone inside. Another movement, but this time, the creature stopped and stared right back at Jeremy. A big buck, most likely wondering who was invading his space. After a short stare-down, the buck leaped out of sight. Two deer peeked out, glanced his way, and followed the buck back into the stalks. As Jeremy breathed a sigh of relief, something pounded on the car's hood, and the door flung open.

"Let's get the hell out of here. Border patrol is everywhere tonight." Allen looked over at Jeremy, who was staring at him. "I mean it. Let's get the hell out of here. Now."

Jeremy started the engine, placed one arm over the back of the seat, and started backing out.

"Carlo's going to kill me. How the hell am I supposed to know what the Canadian side is doing?"

Jeremy focused on driving in reverse through the cornfield in the dark. "You told Carlo it was all clear tonight?"

"Yeah."

"You're in deeper than I am."

"I've got connections. I'll be fine."

"Will you?"

"Yeah. I'm not worried." Allen held the secret of his uncle's involvement close to his chest.

Jeremy reached the end of the path and carefully pulled out onto the quiet country road.

"David thought he'd be fine, too. That man was probably my only true friend." Jeremy stared ahead. "But I can't ask him anything anymore, like why the hell did he get me into all of this shit."

"We make our choices."

"We make some. We're given a shitty deal and try to make the best of it, which means sometimes we try to cheat the system. You can't beat a royal flush by playing by the rules."

"Can't deny that fact."

"You were born with a royal flush. Why are you screwing it up?"

"No one has a winning hand in this town; if they do, they're not playing a level game. I want more."

"More than your two-story home in town with its white picket fence?"

"No one has white picket fences anymore, and, yeah, man, I want more than that. This town bores me to death. Speaking of homes, do you have a place I can crash tonight? I don't need the riot act when I'm dropped off smelling of alcohol."

"Still with the folks then?" Jeremy asked, amused more than anything.

"I've got a one-year plan. Or rather, my parents have a one-year plan for me."

"Sure. I guess you can crash at my place. I live about five miles from here."

"What got you into this side job?"

Jeremy was quiet for a moment. "David. You can't make shit doing the jobs David and I were qualified for. That is, if someone will even hire you when you have a record. David worked on that farm, shoveling cow manure and milking cows, for peasant pay. We could drink a day's wages in a few hours."

"We sure can," Allen said with a laugh.

Jeremy sighed.

"This world was not made to support the likes of us. School sucked, the teachers hated us just for walking in the door, and most of the students snubbed their noses at us as though their own drunkenness was socially acceptable. Hell, acceptable doesn't even describe it. But let David or me be seen with a six-pack, and we're nothing but losers going nowhere in life. Well, I guess we proved them right."

Allen reached into his pocket and pulled out a joint.

"Mind if I smoke?"

"Not at all when it's not in my damn car, and it's too fricking cold to put a window down."

"Whatever." He tucked it back into his jacket.

"David and I were just trying to even the scales, get a little money to get the hell out of this place and start over. That's how it started anyway. And the money was good. Of course, we had to stash it away since we couldn't suddenly start a bank account and add anything of worth to it. It's a small town. People would talk. Investigators would be on our backs. So, we stashed the cash."

"Where?"

Jeremy laughed. "If I knew, I wouldn't tell you."

"I don't suppose you would."

A cold sweat overtook Jeremy as he realized his mistake. Why had he mentioned the money to anyone, especially someone he didn't trust?

"You don't know where the money is?"

"No, I don't. David thought they were onto us, so he hid it. That was right before he went missing." Jeremy swallowed the uncomfortable regret rising inside of him. "For months,

I thought he left town with all of it. Left me to deal with the mess here. But then, the neighbor's dog found his jawbone."

"How much money was it?" Allen asked.

"I don't know. Maybe a couple thousand." But Jeremy did know. At the last count, it had been over ten thousand.

"You seriously have no idea where it went?"

"No clue."

"You checked his house?"

"The best I could. David kept the cash in his room while looking for a new hiding place. After David had gone missing, I visited his mother, pretending David had a favorite jacket of mine. She let me search his room while she sat on her porch the way she always does. I searched everywhere. The money wasn't there."

Jeremy hoped Allen believed him and would never go near David's home searching for the cash. Jeremy wasn't close to David's mom, but he also didn't want to endanger her.

"The cash could be somewhere else in the house. I'm sure there's an attic or closet she never goes into."

"No. David wanted the money somewhere he could grab it if he got in trouble, and we had to leave fast. Whoever was looking for him, the police or mafia, would know where he lived."

Allen ingested the information for a minute. "It's somewhere in that barn."

"What makes you say that?"

"It's unlocked. There's no surveillance, and the border is just across the field. If he's in trouble in the US, he jumps over to Canada. If he's in trouble there, he disappears into the mountains."

Jeremy didn't want to admit that Allen was probably correct. His reasoning made perfect sense. If he was correct about the money being hidden on the farm, Allen could search for it unnoticed until he found it. Jeremy wouldn't be aware that it had been found since he didn't know where it had gone missing from.

Allen reached for the joint again. "Are you sure I can't have one hit?"

"Have all you want when you get out of my car. I don't need to get pulled over with pot smoke rolling out of my windows. I've had enough run-ins with the law."

Allen removed his hopeful hand from his jacket pocket.

"Do you know the guy I was supposed to meet tonight?"

"I've never met him. David did once, but mostly, the guy lurked in the distance during the transaction. When David was alive, I drove the car. That's it. Sometimes, I would meet David for lunch at the farm after he had worked in the back fields. Sometimes, we would come back at night. We tried to change it up. The border patrol is everywhere out here. You can't have a routine."

"So, you would get the drugs from David, and then what?"

"We'd take them to Carlo, who would pay us our share for the delivery. Just like what we're doing. Same deal, different partner. It was easy money for a while." Jeremy slowed and then turned onto a gravel driveway. A trailer sat back in some trees. Not even one light was on, making it hard to see the property well, but the headlights showed enough: a crumbling makeshift front porch, an old couch in the front yard, and beer cans lining an overgrown path to the stairs.

"You live here alone?"

"Are you kidding? I'm too poor to afford even this piece of shit house. It's my dad's place. We do our own things and bump into each other occasionally."

A dog ran to the length of its chain, barking and showing teeth.

"As I said, I wasn't dealt a royal flush."

CHAPTER 22

Eli Simmons
Present Day

CLAIRE HAD ASKED ELI his story, but even if there had been time, he wouldn't have shared it. There were too many characters, too many scenes, and to be honest, they all belonged to him. He would share pieces. It wasn't as if he had something to hide, but he considered them his own. No one got to travel his whole life trip with him, either at the time of the events or after the tale had ended.

Eli Simmons was born a drifter. He couldn't remember when he wasn't an outsider, watching and learning but never fully belonging. As with most humans, Eli had little to no memory of his early years, the ones before the age of five. However, one memory haunted him. He wondered if changing this single moment would alter all the subsequent moments of his life. In his memory, he was a boy of about five years old playing with a yellow Matchbox car on a dirty beige carpet. A slender woman wearing jeans and a tattered yellow T-shirt watched him as she sat at a kitchen table, smoking a cigarette, and blowing puffs of smoke into the air. She was barefoot and Eli recalled the boniness of her calloused feet.

Occasionally, he glanced up from the paths his car created in the carpet and locked eyes with her before refocusing on the toy. Her contemptuous stare made him feel uncomfortable. What had he done? How could he make her stop staring at him that way? Eli stood, his belly full of butterflies, and walked toward her. She blew another puff of smoke. With a shaky hand, he reached out to her, offering his cherished toy. She didn't take it. Instead, she watched him, again with the same disdain in her eyes, and then blew the smoke in his face. Eli coughed, causing the woman to chortle. She then mashed her cigarette in the ashtray, stood, and disappeared into a bedroom. This memory was the only one he held of the nameless woman. He couldn't recall if she was his mother or one of the many foster parents he would have throughout his childhood. Still, something about her was different, and different had to mean important.

The memories he could recall after that one came in blips rather than a linear pattern. He could not remember which foster family took him on first, nor how many there had been. He stopped counting his families after about six of them had handed him back to the system. Eli never understood why they didn't let him stay. Never having experienced a stable home, he once believed all children were shuffled from one place to the next.

The children at his various schools never invited him to playdates, so he wasn't privy to the intricacies of their family lives. Little things, however, made him aware that his life differed from the others. The parents huddled in the hugs and kisses zone in front of the school. This was the designated area where the parents transferred their children's care from themselves to the school personnel. The parents were not allowed to walk their kids to the classrooms.

Eli watched as the moms and dads said their goodbyes. He noted a tenderness between the parents and children that his varying families did not share with him. Some children clung to their parents, a desire he did not understand. Eli noted the relationships with siblings as they passed in the hallways. The teachers embraced students from the previous years. Eli never stayed at a school long enough to see last year's teachers.

Some of the foster parents spoke kindly and seemed to like him, at least for a while. Then, they got bored with his quiet ways and stopped trying to interact. Some of the homes were filled with yelling or strict rules. He didn't mind the rules. He liked routine, but the yelling was unsettling. He ate his afterschool snack, did his homework and chores, and went to bed on time. In his opinion, he demanded little of his families, yet within months, they would send him back, and a new family would eventually take him in.

Sometimes, Eli would overhear conversations. "He's so quiet. It creeps me out. He's always watching us." Why were those things so bad? It's how he experienced the world. He learned more that way, and even if his families never really got to know him, it's how he became a part of them. It's the closest he felt to belonging. It's not that he couldn't speak or never spoke. He answered questions with simple phrases. He could have gone on, but he didn't feel the need. Some people entered a room needing to turn on the television for noise, but the noise felt like an intrusion for Eli. That's how his voice was to him: an intrusion. Not that he didn't like himself or his voice, but why turn on a device when the quiet had felt so comfortable?

When he was sixteen, his foster father had pushed him against the wall. Eli smelled alcohol on his breath as he spewed ugly words at him about being deaf and dumb. Eli ran from the house and into the night air. For hours, he wandered the streets, hearing the words of his drunken foster father mixed with the voices of past foster parents. Words he'd heard through closed doors and sometimes to his face. "That kid's as bright as a two-watt bulb. What job could he do even if he did manage to graduate? He's going to end up on the streets."

Their predictions became true. Two days after running away, Eli was starving and sitting on the sidewalk in town with his back against the brick wall of an office building. Black billowing clouds rolled in from the west. For the first time, Eli had no idea what the future held. Without the foster system, he was homeless. To his knowledge, no one from the system came looking for him, even though they must have been aware of him running away. The fact made him both relieved and a bit surprised, but Eli was more curious than afraid. Change was coming, and he watched the clouds as if they would open and share secrets with him.

"What are you doing out here, boy? This storm's gonna be a doozy. Best get yourself inside."

Eli looked up at the man but didn't speak.

"How old are you, boy?"

"Sixteen." His throat tightened around his response. Was he saying too much? Too little? Could he trust the man before him wearing old khaki pants, a raincoat, and beaten-up work boots?

"You got a place to go?"

"No, sir."

The man stood with his hands on his hips, looking up and down the sidewalk. After a long moment, he looked back at Eli.

"You need work?"

"Yes, sir."

"I need some help on my farm. You willing to do farm work?"

"Yes, sir."

"You can stay with our family for the night. We'll give it a try." He gestured toward the pick-up truck parked down the road a bit. Eli followed the man, glancing back at the looming storm. The skies had spoken, and Eli had listened.

Mr. Bates and his family let him stay in a room above their garage and taught him how to drive a tractor and milk cows. They also taught him how to drive the farm truck and helped him get his license. Eli never knew if the man researched his history, but the boy and man were what each other needed. Eli stayed until Mr. Bates took a payout, and the farm was eaten up by a larger corporation. The family showed Eli how to use a bank account and gave him a generous bonus. He added to the account the money he had stashed away while working there, minus enough to buy the cheapest car that would run, an old gray Chevy with a rusted-out floorboard. They shook hands and parted ways.

He mostly slept in his car and only occasionally splurged on a hotel if the weather was too cold, or the storms were bad enough to frighten him. But mostly, he liked the storms and the feeling of change in the air.

It wasn't long before another farmer needed a hired man and then another. Each experience either made him stronger or showed his weaknesses. In his earlier years, his shortcomings sometimes led to him politely being let go. The farms, although similar, had their own ways of doing things, and the steps blended and blurred together. After one too many mess-ups, or when a more able person would come along, the farmer would sit him down as if he were his own child and tell him he was no longer needed. Eli didn't hold a grudge. He let the wind take him to the next stop. As he aged, he no longer lost jobs in this manner.

Sometimes, he took short term seasonal jobs that ended when the harvesting was complete. He enjoyed this type of employment. As time passed, he became more comfortable with his life. Once, when passing through a small town, he stopped at a flea market. He was not one to waste money on material things since he had no room for anything but necessities, but he ran across one sign that spoke to him. The sign read, "Not all who wander are lost." The sign rode around in the back seat, reminding him that his life, albeit different than most, was not a failure. He was not a failure. In fact, he couldn't picture a life that had him strapped to one place or one group of people.

Each stop was a short story, with its own beginning and end, rather than a chapter building up to one big novel. But with each new story, just as a writer fine tunes their skills, he became a stronger, more confident character. As much as he enjoyed experiencing each one, some more than others, just as when reading a series of short stories, he didn't want them to go on. He had learned to be comfortable with the quiet solitude of his life. The peace that he had discovered took shape when his life led him to one farmer and his wife.

Long before heading to the Phillips's property, he worked on a farm owned by Mr. Lyle Burkett, who helped Eli discover his faith. As most of his jobs began, he saw an ad in the paper and drove his rusty Chevy down the dusty dirt road to an old farmhouse. The buildings were in disrepair, and the lawn needed tending. When he met Mr. Burkett, he realized why. Eli suspected the man to be in his eighties. His back was hunched, and he moaned as he bent to milk each cow. Mrs. Pauline Burkett was a round, jolly woman who baked cookies all day, wrapped them in ribbons, and passed them out to their few neighbors and friends. She couldn't eat them on account of her diabetes and, since she always had her husband's health in mind, held him to a strict diet of one cookie a day.

The Burketts helped him settle into the camper that would later become his home on the road. He lived in their backyard and woke up each morning to the sound of their rooster crowing. Mr. Burkett enjoyed sharing stories about his life, his faith, his children, grandchildren, and his experiences running the farm. When he talked, his eyes sparkled in a way that only elderly eyes do. Eli didn't know the name of the condition that made old men's eyes shine as if they were about to cry, but Mr. Burkett had it. However, Mr. Burkett never displayed any sadness. With a voice full of joy, he recounted the tales that shaped his life.

Eli loved hearing them, how Mr. Burkett referred to him

as a son, and how Mrs. Burkett snuck him cookies when her husband wasn't looking. "We don't want to tempt Mr. Burkett. He already had his share," she would say with a smile.

Their herd had dwindled down to thirty cows. Mr. Burkett had sold off much of his machinery and rented his fields to neighboring farmers. In return, the farmers would fill Mr. Burkett's silos and haymow with enough food for the winter months. Whether or not this was an even trade, Eli wasn't sure, but everyone seemed happy.

On Sundays, their grown children would come to visit. There were three of them: a boy and two girls. Between them, there were five grandchildren who raced around the farm, squealing in delight, until their parents called them in for Sunday dinner. Mrs. Burkett always invited Eli to join them for their meals, an invitation he often accepted. He never missed a Sunday dinner though, not just because of the quantity and heartiness of the meal, which was always followed by dessert, but because of the beautiful chaos of family and laughter. The raucous harmony only quieted when Mr. Burkett bowed his head in prayer before the meal. This quiet reverence made Eli curious enough to join the family at Sunday service, and it was the peace he found there that he clung to in the passing years.

As much as Eli had learned to trust life's journey, he had not been introduced to the belief that God was the one behind his steering wheel. That He was the one responsible for chance encounters and the peace Eli had found with each one. When Eli attended church with Lyle one Sunday, a curtain was drawn back, revealing the backstage crew so to speak. From that day, Eli knew he wasn't a drifter in the same sense of the word. He was a man standing on a rock, and watching the waters pass him by. He had found solid ground.

The Burkett farm was the only farm that had tempted Eli to stay forever. Still, maybe he only allowed for this temptation because he knew what he had with this family would not last. This story ended when Mr. Burkett leaned down to pick up a towel and kept falling. Eli heard the washing bucket tip as the old man's body slammed into it. He raced to the house, seeking the words he needed. He only uttered "Help," and Mrs. Burkett was on the phone, somehow knowing they would need an ambulance.

Eli watched as strange men loaded Mr. Burkett's body into the back of the vehicle. Their children came from nowhere, it seemed, sobbing as they held their mother. The next morning, Eli did the chores alone. And the next day. Mrs. Burkett called him inside when chores were finished and presented him with the dressiest clothes he had ever owned.

"My son thought you might need these to wear to the service. I hope you will come."

He thanked her politely, took the clothes, and wore them to say goodbye to the closest thing to a father figure he had ever had.

Mrs. Burkett warned him that they were selling everything except the camper. She wanted him to have it. She only asked that he stay until after the auction. Within days of the funeral, Eli woke to the sound of trucks. When he opened the camper door, the driveway was filled with large cattle trucks. One by one, the cows walked up the ramps. The large trailer doors slammed shut, and the metallic clang resonated in Eli's ears. Farmers from nearby farms hopped up into the different vehicles and drove away with Mr. Burkett's cattle. A tear rolled down Eli's cheek for the first time in his memory. For days, he stayed in his camper parked in the yard. Mrs. Burkett went to her daughter's house so she wouldn't have to be alone. Before leaving, she told him to stay as long as he wanted, and when ready, he could take the camper with him, but the farm was ghostlike without the Burketts and their animals. He needed to begin a new story.

He drove his Chevy into town, traded it for a used pick-up truck in far better condition, and returned to hook up the camper. He drove until something told him to stop, and he began the next story with the next family. Years passed this way, and then a decade passed before he reached Derby Line and parked in an old unused parking lot where he drank coffee and scanned the want ads. The next day, he pulled into Mr. Phillips's farm, his file of references on the seat of his truck. He had no idea how this next story would challenge him.

CHAPTER 23

Dylan Phillips
Past

IN THE FOLLOWING WEEKS, Marybeth became a constant figure at their home. Lady Bella was the only lucky hen who kept her eggs rather than having them taken for use in the kitchen or placed inside the incubator. Each day, the girls candled the eggs by going into the dark pantry and holding a flashlight against the shell. They noted how a small blood sack formed in most of them. As the weeks passed, the blood sack evolved into a little being with a beating heart. Even Dylan's family members became curious, although her father watched from afar and tried to hide his interest. Dylan and Marybeth's enthusiasm even gained the attention of their classmates. Soon, Olivia and Christina were following the daily progress. With the help of Marybeth's cell phone, the girls could share pictures and videos.

Dylan could not be sure whether it was the baby chicks or Marybeth, but her classmates began noticing her. Olivia and Christina waved the two of them over at lunch to sit with them. Dylan smiled when it seemed appropriate but remained as silent as she could. The fewer words Dylan used, the less chance for them to remember she didn't fit in at all. Marybeth spoke some, but she, too, was careful around the girls. The others still judged them, seeing if Marybeth's presence was worth bringing Dylan into the mix. Dylan had not noticed them trying to get between their friendship, at least not yet.

On Friday, Olivia mentioned their plans to go to a movie. Dylan noticed

Christina's expression of warning aimed at her friend, but it was too late. If they did not invite Dylan and Marybeth, the moment would turn awkward.

"You two are welcome to join us," Olivia said.

"Are you sure?" Marybeth asked, aware of the tense glance that had passed between the girls.

"Of course." Christina smiled; the tension eased from her shoulders as she accepted the change in plans.

"What movie?" Marybeth asked.

"I have no clue." Olivia laughed. "We go to see whatever so we can escape our parents' prying eyes."

Marybeth glanced at Dylan. She shrugged as if to say, I will go if you do.

"We're in then. Where should we meet?"

"In front of the theater. Seven o'clock," Christina confirmed.

Hours later, after switching nights in the barn with Jessie and working out the rides with Marybeth, they pulled up to the theater.

"You two buy the popcorn. We brought treats to share." Olivia tapped her purse with a wink.

"Okay," Marybeth replied.

"We'll meet you inside," one of them called over her shoulder, but Dylan was too distressed to tell which one.

"My parents only gave me enough for a ticket," Dylan whispered.

"Don't worry. I have money."

Marybeth ordered a large, refillable bucket of popcorn and a gigantic cup of diet soda. With full hands, they walked down the dark theater, looking for two familiar heads. Once they reached the front, without luck, they turned back. Olivia and Christina sat in the back row, giggling.

"You two looked so dumb." Olivia laughed.

Marybeth giggled back as if sure their banter was friendly. Dylan suspected something darker. As soon as they sat, Christina grabbed the bucket.

"I love popcorn." Her voice was too loud for a theater. She stuffed a

large handful in her mouth. The woman in front of them turned and gave a threatening glance. "Sorry," Christina said, flipping the bird as soon as the moviegoer turned around.

After a few moments, Marybeth, who had sat closest to Christina, whispered, "What snack did you bring?"

The two girls snickered again.

"One you'll like." She reached into her purse and pulled out two small bottles.

"What's that."

"Cinnamon liquor. It's delicious." Christina handed it to Marybeth who only stared at the bottle. "Well, take it already." Marybeth took the bottles. "I only have one for each of you."

"I...," Marybeth began and then stopped. "Thanks."

She handed one to Dylan, and they stared into each other's eyes, mouths agape.

"Should we?" Marybeth mouthed the words.

"I think we have to," Dylan whispered.

They unscrewed their bottles and put the spicy liquid to their lips. As it slid down Dylan's throat, it burned, making her cough. The woman in front of them turned around again as Dylan dropped the bottle onto her lap. Had she done it in time? Once the woman's attention fell back on the screen, the girls compared their progress. Only the necks of the bottles were empty.

"That was kind of yummy," Marybeth whispered. Despite Dylan's fear, her friend's beaming smile made her chuckle.

"On the count of three." Dylan raised her drink. "One. Two. Three." Together, they tossed back the rest of the beverage.

By the time the movie ended, the warm sensation of the forbidden drink had vanished. Christina handed Marybeth a cinnamon candy.

"In case your mother suspects something," she said with a smile.

The three of them huddled together, with Dylan a few feet from them.

Should she try to move into their huddle? Had Dylan drifted from them, or had they drifted from her?

"That's pretty brilliant," Marybeth exclaimed as she unwrapped the sweet and popped it in her mouth.

"This isn't my first rodeo," Christina said with a proud smirk.

Dylan looked on, waiting for Marybeth to remember she was standing there as well. Finally, they locked gazes, Dylan unable to keep her hurt from her eyes. Was this where their friendship crumbled? Dylan glanced down the road, hoping to see Marybeth's mom pulling up. She needed to get away from Christina and Olivia and the feeling that the one good thing in her life was about to slip away.

"Do you have another candy for Dylan?" Marybeth's afterthought came too late to make Dylan's fears ease.

"Let me check." Christina dug through her purse.

"I love that purse," Marybeth said in a voice too high and fake. Why was she acting this way? Marybeth didn't care about purses. She cared about chickens and cows and science experiments.

"I found one," Christina exclaimed just as Marybeth's mom pulled up to the curb. "The wrapper fell off." She laughed. "You might need to wipe it off."

"Hello, girls. How was the movie?" Marybeth's mother asked. Her smile concealed the tiredness in her eyes.

"It was great, Mrs. O'Brien. Thanks for letting Marybeth come," Olivia answered.

"Wonderful. Let's get going, ladies. It's late."

Dylan looked down at the dirty candy. She could still taste the cinnamon drink on her tongue. Glancing at Olivia, who was staring at her with a smirk, Dylan popped the filthy candy into her mouth, letting the rough surface scrape against her tongue. What was the debris from the bottom of Olivia's purse now swirling around in her mouth? Dylan wanted to spit it out, but how could she? She swallowed hard, forcing most of it down her throat.

That night, Dylan tossed and turned. Not only did she fear she was losing her friend, but she also feared someone had seen her drinking, and that someone would tell her parents. A piece of her wanted them to know. She wanted them to sit her down and yell at her. At least then, they would recognize her existence. But the anger at them transformed to a pit of guilt. As frustrated as she was with them, she still feared disappointing them. She was caught between two colliding worlds. She needed to fit in with her peers, and she needed her parents to be proud of her. One of those worlds would need to give way for the other to survive.

She wished she had a phone. Maybe Marybeth tossed and turned in her bed as well. Or maybe she was texting Christian and Olivia, making bonds Dylan could not be a part of. This intruding thought bothered her even more than the guilt of sneaking drinks and the fear of getting caught.

The following day, Dylan needed to wake up early for chores. Her mom was already in the kitchen. She held a piping hot mug of coffee close to her lips as she scanned her nursing notes. They made small talk as sleepy Dylan slid on her coat and boots. Before she walked out the door, her mom stood, placing her hands on Dylan's shoulders. She then brushed the bangs from her eyes.

"You look tired."

"I didn't sleep well."

Her mom smiled softly as she gazed into her eyes. "I love you, Dylan."

Dylan's gaze drifted to the floor, and her weight shifted from foot to foot. She wanted to run. "I love you, too."

CHAPTER 24

Eli Simmons
Present Day

Frost coated the grass, and gray clouds floated across the sky. Eli's boots crunched through the ice as he walked across the pasture to the barn. Conner was coming out of the shed, where he had been spending more and more time lately. Conner locked the door and turned to watch Eli walk up the driveway.

"Is that your man cave?" Eli asked with a grin, but when he looked closer at his boss's drawn expression, he wanted to bite back his words. "Is everything okay?"

"It's as it always is."

A bitter wind gust pushed Eli. Unspoken words lingered in the air between them. Eli studied Conner's dark circles beneath his eyes and the stubble on his ashen face. Life's problems were eating away at this man.

"Is there anything I can do to help?"

"Did you see her? Was Claire in the bar last night?"

"Yeah, she was there."

"Was she with a man?"

"Not when I was there." Little lies, little holes in the story, were necessary at times. At least, that's what Eli told himself.

Another gust cut through the air, and Eli wrapped his jacket around him. "She sat at a table with several female students. When they got up to dance, she headed to the bar for a drink. That's when she noticed me."

"Did you talk?"

"Small talk. Claire asked if I liked farming. It was a very surface-level conversation, and then she left. I never saw her with a man."

Conner's shoulders eased as the tension melted. He nodded. "Good to know." The smell of whiskey wafted in the air as Eli followed him to the barn.

"If you ever need a night off, I can handle things. Grab a nice dinner and movie with your wife," Eli said to his boss's back.

"And how many relationships have you had? You don't know the first thing about my situation." Conner spit out his words, causing Eli to freeze in his tracks. However, Conner never turned around to face Eli. He remained his cold, impenetrable self, and Eli followed his lead, becoming careful and watchful.

Not able to bear sitting across the quiet kitchen table from Conner, Eli excused himself from lunch and headed into town to eat fast food in a parking lot and watch the people in town through his truck window. Afterward, he drove around, checking areas he had never seen and staying away from the Phillips's farm as long as possible.

When he could no longer stay away without being late for chores, he headed back to the property. He stopped to wait for a passing car before turning into the field where his camper was parked. A figure moved at the cornfield's edge.

Before he could give the person his full attention, a passing vehicle blocked his view momentarily. Whoever was there had disappeared too quickly to be identified beyond having long dark hair.

Eli could not be sure which one of the girls hid in the stalks. Were they spying on him? But why? Or were they more interested in the cornfield? How many times had the teenagers strolled through the rows looking for what he could only assume to be the rest of David Miller's body? Why would they do so? Did they know the land was a designated crime scene, and they weren't supposed to wander without police supervision? Of course, the girls knew these rules. Curiosity can create powerful, irresistible temptations for teenagers. As a teenager, Eli would have snuck out there as well.

Adolescence was a time when death seemed distant, or so they thought. The creepiness of death fascinated young minds, and for the two girls Eli struggled to understand, their interest might have stemmed from something deeper.

A gothic air seeped from them, almost inviting darkness into their lives. The local police's demands would not be enough to deter their desire to surround themselves with the mystery of death. The police department lacked enough officers to watch over hundreds of acres, making it easy for people to wander. As Eli pulled up to his camper, the hairs stood on his neck. What other circumstances besides youth would tempt a person to break laws and search the fields for the evidence the investigators were sure to find in the coming weeks?

The rest of the day passed uncomfortably. Jessie came out to help with evening chores but mimicked her father's mood, which Eli noticed often happened. Conner dictated so much yet he either didn't notice or didn't care about his influence. When the chores were finished, Eli dragged his tired body across the road and through the pasture. The atmosphere in the barn had exhausted him more than the work itself.

The volunteer fire department's siren blared in the distance, setting off the coyotes. Their yippy calls echoed in the chilly air. They were close, but not close enough for him to be afraid. He rather enjoyed their haunting music. He grabbed the kerosene from under the camper, poured some over the dry wood he had collected in his firepit, and threw a match into the pile. The blaze shot up quickly and then eased. He found a thicker log and placed it in the middle of the stone circle. Once a solid fire roared and crackled in the pit, Eli pulled up his lawn chair and poked at the embers with a stick.

His mind drifted back to the many families he had met through the foster care system and the stories the children had shared with him while they lay in rooms lined with bunk beds as they waited for their next temporary home. Not every foster family was looking for a paycheck and willing to tolerate but not enjoy the extra mouth they had to feed to earn one. Some families were kind and wanted to make a difference in someone's life. Some homes had one foster parent, while others had couples. The marriages were sometimes strong, while other times, they seemed strained. Sometimes, the strain was caused by not being able to have children of their own. Sometimes, it was created because one adult wanted children while the other partner did not. A foster child served as their happy medium.

Eli had met many children through the years who watched as their foster parents' excitement about their temporary child tapered when the woman found out she was pregnant. The temporary child was returned to the home to wait for a new family, a new chance.

But in the Phillips's case, the loss of a child was more traumatic than never having had one at all, Eli supposed. Those who had never experienced pregnancy, baby kicks, the moment of birth, the first steps, the first words, and all the wonders of bringing children into the world might disagree. Eli had read once that eighty percent of marriages ended after the loss of a child. The results varied, but if the parents blamed one another or found it too difficult to share their feelings with each other, the days, months, and years following the loss could be detrimental. Dylan and Jessie were watching the loss of their parents' marriage every day. Again, his heart filled with pain for the two girls. Eli recalled the times when he believed he didn't matter to anyone. If he disappeared, would anyone notice or care? The question had haunted him for years.

The coyotes howled again. This time, they sounded like they were standing at the edge of the woods. The threat of something ominous lingered in the air. He poked the fire again, wanting more light in the darkness. As he did, that image of the figure drifting back into the cornfield forced itself into his mind. He needed to help the family. Conner and Claire needed to come back to life and see their two daughters suffocating in sadness. The girls' lives had to matter as much as the death of their son. They had to choose the light in their lives over the darkness before more damage was done.

CHAPTER 25

Claire Phillips
Present Day

CLAIRE STRETCHED OUT BENEATH her heavy quilt. The spot beside her had already cooled. Conner had been up for hours. She placed her hand on his side of the bed, missing the days when they would snuggle into each other before starting their day. But the memory only saddened her. She pulled her hand back to her chest and stared at the ceiling. The house stood silently around her, and the sun beamed through the windows. She guessed the time to be nine or close to it. Rarely did she ever sleep in so late, but it was Sunday, a day of rest, at least for her. Conner and the girls would be deep into their chores by now. Guilt over her moment of laziness threatened to wash over her, but she pushed it from her mind. Maybe she would surprise her family with hot cocoa. The idea warmed her, if only for a moment.

Eli had the day off as he did every Sunday. He seemed nice, but she wouldn't be fooled. After Claire caught one of the hired help smoking weed in the driveway, she started complaining to Conner. She couldn't have these men around her children. The first time Conner hired an ex-convict, they had one of the worst fights of their relationship. After that, he stopped telling her about the men's so-called resumes. And now, a jawbone belonging to one of their former hires had shown up at their neighbor's house. What was she to do if somehow the authorities blamed Conner for David's death. What if he went away to prison even for a short time? They would lose everything. She had lost all control of her marriage, her children, and the farm. Despite knowing he wasn't entirely at fault, she hated Conner for her helplessness.

Claire pulled the blanket back, and the cold air stung her skin. The heat never reached their back bedroom the way she had wished it would. She wrapped her faded blue housecoat around herself and slipped on her fluffy slippers. The old stairs creaked under her weight despite her tiny frame. She entered the kitchen and searched the pantry for hot cocoa mix. An empty box sat on the shelf. Claire sighed heavily and tossed the box into the recycling bin. Still, the longing for something comforting stuck with her.

Cookies. Claire pulled out cookie sheets. Baking, she hoped, would bring back a feeling of normalcy. Dust floated to the cracked linoleum floor, tempting her to return the cooking supplies to their spot in the cupboard. She was the mom. She could cast light into her family's darkness, but even as she gave herself the pep talk, exhaustion, deep-rooted to her core, fought to drown her. Still, she took ingredients out of the pantry and found a mixing bowl.

If only she could start all over and never marry a farmer. What had she been thinking? She hated the lifestyle, the poverty, the smells, the work. But she had loved Conner so much, and because of that love, she thought her feelings for the lifestyle would change. Someday, she would come to love the land as much as Conner did.

When Conner proposed, Claire only agreed to become a farmer's wife once he promised to keep her out of the barn. She could and would share his dream with him, but her part would be watching the world of farming through the kitchen window, where she would make their house a home. Conner smiled and promised. And for a few years, their lives unfolded exactly as he assured her it would. Claire gave birth to Dylan, and Conner and Claire fell further in love. Then she gave birth to Jessie, and their love deepened despite the bills and obstacles. Claire filled the house with the smells of freshly baked cookies she had created with two giggling girls who licked more batter out of the bowls than made it onto the pan.

As Claire mixed the chocolate chips into the batter, she heard the whispered giggles of the past chirping in her ears. A soft smile tugged at the corner of her lips, but guilt forced the emotion away. How could she be happy when such a big part of her life was now missing? What kind of mother would that make her if she moved on? Claire plopped the globs of batter onto the prepared pan, and her mind drifted to the past again.

Fall was her favorite time of year. She used to line her old farmhouse porch with pumpkins and mums. Apple pies would cool on the windowsills as fall leaves drifted softly to the ground, coating the world in red and orange. At night, Conner and she would sit on their front porch swing, holding hands and watching the stars. She would drape a blanket across their legs and feel their combined warmth fight against the cool autumn air.

Claire placed the cookie sheet in the oven and began washing the dishes. The aroma of chocolate chips filled the kitchen as it had so many years ago. They'd been good years, better than good. But they hadn't known that. How could they have known? Instead of cherishing those times with their girls, they felt something was missing from their lives, and without it, the pressures of farming began to weigh on them. Conner's positive attitude dwindled to a half-hearted enthusiasm. Lines were forming on his face, and his smile was fading. However, one blessing could reignite his spirit if only it would come.

For Conner, true happiness awaited the granting of one prayer. The years passed—two, then three. Each week, Conner knelt in the church pew, offering his desire to the one he held in such faith. With each passing month, Claire's inability to give Conner the boy he prayed for made her feel small and incapable. Conner's moods would darken for periods, increasing the pressure she felt. Eventually, he would return his gaze to his wife and young girls, four and six at the time, seeming to accept that the son he wished for would never become reality. The acceptance would sometimes last for weeks and even months.

By this point, the farm devoured any profit they hoped to earn, and her and Conner's quiet moments under the stars became more strained. The paint job that the house needed cost far more money than they could afford, and with all the chores, Conner only had time to repair what was vital to survival. But each morning, Conner kissed her forehead and promised that next year would get better. But the following year, they didn't pull a profit, and the emptiness in her womb grew heavier. They were both failing.

When the third pregnancy took hold, she held her breath in anticipation for twenty weeks, waiting for the sex to be revealed. Conner didn't go to the ultrasound with her, but he was waiting in the driveway when she returned. When she stepped out of the car with a beaming smile, Conner knew his prayers had been answered. Months later, Claire gave birth to a boy with golden brown hair. As he grew, his eyes turned bluer and his hair wavier. He didn't look like any of them, yet he was the best of all of them. If Claire hadn't believed in angels before, Hayden was proof of a divine world that was always within reach despite her inability to see it.

The memory of her son punched Claire, making breathing difficult. She fumbled for a kitchen chair and let the tears fall into the palms of her hands. She didn't notice the smell of burning cookies. She didn't hear the door squeak or hear her husband and two children enter the room. She only saw her son, her sweet and perfect child, who was loved beyond measure. Only when she heard Dylan whisper, "Mom," did she raise her chin and reveal her tear-stricken face. Her remaining family stood so close, but they couldn't touch her. She was lost to the past, to the one they'd placed on a pedestal.

CHAPTER 26

Eli Simmons
Present Day

ELI'S SUNDAY GAVE HIM a slight reprieve from his concerns. He attended service at a small chapel, bought a few necessary items, and did his laundry. Once home, he hiked the property, keeping away from the unsettling cornfields and as far from the farm as possible. Weeks before, he'd discovered a flat stone that sat on the edge of one of the fields and had visited the spot frequently during his breaks. Deer would occasionally strut across the fields. When they noticed him, they would stop and watch him in the same curious way he watched them. When he locked gazes with them, a sense of peace settled over him.

Eli found peace and sometimes answers in the calmness of nature. Prayer was like that to him as well, and the rock he sat upon became his church on days when he could not or chose not to attend. Sometimes, he prayed as he gazed out over the field, and other times he listened for direction that came to him in unexplainable ways.

Today, he prayed. He prayed for a peace to wash over him, to fill him to the brim so that it overflowed to the family that teetered on destruction. But Eli knew there was still hope.

He had found it for himself at the age of sixteen when he'd sat on the cold sidewalk in the rain with not a soul in the world to care about him.

The farmer who had put out his hand in kindness had given him that hope, like a candle in the darkness. And that light lived within Eli now. He thought about a Christmas Eve candlelight service with the Burkett family, and how Mr. Burkett held a candle and passed the flame to him. Eli then passed the flame to the person next to him. The flame continued to spread from one candle to the next, making the church fill with warmth and wonder. He wasn't sure how he could pass the flame to the Phillips family, but he also knew he didn't need to know how. Where there was prayer, there were answers.

After spending a peaceful afternoon on the sun-warmed rock, Eli returned to his camper. He made a small fire in the fire pit using some dried logs he had piled nearby. As the smell of burning wood filled the air, he settled into his lawn chair and opened the local newspaper. While he read about community events and local happenings, he roasted a plump hot dog over the crackling flames as they danced in the air, creating a warm glow. Even though the family allowed him to download his programs onto his phone using their passwords, the distance from their house and the spotty Wi-Fi connection made the service struggle to maintain a steady stream. That wasn't a problem for Eli, though; he relished the moment's serenity, finding more joy in reading the paper than in the distractions of a television or phone. He even appreciated that he could use the paper as kindling once he finished reading the day's news. As night fell and the stars twinkled in the clear sky, Eli prepared for bed, feeling content and relaxed. The gentle sounds of nature surrounded him, and he drifted off to sleep without a care in the world, undisturbed and untroubled by what the next day might bring.

The alarm woke him at five-thirty the next morning, giving him enough time for a coffee before crossing the street and beginning his workday. When Eli reached the Phillips farm, the moon still hung above the barn. For a short time, he went about his chores to only the quiet sounds of animals standing and stretching, waking to another monotonous day of eating and being milked.

At one point, he heard the school bus halt in front of the house. Soon after, Conner entered the barn. They completed the morning chores with only necessary conversation. After lunch, Eli returned and cleaned the barn, letting the gutter cleaner carry fecal matter to the awaiting spreader. When the spreader was full, he jumped on the tractor and pulled the machine from the barn. He found comfort in the routines of his daily chores.

As he rode out into the field, something on the edge of the worn path caught his eye. Something white and rock-like peeked out from under the outer branches of a group of bushes. His mind fumbled for recognition, but it kept returning to one dreadful thought. His heart raced in anticipation. He stopped the tractor, leaving it running to not draw attention, and jumped to the ground. Eli forced his feet to move closer, hoping the object would take on a new form, but it remained the same.

The grass leading to the area had been disturbed, but not recently. The vegetation had already made gains in reverting to its natural state. He edged closer. One object became two. He looked over his shoulder for any sign of Conner in the distance. Nothing. He crept closer until he hovered over what he could no longer deny was a bone, maybe a leg. His stomach turned. Could this be David Miller?

His heart raced within his chest as he bent down and split the grass to reveal more. Attached to the bone were pieces of black and white hide. The bone was a leg bone, but not that of David Miller. It had been picked away by predators and left to decay slightly away from the rest of the remains. He gazed around the area and found other remains, but much smaller. Calves. He could count three. What the hell had happened here? He took out his phone, snapped pictures, and climbed back onto the tractor. The farm was a crime scene, and who knew if he would someday be interviewed by police. They may need this evidence if that is what it was. A chill raced up his spine like a spider.

That evening, when Jessie walked into the barn for the second daily milking, Eli sighed in relief. If he wanted any answers, she was his only hope. If all went as it usually did, he would have approximately fifteen minutes to pry before Conner joined them.

"How was school?" The question was so typical that Eli cringed before seeing Jessie's eye roll.

"I get it. School was never my thing either."

Nothing.

Eli scrambled to find words as the precious time ticked

away. What was a good segue for the questions about the graveyard in the back pasture?

Conner would be there any minute. Hell, there was only one way through this. "I saw a strange thing while spreading manure today."

Jessie glanced his way but said nothing.

"There's a bunch of carcasses out there."

She squinted at him, making him feel suspect. But of what? Simply asking where questions weren't necessary?

"Animals die on farms. Do you think my dad is going to dig holes and put gravestones up for all of them? They decay and go back to nature." Jessie dipped a towel in the bucket and shrugged. "You get used to it after a while."

"That happens a lot?"

"Not a lot, but sometimes. Calves get sick, or now and again, they're stillborn."

"I guess that makes sense." He had never seen a graveyard of animals on any other farm, but he did know that calves sometimes passed away. "But what about the cow? How did she die?"

Conner entered the far end of the barn. He stooped to pet one of the dogs that roamed the property.

"We shouldn't talk about that. Not right now, anyway."

Conner stood, becoming a looming silhouette in the distance, growing larger with each step he took toward them.

"Later?"

"Maybe." Jessie glanced toward her father with fearful eyes. "Please don't ask Dylan about it. She won't talk about it, not even with me."

"What's all the whispering about down here?" Conner studied the two of them as he spoke.

Jessie ducked between two cows, massaging the last drops of milk from the udders. Eli looked in Jessie's direction only to see her giving him a warning shake of her head.

Eli struggled for a response. "The dog you were petting. Bandit."

Conner's eyebrow raised. He needed more.

"Jessie's not a fan." The statement was lame, but Eli never claimed to be quick-witted or a good liar. He held his breath, hoping it was enough to quelch Conner's suspicious tone.

"The girls aren't a fan of much anymore." Conner looked at Jessie. "But Bandit used to be a favorite of theirs."

"Teenagers. They can be fickle. Friends one day, enemies the next."

"You can say that again. Well, at least Bandit does his own thing and doesn't cause problems. His only guilty pleasure is chasing some deer now and then."

"Sounds like a typical country dog to me."

Conner grabbed a hoe and scraped a fresh pile of manure into the gutter. The pitiful response had sufficed, but Eli's lingering questions hung in the air. How long would he have to wait to understand this family and the danger he may be in?

CHAPTER 27

Jessie Phillips
Present Day

J ESSIE TOSSED AND TURNED in bed, begging for sleep to overtake her. Eli would ask about the bones again tomorrow. If not tomorrow, soon. A piece of her wanted to keep the secret about the cow tucked in the family vault, but another part needed to share the truth because not sharing this one detail was eating away at her. Still wrestling with her decision whether or not to confide in Eli, her eyelids grew heavy. She drifted off to sleep and was soon awakened by a crash, like a dish hitting the wall. Her eyes shot open, and she rushed to the vent on the floor leading to the downstairs kitchen. She could only spy on the center of the table, but if she laid her ear against the metal, she could hear almost as well as being in the room. It wouldn't be the first time one of her parents had thrown a dish, but it had been forever since they had fought this badly. At least when they fought, they were communicating. There was hope for them if they spoke or even yelled. What scared her the most was the silence between them.

Then she heard muffled crying and envisioned her mom downstairs, trying to smother her sadness into the palms of her hands again.

"I wasn't accusing you." Her mom's voice cracked.

"It sure as hell sounds like you are."

"I was only asking what happened."

"I already told you what happened. David killed our freaking cow. Over a thousand dollars value dragged out to the bushes to rot."

"I know that part. I was here when Dylan ran into the house crying. I saw the poor animal lying in the manger."

"Then what?"

"What did you say to David before he left the barn?"

"I told him he owed me wages for the cow, which I never even took out of his last paycheck."

"Why would you have paid him then?"

"I don't like your questions."

"We're so short on cash. Why would you pay David if he owed us the money?"

"There you go again, Claire. Are you insinuating that I paid him because I knew he wouldn't be around to cash the check anyway?"

"Please, help me understand. For once, don't clam up when it gets difficult. Talk to me, please."

"I contacted his mother about the last paycheck, hoping she would know his whereabouts."

"The girls said you were really angry. Jessie thought you had scared David, and that's why he didn't come back."

"I had a right to be angry." Conner slammed his fist on the table, making it rattle.

"We were all upset about the poor cow dying like that. Hit over the head with the hoe just because she wouldn't go back in her stanchion. It makes me sick. And poor Dylan had to see Betsy die right in front of her. That's all Dylan needed, another traumatic experience."

Quiet fell over the room. Jessie could hear her heart beating against her chest.

"It's not what any of us needed." Conner's voice sounded calmer. "I'm not sure why I didn't deduct his paycheck. Maybe it was because I was so mad that day. Maybe I thought if I paid him the full amount, he would come back to work, and I could just deduct a portion at a time. I don't know. Paying him just seemed like the right thing to do at the time. I never thought doing a good deed would make me look guilty of murder to my wife." Jessie waited for her mom to her respond but heard nothing. Had they made eye contact? Had she nodded in understanding? "I'm sorry about the plate. Let me help you pick it up."

"No, I have it."

Jessie stared down at the middle of the table as her father's hand reached for her mother's. The room was silent as the two hands lay entwined. Why did the image hurt her so much, like pushing on a bruise? A minute ticked by, and then her mom's chair scratched across the floor as she pulled away from the table. The pantry door squeaked opened, and then Jessie heard the broken ceramic pieces being pushed across the floor and scooped into the dustpan.

"I'm sorry, Claire."

In a cracked voice, her mom asked, "For what?"

Jessie held her breath. Her father had the chance to say so many things. Tick, tick, tick.

"For everything."

His chair slid from the table, and then his heavy footsteps

climbed the stairs. Jessie raced from the vent and climbed back into bed. As she pulled the blankets to her chin, her door opened slightly. Her father hadn't checked in on her before bed in so many years. She had almost forgotten how he would kiss her forehead when her mind was half asleep. The memory comforted and burned at the same time. Could it be her father's plan tonight, to kiss his daughter as he once did, to show affection that had been withheld for years, or was he checking to see who might have overheard his confession?

Jessie squeezed her eyes shut and fought to calm her breathing. She counted one thousand one, one thousand two, one thousand three until she reached one thousand ten. The door closed, and her father's footsteps sounded down the hallway. The memory of their old forgotten nighttime ritual made Jessie ache for what once was. She closed her eyes wishing him back down the hallway, but the house remained silent, as she silenced her cries into her pillow.

CHAPTER 28

Jeremy Biggs
Present Day

WHEN JEREMY WOKE, HE stumbled out to the kitchen to make coffee. The couch was empty. Allen must have called for a ride, maybe even before closing his eyes, or maybe Jeremy's father had woken him in the night. He heard snoring coming from his father's bedroom but had not heard him come home.

Jeremy poured out the coffee sludge from days ago and rinsed the pot. He went to the pantry and found the bag of generic brew. Empty. Speaking a few profanities, he tossed the bag into the garbage. His dad's wallet lay on the counter. He glanced down the empty hallway and then turned his back to it while opening the tattered leather wallet. Empty. "Damnit," Jeremy muttered. After grabbing his wallet and keys from his room, he headed to his car and into town.

When he returned half an hour later, his father was watching a documentary from his recliner. He looked up at Jeremy with questioning eyes. "Who was the kid passed out on our couch last night?"

"A friend."

"That's just what you need. Another loser to mess up your life with."

Jeremy headed to the coffee maker and scooped the grounds into the machine.

"Make enough for me." Jeremy still didn't answer. "Is that bread in the bag? I'll take a piece of toast."

"Whatever."

"Don't you whatever me, or you'll find yourself on the street." His dad turned his attention back to the documentary and awaited his breakfast.

What his father said was true. Jeremy had nowhere else to go. He was twenty-four and still living in this run-down trailer with his parent. It would be one thing if he attended classes at the local college, but he didn't. Jeremy didn't have the grades, money, or intelligence to get into college anyway. Nothing he would do today could change his tomorrow for the better.

His dad thought he was nothing more than a slug despite the fact he was following in his footsteps. The difference between Jeremy and his father, and to be honest, between Jeremy and David, was that Jeremy had wanted more. He did want a different future. The problem was his inability and lack of knowledge of how to move forward. He couldn't imagine himself in any role besides a loser, already in trouble with the law, already far behind the peers he'd graduated with years ago. And if he couldn't imagine a better future, how would one magically form?

Sometimes, he wondered if his father wanted him to fail, like his failure was less threatening than having a successful child. Jeremy's mother had run off too quickly for her to be disappointed. But it wasn't until his arrest that Jeremy stopped believing in a better version of himself. To be honest, the first arrest had pissed him off. He hadn't even smoked that much pot at the time, but he and David had already become targets.

"You hear what they're saying about the musk ox? They're born with a skull three inches thick. That must be how thick yours is, as thick as a musk oxen's skull."

His dad enjoyed documentaries. Watching them and filling his mind with useless facts made him believe he was bright. Jeremy rolled his eyes as he slapped butter on a couple of slices of toast. Then he stepped over the beer cans sprawled across the filthy carpet and gave his father his food.

His dad eyed the plate. "No peanut butter?"

"We're out." Jeremy envisioned taking the toast and throwing it in his father's face, but nothing good would come from the behavior, so he swallowed his bitterness as was his general tactic.

"Weren't you just at the store? Like I said, you're as thick as a musk ox." Jeremy's fists clenched as he walked back into the kitchen, biting his tongue. "Let's see. You were arrested with that no-good David kid, and if that wasn't good enough, you got arrested again." His father shook his head and took a bite about half the size of the slice.

The coffee machine beeped. Jeremy stood with his hands on the counter, staring at his father as he shoveled in the last bite. "You bringing the coffee, or you gonna let me choke on the dry bread?" The words were understandable despite being spoken through a mouthful of food.

Jeremy poured the hot liquid, never taking his eyes off

the man he struggled not to hate. "Musk ox about sums it up. How long will it be until you and this new friend are wearing cuffs?"

Jeremy tossed his half-eaten toast into the garbage, and headed to the door, letting it slam behind him.

"Where the hell's my coffee?" His father shouted at him through the closing door.

On the front porch, he closed his eyes and took a deep breath, breathing out his anger. He had to get away from his father. Somehow, he had to get away.

Jeremy stomped off the porch and across the driveway to his truck. He turned the key in the ignition, and the engine fought for life. As soon as he heard the steady hum, he sped out of the driveway and headed down the country road, chased by memories of his second arrest. The night had started with David and him at a party. They were several six-packs in, and one of the kids mentioned he wanted some pot. Jeremy hadn't touched the stuff since his last arrest. Enough time had passed since the arrest that Jeremy pushed the whole thing out of his mind. But some of his past contacts still lived within his phone. His buzz led him to believe searching for Speedo in his contacts would be a good idea. Speedo was not the guy's real name, nor was a name anyone else knew of. The comical name choice came about completely at random one drunken night in high school when Jeremy entered the number into his contacts. "I got this," he said to the group of kids who had somehow allowed him and David to join them for the night. Or had they invited themselves?

"You sure?" One of them said, a warning in his voice.

"I know a guy." Jeremy typed the name in his phone

and then entered the code phrase: *Do you still skate on the weekends?*

Only moments passed before he received the reply.

Sure do. Same place as always. I can be there in ten.

Jeremy grabbed his jacket. "You stay," he said to David. "I'll be back in a few." Thinking back, he probably told David to stay to ensure he would still be invited back into the house.

Excitement raced through his limbs. He had missed this feeling. Speedo had never skated, or at least not to Jeremy's knowledge. The convenience store serving as 'the skating rink' was only half a mile away. The night was crisp, but occasionally, hints of spring lingered in the air. Jeremy felt alive walking under the stars, alone with a heavy buzz that made him believe great things were possible, even for him.

When he reached the store, one car was parked in front of the windowed front, while another was parked off to the side. Even before the headlights blinked at him, he figured Speedo would be sitting in the one to the side. He climbed in the passenger side, looked Speedo in the eye, and, for the first time that night, sensed something was off. Speedo's eyes were shifty, unlike the cocky kid of the past. Jeremy's heart began to race, but he told himself he was being foolish.

"How much?"

"One gram." Jeremy knew to keep the amount under two ounces to avoid prison. He reached inside his coat pocket with a shaky hand and pulled out the money. Speedo handed the bag to him, which he took and tucked in his pocket. Without another word, Jeremy stepped out of the vehicle. That's when the night sky came alive with red and blue lights.

When the cops placed the cuffs on his wrists and tucked him into the back of the police vehicle, Jeremy was alone. He would not make the call to his dad that night. He would wait until the next day to prove his father right yet again.

Jeremy kept driving until the memories quieted and his anger had subsided into despair.

That next evening, Allen and Jeremy worked together again. Jeremy waited until after the dinner crowd had dwindled to a few tables. "What happened to you the other night?"

"I woke up when your dad came in. He looked pretty surprised to see someone on the couch."

"I don't have many sleepovers." Sarcasm was thick in Jeremy's voice.

"I texted this girl."

As if on cue, Amber sauntered into the kitchen. "Great setup you got yourself, Jeremy. You must bring in all the ladies."

She grabbed a pad and pen and walked back into the dining area.

"Seriously?" Jeremy stared at the man he was forced to befriend.

Allen shrugged. "What can I say?"

They washed the pots and pans in silence. Jeremy sensed a heaviness in the air in warning that a heavy conversation was on the horizon. Allen cleared his throat. "Listen. I wanted to ask you. What happened that day?" Allen glanced over his shoulder. No one was around. "Be square with me. Do you know what happened to David?"

Jeremy hesitated. What instigated this question? Was it

Allen's fear or Amber's curiosity? He took a deep breath. He had nothing to hide, and hell, he would want to know if he were Allen. "I can't say for sure. I only know that I dropped David off at the farm that morning. I can't remember if I watched him walk into the barn or not. By the time they found his bones, months had passed. I can't remember every detail from a day that long ago." Frustration flared in his voice. "The investigators make me feel like I'm a suspect when my story changes slightly. Whose memory is really that clear anyway? Do you know who they should worry about? It's the guy who pretends he remembers anything one hundred percent. You show me that guy, and you're showing me a liar. Our minds just don't work that way."

"Ain't that the truth. I can't remember what I had for breakfast yesterday."

"I know I dropped David off. He was acting weird. Very quiet. I came right out and asked him if he was planning on bolting."

"What'd he say?"

"At first, nothing. I got pissed. David got me involved in this shit show, and if he planned on taking off and leaving me to pay the price, well, let's just say I wouldn't feel any loyalty to the bastard. But we'd been friends since grade school. I wanted to believe he wouldn't screw me over like that."

"You said, at first, he said nothing. Did David say something after?"

"Yeah, he looked me in the eye and said, 'Now, would I do something like that?'"

"I told him, 'You've taken off a ton.' David laughed and got out of the car. He looked back, took his hat off, and gave me one of his usual smiles. That's all I remember for sure. The rest is hazy."

"What made this time different? If David had taken off in the past, why not now?"

"I wasn't in the mix the other times. His leaving didn't put me in any kind of danger. I wasn't sure what they would do to me to find out information."

"And did they? Do anything?"

"No. For months, I held my breath, waiting, and nothing happened. Our boss would occasionally refer to David as some undependable scumbag. Did that mean Carlo knew David had been killed due to his lack of loyalty, or was Carlo angry that David had left him without help? I never asked. I didn't say a word. I figured silence was safer."

"Why did you think David wanted to take off then?"

"Because something happened a few days before he went missing. The deals we made took place in the back of the Phillips's property. Some were in the day when David would be driving the tractor in the back field. All he had to do was stop, grab the supply, and stash it in the barn by the manure spreader until I came by and had lunch with him. I would drive the supply to the restaurant or Carlos's other house. But sometimes, someone would get wind of border patrol in the area, and the drop would be switched to the nighttime. If it was at night, I drove him down the tractor path in the cornfield, waited while he went to the spot, and then we hightailed it out of there before we were spotted.

"We never knew the actual name of the guy who brought the drugs, but Carlo referred to him as Lupo, which means wolf in Italian, a fitting name since he was a creepy stalker.

David said he had only seen him from a distance, and even then, Lupo wore a face covering. The guy really wanted to be incognito. David's job was to drop the money and retrieve the drugs. He would then back away, Lupo would move in, count the money, and then return to the trees. This was David's only sign that Lupo was happy with the exchange.

"But we didn't have anything planned the day the weird thing happened. David was spreading manure and saw a man standing at the Canadian border, which began at the end of the field. At first, David thought the guy was with border patrol, since the man wasn't wearing a face covering, but he wasn't wearing a uniform. David stopped the tractor and stepped down. He said he was scared as shit, even though he was trying to laugh it off while he was telling me.

"David said he was a skinny Italian man. At first, the guy made David squirm for a bit, looked him straight in the eye until the situation got awkward, and then said, "'Did you get a good look?'

"David asked him what he meant, and Lupo said, 'Won't you need a description when you report back to the police?'"

"What the hell? Why did he think David would do that?"

"David wouldn't. The police had never been his friend. He wouldn't trust them with any information. He asked Lupo again what he was talking about. He just laughed. Then he said," --Jeremy pitched his voice lower, imitating what he thought Lupo might sound like--"'Do you see where I'm standing? I'm so close I could almost reach my hand around your throat from here, yet so far away it takes investigators a whole lot of paperwork to come after me. By the time they find your body, I'll be long gone. I can go places no one will ever find me. Can you say that much for yourself?'"

"He pretty much told David he was going to kill him?" Allen asked.

"Definitely told him he wasn't afraid to if David started talking. David told him he wasn't trying to hide. Then the guy says, 'If you talk, you'll want to. You'll pray to a God who turned his back on you long ago, but he won't help you. No one will.' David asked him why he was saying all that. The guy says, 'We know they have an informant.'"

"An informant?"

"But it wasn't us. David did want out, but..."

"But what?"

Jeremy shook his head. "David wasn't the informant. I wondered about it when he disappeared, but I think I would have known. Either way, Lupo was sure there was one out there. Whoever it is that's talking to the police may be the reason David is dead. Lupo thought it was him, and that's really all that mattered."

"What happened after?"

"The guy just walked off into the woods. David said he ran like his ass was on fire back to the tractor and stayed far away from the field the rest of the day. When I went to the farm for lunch, he was waiting in the driveway, looking white as a ghost. He scrambled into the car's passenger side and told me what happened. A few days later, I drove him to work, and that's the last I saw of him.

"David went missing soon after that encounter, which makes Lupo a suspect in my mind anyway. But I can't imagine David was the one working with the police. How could he be doing that without incriminating me? Unless he had worked something out for me as well. Hell, I don't know how these deals go down. But if Lupo killed David because him and his mafia buddies thought David was the informant, maybe it's why I stayed safe. Maybe they thought they got rid of the problem."

Jeremy grabbed the next pan and watched it drift to bottom of the sink. He placed his hands on the counter and let his head fall forward. "I still see David giving me the last smile. I think he knew something was going to happen that day, but I don't think he suspected his body parts would be rotting in the cornfield by nightfall." Jeremy fell silent for a moment. "I miss that son of a bitch sometimes. I only wish I knew how much of a son of a bitch he really was."

Allen took the pan and ran the steamy stream of water over it, watching the water run red with marinara sauce.

"We just have to be smarter than David Miller. How hard can that be?"

"No, Allen, you have to be smarter than the mafia, which can be very hard."

CHAPTER 29

Eli Simmons
Present Day

An Indian summer was what they called a rare day when warm temperatures triumphed over the encroaching winter. The leaves glowed in vibrant reds and oranges, and the sun beamed through the branches, giving Eli a renewed energy that he hadn't realized the cold had stolen from him.

After the morning milking, Eli and Conner went from stanchion to stanchion, releasing the cows. The gentle giants backed out of their spots and walked to the door leading them outside and into the sunshine. Eli followed them until the last of them had exited the barn. He rested his arms on the half door and watched the animals, now freed from captivity. Some of them, even the older ones with large bags, jumped around as if they were young and full of life. Eli laughed out loud at their playfulness.

He didn't see Conner come up beside him. The older man rested his arms on the door next to Eli, and they observed the sight together for a moment.

"If I were a rich man, I'd tear this old barn down and put in a different system, where they grazed until it was their time to be milked. But I am far from being a rich man." Conner sighed, and his arms fell back to his side.

"Farming can't be easy. No days off, no pay to speak of, and no respect. When's the last time you and your family took a vacation?"

Conner laughed. "A vacation. Are you serious?" Then, he quieted for a moment. "I used to take my family up to my hunting camp for a night here or there. Back when they were young enough to like it, too. Claire and I let them stay up late, and we all played Blackjack under the lantern light. They ate junk food and drank soda. They slept on mattresses that housed mice in the colder months. I would wake them early to drive out of the mountains and back to the farm. The cows still had to be milked."

"I could probably help out sometime if you want to take them up there again and not race home in the morning."

Conner's face softened into an expression Eli had not seen from him. Gratitude mixed with sadness. "I had to sell the hunting camp years back, and let's face it, those girls wouldn't be amused by the low budget getaway anymore."

Conner turned to leave, breaking up their moment of bonding. "Thanks for the offer, anyway." His shoulders drooped as he walked away and disappeared somewhere in the barn.

That evening, Eli entered the barn to find Dylan waiting at the half door where he had stood earlier that day. A few cows stood waiting to come in. How did they know the time? It fascinated Eli.

"Coboss," Dylan called through her hands, drawing out the first syllable. "Coboss."

Eli stood beside her. "Coboss? Where do you think that call came from?"

At first, Dylan said nothing in response, which is what he'd expected from her. Then to his surprise, she spoke.

"It's Latin, I believe. Bos means cow in Latin, and the Co means come."

"And it always works?"

Dylan pointed at the pasture where cows ambled from behind trees and down paths, heading straight for the barn.

"It's pretty amazing."

"You never heard that on the other farms you worked on?" Her voice was neutral.

"Can't say that I have."

Once most of the cows reached the door, Eli began to open the latch.

"No, wait. Dad said to watch them for a bit today."

Dylan stared out over the cattle, and Eli waited. Then, one of the cows jumped on another cow as if they were mating. They stood that way for a moment.

Dylan said. "Number 11 is in heat."

"You know a lot about animals."

As if she noticed that her guard was down, her tone switched, and the wall between them thickened. "Don't tell me you've never seen that process before." Dylan pointed out to the pasture. Eli got the sensation she wanted to scream at him, to cry out something, but instead, she curled into her ball and shot words out like arrows. "Do you see any bulls out there?"

"No."

"Where do you think the calves magically appear from?

Women don't go around nursing babies if they haven't had one. The cows need to have a calf if we're to get any milk."

"Of course." Eli bit his tongue to resist responding with anger. This girl pushed his buttons, but why? He could be certain of one fact, if he caved to his rage, he would never be able to help her.

"We watch the cows. They are in standing heat if they jump on each other and stand still. It means we need to call the breeder. He artificially inseminates them within 12-18 hours. The cow gives birth. We get milk. Got it?"

Eli was aware of all these procedures, but he allowed Dylan to teach him, albeit in a snooty teenage way. At least she was talking to him.

"Thanks for the lesson. All the farms are different."

"This part is pretty much the same on all of them." Her attitude was thick. "Well, open the door already."

Eli swung the door inward, and the cows pushed each other inside. He watched as they walked directly to their spots and placed their heads inside the stanchions. Eli and Dylan followed them up and down the manger, locking their heads in place. Only a few of the younger heifers needed guidance.

It wasn't until later, once his frustration with the snippy teenager wore off, that Eli realized he had just been taught the animal version of the birds and bees by a young girl who hadn't even blushed. These children were older in many ways than their counterparts. They knew things and experienced things that other children were years from understanding. Life demanded they be older. Eli only wished it didn't mean that for that to happen, the child in them had to die.

The following day, Sam Sullivan ambled down to the barn. He was probably six foot, three inches tall and had a full head of gray hair. His slightly hunched shoulders showed his years.

"Morning, Conner."

Conner shook Sam's hand but avoided eye contact. His demeanor reminded Eli of a child who was about to be scolded.

"Thanks for coming, Sam."

"Of course. Who's the lucky lady?"

"This way."

They walked down the barn and stopped in front of number 11. Eli heard a small conversation but nothing of interest. The breeder pulled out a disposable glove and slid it up his arm all the way to his shoulder. The insemination process took under a minute, and before long, Sam had discarded his glove and was pouring sanitizer over his hands and collecting his things.

Eli observed the grandfatherly figure, who radiated warmth. Though Eli had only been in his presence briefly, it evoked memories of Mr. Burkett, creating a cosmic bond between them.

"Listen, Sam, about the last bill..."

"Conner, I know you're doing your best. We'll work something out. Call the office, and they can discuss payment plans with you."

"Will do." Conner sank his hands into his pockets and shifted on his feet uncomfortably. "And thank you."

Eli understood now why his boss could not make eye contact. He was ashamed.

"It's not fair, Conner. The price of grain goes up, and hell, so does the price of milk, yet everyone is getting paid except the farmer."

"You can say that again."

"You know, Conner, I'm hearing rumors around town about farmers getting desperate and doing things to make a quick buck. The unfairness of the world can make a man tempted to cut some corners and help the wrong people."

"What are you insinuating?"

"Just be careful, Conner. There are some bad people out there. Don't go down that rabbit hole to make ends meet. We'll work something out."

"I'll get you the money. That's all you need to worry about."

Sam nodded and turned away before stopping. "I forgot to give the girls their gum." He reached into his coat pocket. "I think they've learned to expect it through the years."

"Sam, they're not five anymore. You can stop leaving them treats."

"Are you kidding me? Behind those hard teenage shells, they still want those childhood traditions. Don't you forget it."

Conner nodded. "Easy to do, sometimes."

Conner stared down at the red pack of cinnamon gum in his hand.

"You have some good girls, Conner. They need you."

Conner's jaw clenched, but he remained silent as Sam Sullivan headed for the door. Eli watched his boss tuck the gum in his pocket. Even over the sounds of the barn, Eli heard a stifled sob catch in the throat of a proud and desperate man.

CHAPTER 30

Dylan Phillips
Past

*T*HE FOLLOWING FRIDAY, THE *girls planned on going out again.*

"You guys bring the treats this time," Olivia demanded as if just by her ordering it, the opportunity would magically present itself. Marybeth's mom occasionally drank wine, but taking a bottle would be obvious. She only had one on hand when she planned on consuming it.

Dylan's father drank whiskey and had bottles stashed in various places. Dylan, and she assumed Jessie, like her, pretended they didn't know about the drinking, but sometimes, during chores, he would walk away, and when he returned, she smelled the potent alcohol as he passed by. Her father would assume he had drunk the missing amount. When she got home from school, she walked straight to the barn.

"Where are you going?" asked Jessie.

"Mind your own business."

Jessie's shoulders slumped, and Dylan could see that her words had devastated her little sister. The realization made her feel sick, but she felt there was no other option. She didn't want Jessie to be involved in her deception, not only because she wanted to keep this secret to herself but also because she felt ashamed. And there was always the risk that Jessie might reveal her secret.

Dylan emptied her water bottle in a bush and headed into the barn. She stopped short when she saw David coming out of her chicken coop.

"What are you doing in there?" Dylan's voice filled with frustration.

"Calm down, twerp. I was just looking at your stupid chickens."

"I take care of my chickens. You don't need to go anywhere near them."

"Whatever." He strutted out of the barn.

Dylan caught sight of his friend's car waiting in the driveway for him. Good. He was leaving for a bit. She would have time to do what she needed to. But what had he been doing in her coop? There was no way he just wanted to see her chickens. Dylan stepped inside. Two hens pecked at the floor while one sat on her nest. The rooster dozed in the corner. There were six nesting boxes, giving room for growth provided the construction held up. The wall supporting the beds was in disrepair, and several boards near the structure wobbled. Her father had built the boxes years before. Due to a lack of time, money, and talent, the boxes were also far from perfect. Dylan generally paid little attention to her father's carpentry, but David's presence in the space made her study the area more closely. What had he been doing in here? Nothing looked amiss.

Keeping an eye out for her dad, she left the coop, walked directly to the secret hiding spot in the haymow, and filled her bottle to the top with her father's whiskey. Some spilled out and dripped over her hand. She licked her fingers, testing her ability to drink liquor, and winced at its potency. If her new friend's main desire was to get a quick buzz, and if they could keep it down, this would do the trick.

When Dylan entered the kitchen, her mother stood at the counter. Guilt and fear swam through her, making her dizzy. Jessie's water bottle sat on the counter, and she sat at the kitchen table with her cinnamon crackers and powdered orange drink, studying her sister's every move.

"Dylan, let me have your water bottle so I can wash it."

The blood drained from her face as she struggled for a response. Her mom glanced over her shoulder toward her.

"Well, are you going to give it to me?"

"I think I left it at school."

Jessie took a bite of a cracker. The sound of her chewing echoed through the kitchen.

"The one I just bought you?"

"I'll check the lost and found on Monday."

Dylan ignored Jessie's glare and the horrible feeling of guilt rising within her. Her sister had watched her dump the water out. She knew the bottle was in her bag. Please don't say anything.

Her mother sighed. "I hope you find it. Those things are expensive."

"I'm sure it's there."

Jessie choked on her drink, forcing her mother and Dylan to glance her way. The girls locked gazes, and Dylan squinted in warning.

"What's up with you two?"

The clock on the wall ticked. Jessie's gaze shifted back to her cracker.

"Jessie?" Her mother preyed on the weaker of the two.

Her sister thankfully only shrugged and took another bite of cracker.

"I'm going to my room." Dylan forced her legs to carry her out of the kitchen and up the stairs. She stood, back against the door, calming her heart rate and waiting for her mother to call her back to explain herself. She never did.

Claire didn't check Dylan's bag when Mrs. Obrien pulled into the driveway to pick her up. She was, no doubt, simply thankful that her daughter had plans. Not to mention, Dylan had never given her any reason to worry. Despite her enigmatic demeanor, Dylan had never gotten into serious trouble at home or at school.

Dylan kissed her mom on the cheek as she said goodbye. How long had it been since she had dared to get that close? To show that much affection? Her mom's skin radiated warmth, and she smelled of an inexpensive floral perfume—one that was too cheap to notice from the distance usually kept between them.

"Have fun, Dylan." Claire's voice was soft, and her eyes glossy. Her mom had missed her, too. Dylan looked away. Forgive me.

As they pulled up to the theater, Olivia and Christina stood on the sidewalk and shouted, "Hi, Mrs. O'Brien," in high-pitched, fake voices. Mrs. O'Brien waved and blew a kiss to Marybeth, unaware of their insincerity. They weren't good people. The knowledge should have terrified Dylan, and in a way, it did. But her heart betrayed her by pounding with a rush of adrenaline.

Mrs. O'Brien turned the corner, and the pasted smiles melted from Olivia and Christina's lips.

"Okay, ladies, time to ditch the movie," Olivia announced with a sneer.

Marybeth shot Dylan a look before stammering, "My mom's going to ask me about the movie."

"No worries; Colby and Austin saw the movie last weekend and will tell us all we need to know to pass the parent test. Now follow me."

Olivia and Christina shot across the road and into the parking lot across the street. They kept running until they entered the group of trees on the back side of the paved area. The night sky shone with stars, blanketing them in a cool, magical air. The warmth of Marybeth's hand wrapped around Dylan's chased away the chill in the air.

"Do you want to go?" Marybeth asked.

"I don't think we have a choice."

"Me either. But the minute you want out, tell me. We can go into the movie theater late."

The idea tempted Dylan, but it would be social suicide. "No. I'm sure we'll be fine if we stay together."

Marybeth lifted their joined hands and smiled warmly. "Together to the end." They raced across the road and entered the group of trees that had swallowed their newfound friends. Four boys mingled in the shadows. Dylan recognized all of them, including Colby and Austin. Colby was tall with blond hair and blue eyes while his best friend, Austin, was shorter and had brown hair and brown eyes. *They were both on the football team and were the most popular kids in school.*

Olivia stood by Austin and Christina by Colby. They had already stolen beer from the boys and were pouring large gulps into their mouths. They whispered to each other and giggled afterward.

As Olivia faced the boys, she flipped her long blonde hair in a show for them. "Dylan and Marybeth bummed off us last time." She faced Dylan. "Did you bring something to share?"

"Yes." Dylan's voice cracked despite her efforts to sound calm. Christina looked her up and down with an upturned lip. Dylan would have never been invited to join them if Marybeth hadn't been with her. With every word and glance given, they made sure Dylan was aware of it.

"Dylan, what did you bring?" Colby had never uttered two words to her in her life, and her name sounded strange on his lips.

"I brought whiskey."

"Whiskey?" Olivia's voice filled with distaste. Shaking her head, she turned to Colby. "Can I steal a beer?"

"Whoa!" Colby's smile lit his face as he eyed Dylan "Look at you, bringing out the big guns."

Dylan laughed nervously, feeling alive and petrified as she became the center of their conversation. Christina rolled her eyes and turned her back on her, sending Dylan crashing back to reality. Heat rushed up her neck, and a tear threatened to form in her eye. She silently begged that her glistening eyes would go unnoticed, but Olivia studied her over Christina's shoulder. The sneer on Olivia's face made

Dylan shiver. She wanted to grab Marybeth's hand and run, but that would destroy any possibility of a friendship. Olivia whispered something Dylan couldn't hear, but it made Christina laugh.

"So, are you going to share?" Colby asked.

Dylan reached into her bag and brought out the water bottle. A memory of her mom handing the cashier money as she smiled at Dylan forced itself into focus. The twenty-dollar bottle was a splurge, one her mom seldom made. Dylan pushed the image from her mind.

"The whiskey is my dad's. He has a lot of it hiding around the house."

"I've heard he's a drinker," Olivia said.

Dylan went silent. What did they know about her family? In that moment, she hated them for judging her father more than anything else they had done.

"Ignore her," Colby said. "I respect it. Really." The group snickered again. The sound didn't feel like respect.

"He's not a drinker like that. He just has some every now and then." Dylan's voice cracked. Somehow, despite her desire to protect him, she also felt embarrassed. And how did they know? He was never in the bars. If it weren't for the smell on his breath, Dylan wouldn't even know he drank.

"You first," Colby said. "Take a big swig."

Dylan's skin crawled under the weight of his smirk. Colby was in eighth grade, but with his muscular frame, he could compete with the high school sophomores. He was the quarterback of the middle school football team and a person the world seemed to revolve around whether it chose to or not. Dylan did not choose to, yet she unscrewed the top of her water bottle and chugged three giant swallows. Her eyes teared as she coughed up fumes, making the crowd laugh.

Colby looked Marybeth in the eye. "You next," His sneer faded into something laced with interest and peppered with desire. Christina watched Colby's expression from inches away before turning toward Marybeth with an icy glare.

Marybeth smiled nervously at Dylan as she reached for the container. Slowly, she lifted the bottle to her lips and let it linger there before slightly parting them. Dylan watched Marybeth's throat as it forced down two swigs.

"Done." She wiped her mouth and handed the bottle to Austin, who took the bottle and chugged his share.

This process lasted until most of the crew of people had had their turn. The last, a boy Dylan did not know, forced out a dribble. "Thanks for nothing." He tossed the bottle to the ground and then kicked it. Dylan watched it roll into the darkness. She wanted to chase after it and gather it safely into her arms, but she didn't dare move.

The boys returned their attention to their bags, digging out more cold beer and offering some to their girlfriends. Marybeth and Dylan stood empty-handed. As Austin yelled shotgun and jammed a hole in the bottom of his can, a pair of headlights shone into the woods.

"Cops! Run!" many voices yelled in unison.

Marybeth grabbed Dylan's hand, and they darted farther into the trees. They kept running, despite fear and whiskey blurring their vision, until they found a clearing and then walked casually, hoping they had distanced themselves enough to look innocent.

"Holy shit," Dylan whispered.

"I know," Marybeth said breathlessly. "Now what? We still have an hour before we get picked up, and I have no clue what the movie is about."

"We can know the end."

For the movie's last hour, Dylan and Marybeth sat in the back eating peanut butter cups, hoping to cover the smell of whiskey.

"Don't you see why life is better with animals?"

Dylan and Marybeth laughed until they were hushed by an annoyed man in front of them. They didn't see the others the rest of the night and didn't care to. But Dylan knew that come Monday, the battle of surviving would begin again, and they would find themselves doing anything to fit in.

CHAPTER 31

Eli Simmons
Present Day

THE FOLLOWING DAY, IT was Jessie waiting by the barn door and calling to the cows. When all the animals had entered the barn and the stanchions had been closed around their necks, one stall stood empty. Bessie, an older cow, never returned with the others.

"We need to go look for her before the sun sets. She probably gave birth out there." Concern filled Jessie's voice. "It's too cold at night for a newborn."

"Okay, so where do we start?"

"She probably headed into a group of trees for shelter. Listen for the bell. Dad tied one to her neck in case this happened."

They headed toward the back pasture, not far from where Eli had found the cow carcass, along with the deceased calves. It was time to press the conversation.

"Do you want to share how the cow that I found died?"

Jessie sighed. "Not really."

"That kind of sounds like you don't want to, but you will."

"Listen, there's a reason I didn't tell you. The reason didn't go away."

"I don't want to pry, but I can't pretend that I'm not curious either."

"It's not what you think," Jessie said nervously.

"I'm not thinking anything. In fact, I can't even imagine what the big secret is."

They walked in silence, listening for the sound of a bell. Jessie snapped off a branch that threatened to wipe across her face.

"Can I trust you?" she asked.

"Of course."

She swatted at trees with her branch, taking her time before speaking. "David killed the cow."

Eli stopped in his tracks.

"David Miller? The dead guy?"

"Yeah. He killed her the day before he went missing. My dad and him got in a big fight."

"But why would he kill her?"

"He lost his temper and hit her over the head with the hoe. Dylan saw the whole thing. She was really upset."

"I bet. Did David always have a bad temper?"

"Not that I saw." Jessie was quiet. "Dylan hated him. She kept telling me he was a really bad guy and not to talk to him. She warned me I should do my chores and say as little as possible to him."

"Why didn't she tell your father David was such a bad guy?"

Jessie laughed. "Because all the hired men are bad guys. What difference would it have made? If David got fired, then another terrible person would fill his place. They all had their thing to fear. Dylan and I are still trying to figure out yours."

Eli swallowed hard. He was still trying to figure out how to respond when she continued.

"Sometimes Dylan and I found some of it amusing. We would play hired men charades."

"Hired men charades?"

"Yeah. One of us would act out a hired man, and the other had to guess." Jessie got quiet. "Dylan used to make me laugh really hard. She doesn't do that anymore."

"What do you think changed?"

"Who knows?"

They walked silently for a bit, listening for the sound of the bell.

"And how would you act me out?"

"We don't play that game anymore."

"And if you did?"

Jessie thought for a moment. "You haven't given me very good material to work with."

"I guess that's a good thing."

"Yeah, I guess it is."

"You have me intrigued about these men. What would they do that was so crazy?"

Jessie huffed a mock laugh. "You really want to hear about them?"

"Yeah, I think I do."

"Okay. Well, we had the one who got mad and threw a pitchfork that pierced Dylan's foot. Then there was the ex-convict who didn't put his parts back into his pants after using the bathroom. Another one hid candy dishes to lure us into secret parts of the barn. There was a pill popper who told war stories. We also had the one who liked to trap us in the haymow—"

"Wait! Stop! Are you for real right now?"

"One hundred percent. And that is why we stopped complaining, and that is why Dylan hates you."

"Did you ever go to your parents?"

"Sometimes. The hired men didn't usually last long enough for my dad to fire them anyway. Sometimes the unknown was scarier to deal with then the problems we had."

"How did you laugh at any of that?"

"I can't explain it, but we did. We had our charades and private jokes. They made the weirdness not seem so scary." Jessie's expression turned thoughtful. "For one, we had this hired man who stole our metal stool we used to milk the cows. You know how bending by the cows hurts your legs after a while. We would take turns using it, but the one hired man tied it around his waist. He would walk around with it dangling behind him." Jessie, in imitation, strutted with her hands swinging behind her. "Every time he sat down, he adjusted the metal stool so he could sit on it. We were so mad at him that we tossed it up in the hayloft above the granary one Sunday when he wasn't there. The floor is weak there, so even if he found it, he couldn't get it because he would fall through the boards." A rare smile lit up her face. "We laughed a lot about that one."

Eli shook his head and chuckled. "I bet."

"Let's head over to those trees. The sun's setting so we have to hurry."

They picked up their pace.

"What was David like?"

"He seemed stoned half the time, or tired from being hung over. He wasn't a perv that I know of."

"What do you mean, that you know of?"

"Dylan hated him. At first, she hated him the normal hired-man amount, but something happened that made her hate him even more."

"When he killed the cow?"

"No, something before that. I asked her why she was so angry with him, but she only said that he was scum. I know my sister. There was something."

"Can I ask more about the cow David killed?"

"There isn't much to say. David got mad because the heifer wouldn't get to her spot. When she went to run in the wrong direction, he hit the top of her head with the hoe. Dylan said the poor thing fell right down and started to swell up immediately. Dylan ran into the house crying. She never cries. She usually just gets quiet and hides in her room when she's upset."

A bell jingled from within the clump of trees. "She's in there. Let's hurry."

Eli kept pace. "Why is what happened to the cow so secret? David is the one who's to blame."

"My dad was pissed." Jessie gave Eli a sideways look, as though waiting to be corrected for her language. He didn't react.

"Your dad had a right to be angry. Everyone would understand if he yelled at David."

"Yes, but David went missing the next day and then his jawbone was found on our property months later."

"Do you think your dad had something to do with David's disappearance?"

Jessie's expression deepened. "In the movies, yelling at someone the night before they end up dead causes concern, don't you agree?" Jessie stared at Eli, clearly waiting for an answer.

"I suppose so."

"You said I could trust you. Please don't tell anyone about my father being angry with David. He's my dad."

"You can trust me." Eli wanted to be telling the truth, but in truth, he didn't know what he would do if he learned that his boss was a murderer.

"Dad had a right to be mad, and as I said, David was a bad person." They walked under the canopy of the trees. A mother and calf hid in the shadows. "There she is. Let's get her home before dark."

"You didn't answer me. Do you think your dad killed David?" A chill shot up Eli's neck. Speaking the words made the possibility more real.

"I hope not." Jessie ran a hand down the back of the small calf as it suckled from its mother. "No one wants to find out one of their parents murdered someone."

That evening, when Jessie and her father scrambled to get milking going, Eli wheeled the wheelbarrow back in place after the last load of grain had been distributed. As he turned to leave the haymow, he saw the ladder leading to the loft above the granary. The ladder was merely boards, old and worn, nailed to the side of the wall. He placed one foot on the ladder's bottom rung and tested the strength of the old wood. Slowly, he crept to the top and peered over the ledge. In the far back, he saw the metal stool, hidden there just as Jessie said it would be. But something else hid beside it, sticking out merely enough for Eli to see: a long wooden handle with a metal hoe at the end.

CHAPTER 32

Dylan Phillips
Past

*T*HE CHICKS HATCHED ON *a Thursday night. When Dylan got home from school, the eggs under the hen had hatched, and the ones in the incubator weren't far behind. Marybeth stayed the night. They listened to the chirping coming from within the shells. They watched the eggs dance, and using little beaks, the chicks began to peck themselves free. One by one, the wet little chicks rolled out of their shells. By morning, they were fluffy and adorable, the way the girls envisioned they would be. Of the dozen eggs, seven hatched, four from under the chicken and three from the incubator. Everyone wanted to see the pictures and videos, and for a short time, Dylan and Marybeth were celebrities who aced their science project.*

"We should celebrate," Olivia cheered at lunch.

"Yes," Christina exclaimed. "Let's all have a sleepover. Can we stay at your house, Dylan? That way we can see the chickens."

Dylan froze. No way was she letting these girls into her home. Somehow, Marybeth understood without Dylan saying a word.

"I think we could do the sleepover at my house. We can

bring the baby chicks and the heat lamp to my place for the night."

"That would be awesome," Olivia said.

"I have to check with my mom," Marybeth added. "I'm sure it will be okay, but we'll probably have to do it tomorrow. We can sleep down in the basement and watch movies."

"You have a basement?" Christina looked at Olivia and smiles spread across their faces. "Do your parents come down and check on you?"

"They go to bed around ten. They come down and say goodnight if I'm down there."

"Ten is good." Christina smiled. "You provide the place; I'll bring the goods."

"Goods?" Marybeth's voice shook slightly.

"My parents have an extensive liquor cabinet that they don't lock. I can get just about anything from there. Not only cheap whiskey." Her eyes darted to Dylan.

"We can actually have a good time without being chased off without a buzz." Olivia rolled her eyes in disgust at the weekend's fiasco while Marybeth's gaze begged Dylan for a way out. There wasn't one.

"What's wrong? You two are all in, aren't you?" Olivia's asked.

"We're in. Aren't we, Dylan?"

"Yeah, Marybeth. Of course." Dylan's heart raced. Mrs. O'Brien trusted them. Drinking under her roof meant risking more than just being caught with alcohol. It meant losing that trust.

"Do you think I can stay the night at your house tonight?" Marybeth whispered to Dylan. "We should plan for tomorrow."

"My parents won't mind as long as I do my chores."

"I'll help."

For the first hour of milking, only the girls and David were in the barn. Conner attended to a broken piece of machinery. The girls attempted to have a private conversation, despite David staying close by them.

"I can't believe they're bringing alcohol to my house," Marybeth whispered. "If we get caught, my parents will kill me. Like actually kill me." Her face looked pale.

"We'll only drink enough to keep them happy but stay sober. If your parents come down, we'll tell them we didn't know the girls were bringing alcohol."

"I'm so nervous. They're going to want us to get drunk."

"We'll fake it."

"Fake it? I've never been drunk, and, let's face it, neither one of us are that entertaining in a group."

Dylan's mouth opened, ready to disagree, but she couldn't.

"Maybe we could fake it a little and then go to bed early. People pass out from drinking."

"Seriously? I can already hear them telling all the kids about how I passed out by eleven after two sips. They'll probably take pictures of us and show everyone at school. What are we going to do?" Marybeth's voice cracked.

David stood from between two cows and cleared his throat. "Sounds like you two ladies have a real dilemma."

"No one asked you." Dylan glared at him. "Why are you listening to our conversation?"

"Boredom." Dylan took several steps toward them. "I have two ways out for you."

The girls stared at him, neither stopping nor encouraging his next words.

"I could tell your father your dilemma, and I'm sure after a nice chat with Marybeth's parents, the sleepover won't happen."

"No!" Both girls yelled in unison.

"Or I can offer you a little something that knocks the edge off, doesn't give you alcohol breath, and won't leave your new friends bored to death with you two animal-loving geeks."

Dylan and Marybeth looked at each other.

"What are you talking about?" Dylan asked.

"I have a little pink pill that will do the trick. One pill, and you'll be the life of the party—laughing, dancing. No one will know that you're nothing but a couple of dweebs faking your momentary popularity. Maybe they'll even invite you to the real parties someday."

"I don't want your drugs," Dylan retorted.

"Suit yourself."

The next ten minutes passed in silence. Then Marybeth whispered, "We could just take them and have them on hand if things get really uncomfortable."

Dylan glanced at David who smirked back at her.

"David's bad news, Marybeth. He's been in jail." Dylan whispered her desperate warning.

"It's only a little pill. Do you really think he'd give it to us if it was that dangerous?"

Dylan crossed her arms in defiance, but her words betrayed her. "What's in your stupid pills?"

"It's a Molly. People used to be able to buy the stuff right in the bars in the 70's and 80's."

"And where did you buy it?" Dylan asked.

"How I got it isn't a concern of yours."

"Well, it's kind of my business if you want me to take it."

"Let's just say I have some good, honest sources."

"I doubt any of your sources are good or honest."

"Whatever, kid. I'm only trying to help you out."

"We don't need your illegal junk," Dylan spat.

"You have many years to live before you hit twenty-one and can drink legally, and by then, the world will know you are socially inept. The ship will have sailed."

"We'll take two," Marybeth blurted.

"Marybeth!"

"It doesn't mean we have to eat them. We will just have them on hand."

"Good choice. When I go to leave, meet me at the car. I'll have my friend bring them."

"So, what will they do to us?" Marybeth asked.

"They just make you laugh. Something one of you has no clue how to do."

Dylan rolled her eyes and turned away. Her one and only friend had just drifted a million miles away from her. She hated David for causing that divide. There was only one way to keep their friendship intact, and that was to follow Marybeth into the dark waters she had waded into.

Dylan didn't read newspapers; only the events happening in her small world concerned her. Problems outside her immediate surroundings existed for others to deal with. She had enough of her own. While she had heard about various drugs, marijuana was the most accepted. Most of the students in her middle school still avoided both alcohol and drugs, and the adults believed their children would never venture into that world. After all, drugs weren't for everyone, and Dylan thought much of the discussion around them was just talk. Still, they were all middle schoolers trying to fit in however they could.

Dylan's dark clothes and long bangs might have suggested to some that she was the type to buy and sell drugs, but she had never considered doing so. She just wanted to be invisible.

When her mom jumped into the shower, Dylan quickly rummaged through the cupboard and found an old plastic pint container that no one would miss. She dashed to the barn to fill the container with her dad's whiskey. Although the other girls had referred to it as cheap, Dylan hoped that by bringing more alcohol, Marybeth and she could avoid David's pills. Could they trust that they were even Molly's? David's friend didn't seem to approve of David's decision, but Marybeth still wanted them even after the friend's hesitation.

After filling the container with her dad's alcohol, Dylan rushed back inside, placed it in a gallon-sized bag to prevent leaks, and buried it deep in her duffel bag. Just as she zipped it shut, Jessie walked into the room.

"I don't like that you hang out with Marybeth all the time now. I have to sit here alone."

Dylan paused, took a breath, and turned to her sister. They had been inseparable until a few months ago, but even if she could, she wouldn't take her little sister down the road where she was heading.

"Jessie, why don't you ask someone over?"

"*There isn't anyone to ask.*"

Hadn't Dylan just been there? Alone. Wanting to connect but not knowing how to break through.

"*I'm sorry. Let's do something tomorrow. I'll be home by noon, I'm sure.*"

"*Dylan, I can take you now.*" *Her mom's voice shot up the stairs.*

"*I have to go, but tomorrow. I promise.*"

"*Dylan?*"

"*Yeah?*" *She stopped halfway out the door but didn't look back.*

"*Is everything okay?*" *Jessie asked.*

"*Of course. See you tomorrow.*"

In the car, Claire had Dylan select the radio station, and the two of them listened to the music while lost in their own thoughts. Her mom sang along quietly; a subtle smile tugged at her lips. Her face glowed with something; promise or hope, Dylan decided. Both of which Dylan knew she could destroy in an instant. She flew out of the car when they reached Marybeth's and heard her mom yell, "Have fun," before she backed down the driveway.

Hours passed, spent watching movies and scanning phones, before Marybeth's mom came down to say goodnight. They waited fifteen minutes and then they all ran for their supplies.

"*You brought that cheap crap again.*" *Christina huffed. "You can drink that. I'll stick to my own drink.*"

"*I don't mind it,*" *Dylan said, forcing herself to swallow.*

"*What did you bring, Marybeth?*" *Christina asked.*

"*I'm sharing with Dylan.*"

"Have at it." Christina took a big swallow of her bottle. "We should call the boys."

"No!" Marybeth yelled.

"I just meant call them. I wasn't inviting them."

"Of course," Marybeth stammered. "It's just my parents have cameras. They would be alerted if someone came by the house, and then they would come down here and check."

"Got it." Christina pulled out her phone. "Video call it is."

Olivia pulled her cell out as well, and before they knew it, the party existed through screens, and Marybeth and Dylan fell to the side, quiet and out of place. Marybeth tapped Dylan's arm. "Come to the bathroom." They both stood. Olivia and Christina showed no sign of noticing their departure.

Behind the closed bathroom door, Marybeth squatted and pulled a plastic bag from underneath the sink. Tape hung from the sides. "There is no way we are going to be able to drink that whiskey. No offense, but it's terrible. I'll get sick. Let's just try the pill."

"I don't know, Marybeth."

"David said it will just make us laugh."

"His friend thought it was a bad idea."

"He just didn't want to get in trouble for it. Look at us out there. We aren't even talking. They're on their phones like we don't exist. It's just a tiny pill."

Dylan hesitated.

"I'll take mine first. If I don't act like an idiot, will you have yours after?"

"Yes."

"Promise?"

"I promise."

"And if I do act like an idiot, will you make sure I get right to bed so my parents don't see me if they come down to check on us?"

"I promise."

Marybeth put the pill in her mouth and swallowed it with a handful of tap water. A large smile lit her face. "Stop looking so worried. It's only a little pink pill. How bad can it be?"

CHAPTER 33

Eli Simmons
Present Day

THE SMELL OF MANURE hit Eli's nostrils, making him wince as he entered the barn the following day. He grabbed the hoe and began scraping the wet slop into the gutter. He would need to do the chore again after the milking as well. He studied the hoe that he held, thinking how one like it had killed the poor heifer he had seen in the field. A sticker from the local farm store was still visible on the implement, which would make sense since the one that killed the cow had been thrown above the loft, or at least, Eli assumed it was the one David had used. Why else would it be there? The memory of the event must have been too much for Dylan every time she picked up the tool. By hiding it, she'd forced her father to buy the new one.

Eli's mind swarmed with images of what Dylan must have seen, making him less in tune with his chores. He stood behind a young heifer the girls had named Feisty because the name, albeit not typical for a cow, fit her perfectly. She would kick someone's head off if given the chance. Forgetting to ease the hoe to the floor beneath her, Eli clanked it down on the cement, causing her to jump and kick until she landed on the handle, breaking it in two.

"Great," Eli muttered to himself.

With all the commotion, he hadn't even heard Conner coming down the barn.

"Sorry, Conner. I'll go into town after chores and get a new one."

"I guess that's all you can do." His boss shook his head and mumbled something about it being "one more expense." After a moment, he added, "You tell them at the store that hoe only lasted months. Maybe they'll exchange it."

"It was my fault. I'll buy it."

"Put it on our account. It could have happened to any of us."

During his afternoon break, Eli walked into the farm supply store and went directly to the section with the hoes. After deciding on one exactly like the previous one, he turned and saw a metal stool. He hadn't gotten a good look at the one up in the loft, but Eli suspected this one was close enough. He grabbed three. One for each of them, but not Conner. He sensed his boss would embarrass him if Eli presented such a gift to him. Not with an overabundance of appreciation, but rather, a disdainful look that told him he wasn't a true man if he had to sit on the stool. Eli didn't need to waste his money to be insulted. He skipped asking for a free replacement and bought the hoe as well.

He'd hoped it would be Jessie's turn to do chores that evening, but Dylan walked into the barn. When she saw Eli standing proudly next to the three metal stools, her eyes narrowed.

"What are those?"

"Jessie told me you used to have a stool, but one of the hired men wouldn't let you use it. I thought I would get you both a gift of appreciation, for teaching me the ropes."

"Why are you buying us gifts? That's just weird."

Eli swallowed hard. Was he being weird? He'd meant it to be a kind gesture. "I was complaining about how hard it was to—"

"Then buy yourself a stool. We don't need your gifts."

"Well, they're here if you decide to use them, but I'd appreciate it if you didn't throw them up in the haymow with the other one. They cost me a pretty penny."

Dylan's face drained of color. "What did you say?"

"They cost me—"

"Why did Jessie tell you about that stool? You can't go up in the hayloft. You'll fall through the ceiling."

"I know. That's why I went and bought new ones."

Dylan reached into the bucket that Eli had already prepared for the milking. Her hand shook. Why was she so upset over a stool or Eli knowing about the silly story? Then he remembered the hoe. He must have triggered the memory of David killing the cow. His heart sank. He had only wanted to help.

"I'm sorry if I upset you with the gift."

"Stop talking to me."

"I'm just—"

"Don't you think it's weird for a grown man to try to be friends with middle schoolers? All I want is for you to leave us alone."

"I'm sorry if I made you uncomfortable."

"I don't need your gifts, and I don't need to discuss my day with you. Do your job. That's it."

"We all need other people. It's a lonely world if you try to exist in it by yourself."

"This isn't a therapy session. Stay away from us."

Jessie appeared at the barn door. "Mom wants you," she said to Dylan. As her gaze found the stools, a smile lit her face. "Where did they come from?"

"I told you to stay away from him, and you keep talking to him."

"I'm only trying—"

"No, you don't understand." Dylan breathed in deeply, choking back a cry. "We can't trust them. We can't trust anyone."

She ran from the barn toward the house, leaving Eli and Jessie to stare at each other in bewilderment.

CHAPTER 34

Dylan Phillips
Past

MARYBETH LEFT THE BATHROOM first, giving Dylan time to secretly pour half of the whiskey into the drain. She planted a fake smile on her face and walked out behind Marybeth. The pill's effects showed quickly. Marybeth laughed at everything, and Olivia and Christina bent over in laughter with her. Dylan smiled and sipped from her container. She was an outsider, but once again, she was alone. Marybeth had taped the pill to the bottom of the sink again, well inside the cupboard where no one would find it if Dylan decided not to eat it. But the temptation was growing stronger as she watched her friend drift away from her and into the clutches of Olivia and Christina. Popularity was a drug more addictive than most. Once Marybeth tasted it, she would give up Dylan to keep enjoying the effects of it.

Dylan set down the whiskey container that had let her down. She needed the pill. She wanted to silence the dull, scared child within her and prove to the other girls that she could be fun, just like them, before it was too late. She stood and looked at the three of them, laughing until tears *rolled down their faces. I'm coming, too. I just need help getting there. With that thought, she took a step toward the bathroom.*

"Why is your face so pale?" Olivia said through bursts of laughter.

Dylan turned. Marybeth's laughing had slowed. She did look pale.

"Marybeth, are you okay?" Dylan asked.

"Yes, I'm just so tired all of a sudden."

Dylan rushed to her side. Her skin felt clammy and cold. "Are you sure you're okay?"

"I might get sick. Will you help me get to the bathroom?"

"Beginners," Olivia scoffed.

Dylan reached an arm around her friend and hoisted her up. She guided her limp friend to the toilet's edge and held her bangs while she emptied herself of their nighttime snacks and the Fireball the other girls had shared with her.

After reaching the dry heaving phase and then complete exhaustion, Marybeth rested her head on the cold tile floor. While she slept, Dylan reached under the sink, found the last pill, and flushed it down the toilet.

Outside the bathroom, Olivia and Christina continued to laugh obnoxiously. The floorboards above them creaked. They had awoken one or both of Marybeth's parents. Dylan's heart raced. No one seemed to care that Marybeth's parents could walk down the basement stairs any moment.

"Marybeth, I need to get you onto the air mattress." Dylan tried lifting her friend, but she was dead weight. "You have to help me, Marybeth. Your mom's about to come down the stairs."

Marybeth groaned. Her breathing was shallow and her skin pale.

"Are you okay?" Dylan asked.

Her friend moaned again.

"I'm getting Olivia and Christina."

Within moments, the three girls were lifting Marybeth off the floor and dragging her to one of the blown-up beds.

"This girl cannot handle her alcohol," Olivia said. Her voice was breathless from her efforts.

"Hurry up," Dylan whispered. "We need to get the lights off."

Christina flipped the switch and dove into the other bed just as Mrs. O'Brien opened the basement door. After the creak of the door, there was silence. She must be listening. Dylan heard her pulse beating in her ears. Lying next to her, Marybeth moaned. Please don't get sick again. *Finally, the door creaked shut. Christina and Olivia giggled under their blankets, but Dylan lay silent, wondering what David had done to her friend.*

The sun beamed through the basement windows and directly into Dylan's eyes. By the brightness in the room, she would guess it to be after nine. Christina, Olivia, and Marybeth were still sound asleep. The three of them would most likely be working through a hangover for the rest of the day. Dylan only knew of hangovers through schoolyard talk and the occasional times she'd seen her father moving slowly after a big night, but she didn't fear one today. She had barely drunk anything.

She remembered the baby chicks upstairs. They would need breakfast. After she'd lugged them all the way to Marybeth's,

Christina and Olivia had only showed momentary interest. All Dylan wanted to do was to go upstairs and listen to their quiet chirping and feel their tiny bodies in her hands. She couldn't wait for Christina and Olivia to leave so her and Marybeth could bond through the animals once again. She didn't want all this sneaking around, drinking, and taking strange pills. Her friendship with Marybeth was based on something real, and she assured herself that once they left, Marybeth would remember that as well.

Dylan rolled over and nudged Marybeth. She didn't respond. "Marybeth, let's go feed the chicks." Nothing. She nudged her friend again. "Marybeth." Urgency filled her words. Still nothing, not even the slightest movement. Dylan shot up from her sleeping position. "Marybeth, wake up."

"Shut up, Dylan. My head is killing me," Olivia mumbled.

"I can't wake her up," Dylan cried.

"She's hungover, you idiot." Christina's voice was muffled through blankets. "Let her sleep."

"No, she's not hungover. She won't wake up." Tears filled Dylan's eyes and her heart pounded in panic. Olivia and Christina now stood over them with disheveled hair and shocked expressions.

"What the hell?" Christina only stared on as she spoke. "Get her mom."

Dylan raced for the stairs as Christina and Olivia began tossing their belongings into their bags and dialing numbers into their phones.

"Mrs. O'Brien," Dylan cried into the empty kitchen. "Mrs. O'Brien."

Marybeth's mother stepped out of the laundry room. She

must have seen the horror in Dylan's expression because she had dropped the towel she had been folding.

"I can't wake her." She struggled for more words, but nothing came. Mrs. O'Brien raced past Dylan and ran down the stairs to the basement. Dylan closed her eyes when Marybeth's mom's panicked scream filled the house.

The rest of the morning blurred in Dylan's memory—flashing lights...questions...cries.... Christina's and Olivia's parents pulled up to the curb, unaware of why their girls had both wanted to leave the premises so urgently. The image of their ashen, confused faces as they scanned what was going on seared into Dylan's mind. Dylan's mom stood next to her, but Dylan had no idea who had called her or when she'd pulled up. Dylan only remembered repeating the phrase "I don't know," over and over to endless adults. But she did know. She knew way too much.

EMTs hoisted the stretcher into the ambulance. They had placed an oxygen mask over Marybeth's pale face. She was alive. She would survive this nightmare. They would all survive it, or at least, that's what Dylan told herself. The ambulance sped away, splitting the quiet neighborhood air with the scream of the siren.

When Dylan entered her house, she ran to her bedroom and locked the door. Her head ached from overwhelming emotion. She collapsed onto her bed, tears streaming down her cheeks. She had no idea what she could do to stop the pain and fear rushing through her body. As a small girl, she would imitate her father, who sat in the church pew beside her. Her dad would close his eyes and clasp his hands together.

She would look up to him and try to imagine what he was speaking to God about, and then she would close her eyes and pray the prayers of a little girl.

Sitting beside her father, her mother prayed similarly, but for some reason, her dad fascinated her more. His tough outer shell softened when he spoke to God; he suddenly seemed touchable. Even though he sometimes played baseball in the yard or hide-and-go-seek with them when nothing on the farm needed fixing, those times could not be predicted or expected. He was often too busy with chores to take part in games. Those times were nonexistent now, and she hadn't seen her parents talk to God in a long time. She assumed they stopped believing in the power of prayer, and Dylan's infantile faith stopped maturing when it was no longer nourished.

Dylan sobbed into her pillow. Why hadn't she stopped her friend? Every part of her knew it was a bad idea. She knew they couldn't trust David. Despite her doubts, she began pleading with God. "This is my fault, God. Please help Marybeth. Please help her to be okay." Tears saturated her comforter, but the room felt cold. Maybe she had drifted too far away from Him. Maybe God was punishing her for not speaking up, not stopping her friend. She kept crying out to Him even though she feared His ears had closed to her. After her sobs subsided, she crawled under her comforter and drifted into an exhausted sleep. The ringing of the telephone brought Dylan back to the nightmare. She rushed to the door and cracked it open just enough to listen in on her mom's side of the conversation.

"I know. This must be so hard." Claire's voice cracked. Dylan assumed she was talking with Marybeth's mom.

"Fentanyl. Oh my God. Where did they get drugs?... I know. I just didn't want to believe they were in the kids' middle school.... MDMA?... They think they took drugs?... Dylan has never taken drugs. It must have come from the other girls... I'm sure they are denying it... Well, we'll learn soon enough then. I'll get a test for Dylan as well. Please keep us posted. I know this is so hard... Yes, I'll call you with the results... I'll talk to her right now."

They said an awkward goodbye, and then Claire walked to the stairwell. Dylan clicked the door shut as quietly as possible and ran for her bed. She squeezed her eyes shut and hugged the comforter to her chest. Claire crept to Dylan's door, and the door creaked open. The mattress shifted as her weight settled onto the side of the bed. Claire placed her hand on her daughter's shoulder.

"Dylan, we need to talk." A tear rolled down Dylan's cheek, which she dabbed away with the comforter. "It's really important that you are honest with me right now."

Dylan held her comforter tighter against herself.

"We need to know where Marybeth got the drugs."

"I don't know," Dylan cried. "Will she be okay? Did she wake up yet?"

"She's still in a coma. They found MDMA and fentanyl in her blood."

"What's that?"

"It's a drug sometimes called a Molly, and fentanyl is a drug that some people add to other drugs. It makes people get addicted faster. Dealers will lace other drugs with it, so people buy more drugs from them."

Dylan's body tightened in anger. She hated David.

She wanted to spill everything to her mom and see David handcuffed and taken away forever, but wasn't she as guilty as Marybeth? She hadn't stopped her friend. She hadn't exactly begged her not to take the pills from them.

Instead, she had walked to the car that night and watched the transaction. Then she'd stood by her friend and allowed her to ingest the poison. Everyone would blame her. The drugs had come from Dylan's home. What would happen to her parents? Could they be in trouble somehow? She didn't understand the laws and she had no one to ask.

"Dylan?"

Dylan didn't speak. She couldn't find the right words even if she tried.

"Dylan, Marybeth and you are very close. I can't imagine her keeping this secret from you."

"We snuck in alcohol. I took some of Dad's whiskey, but I didn't drink much. I promise. It made me feel sick. I thought Marybeth was drunk. She drank more than me, and it was so strong-tasting."

Claire stared at her daughter with a hopeless expression. Her hand lay heavily on Dylan's shoulder, keeping the strained connection from snapping. Minutes passed before she spoke again.

"I'm running to the store to buy a drug test. It will show us the truth, Dylan. The other girls are taking one, too."

"They have tests in the store for that?"

"Yes, Dylan, they do. Are you sure you don't have anything you should tell me?"

"No. I promise you; I didn't do any drugs."

Claire released a heavy sigh, and the weight of her hand

lifted from her daughter's shoulder. Dylan listened as her mom walked across the room and down the stairs. Then she crept to the window where dead flies filled the windowsill. Her mom wiped tears from her cheek while opening the car door. After she slid into the driver's side seat, she rested her head on the steering wheel. Dylan watched, frozen, until the car reversed down the driveway and disappeared from her view.

She wanted the test results to rewrite history. When the results told the world she had not touched drugs, people would believe her whole story, including the part where she told them she didn't know where the drugs came from. A weight would lift from her family, and all their prayers would concentrate on the girl lying in the hospital bed. They would be able to focus on Marybeth because Dylan was innocent. They could pass the blame onto someone else.

But, within hours, Olivia's and Christina's parents shared their daughter's negative test results. Dylan and her mother sat side by side on her bed, waiting for the results. The air between them felt too thick to breathe. When the timer went off, Claire reached for the test with a shaky hand and sighed in relief when she read Dylan's results. Now, the adults were back to suspecting everyone, including her. Each family believed that their child would never do such a thing, but if that was true, how had the newest, radiant, shy, shining light in their town ended up fighting for her life in a hospital bed?

CHAPTER 35

Eli Simmons
Present Day

Despite Dylan's general attitude toward Eli, her reaction to the metal stools had shocked him. She had built a thick wall around herself to protect some fragile inner self, but from what? Neglect? Was it the pain of losing people she loved, like when she'd lost her brother? And why would she be so angry that her sister had told him about the stool?

When he finished the morning milking, Eli jumped onto the tractor and slowly pulled the spreader from the barn. Conner stood, hands on hips, watching him. As the tractor emerged into the sunlight, Conner waved and yelled, "Hold up." He walked over to the shaft, connected the spreader to the tractor, and knocked it a few times. "I tightened the belt, but the damn thing keeps coming loose. If it starts chugging again, let me know."

"Will do."

Once in the open field, Eli started the spreader. For several laps, the spreader worked smoothly, but on the last one, it caught several times. He decided to push on, and the machine began working properly. He was used to this behavior. Conner would tamper with it, tell him he'd fixed it this time, and once again, it would threaten to stop midway. Eli had yet to get stranded in the field with a half-emptied load. As he rounded the corner, he saw a man in a uniform walking along the field: Border Patrol. The presence of Border Patrol was something Eli would need to get used to unless someone found a way to stop the flow of drugs into the country, and unfortunately, no one seemed to have the answer to the problem.

Eli finished up and backed the tractor into the barn. Conner waited for him. "How'd she do?"

"Not bad. Gave me a couple of scares, but she picked back up each time."

"Damn thing."

"Border Patrol was out there today."

"What happened to a man owning his land?"

"I believe they were on the Canadian side."

"I don't give a shit what side they say they're on. They're looking for trouble where there ain't any, but if they want to, they'll find a way to make a man look guilty of something." Conner turned to go. "You coming to lunch?"

"Not today. Thanks anyway."

"Suit yourself."

Eli needed space from his boss, who had such a negative presence that Eli felt suffocated just being near him.

He was about to head back to his camper when a sudden urge took over him. He walked into the haymow and stared up the old wooden ladder built into the hayloft wall. He climbed each rung, one by one, until he reached the top. The morning sun shone through the broken window, sending fragmented light beams onto the objects half-hidden in the hay. The stool was old and bent. Cow manure coated the legs, or at least the parts of them that he could see. The hoe settled in the hay in front of the relic. Did he dare cross the fifteen feet of weak boards to get a better look? Would whatever he found be worth risking falling to his possible death? No.

Eli pulled himself up to the side of the loft and sat close to the edge, believing that the wall would make the sides strong enough to support his weight. He reached into his back pocket and retrieved his phone, turned on the flashlight, and shone it toward the objects. The hoe had debris on the blade, most likely manure, but he couldn't tell from that distance. He turned on his camera and zoomed it in as far as it would go before snapping several pictures. Then he sat staring into the piles of decaying hay left there because gathering it would be dangerous. Other objects became more and more obvious, as if they dared to peek their heads out of their hiding places when they thought he had left. Whiskey bottles, several of them. Some still had liquid in them. He couldn't imagine Conner throwing his alcohol away. The only other option was that the girls had tried to hide it from him. This was the first bit of evidence that their father's drinking bothered them. What other secret pains hid beneath the surface of the dusty old hay?

CHAPTER 36

Dylan Phillips
Past

*D*YLAN STAYED HOME ON *Monday and managed to make it through half of the school day on Tuesday. Olivia and Christina didn't skip a beat. By the time Dylan walked into her afternoon classroom, all eyes searched her for answers. The two girls had planted seeds of doubt about Dylan, and those seeds landed in very fertile soil. Her absence on Monday, in their eyes, had only served as an admission of guilt.*

"I heard she tested clean, though." The girl had mumbled the words when Dylan passed by, and then she and her companion fell silent, watching Dylan until out of earshot. The hairs on Dylan's neck stood alert until well after she'd rounded the corner, leaving the girls to continue their gossip.

Why hadn't Marybeth listened to her when she'd told her David was bad news? As pure hatred raged through Dylan's body, bile rose in her throat. She should have insisted they throw the pills away or not get them at all. She'd known better, even if Marybeth hadn't.

Dylan ran to the nearest restroom and vomited into the toilet. She fell to the dirty bathroom floor, too weak from sadness to lift herself from the filth. Her head rested on the stall wall until Mrs. Owens, the dean, knocked on the door and asked her to come out. Dylan pulled herself up and opened the door. She kept her gaze downward.

"Are you okay?"

"Yes, ma'am."

Dylan stared down at the dean's feet. They were stuffed in tight black pumps, making her already tall frame even more imposing. She wore a businesslike beige suit dress which complemented her strict persona. She kept her long blond hair tight in a bun.

"Dylan, will you look at me, please?" She repeated herself and waited until Dylan's chin lifted, and the dean's blue eyes locked her in a trance. The other students had talked about the dean's effect on students, the boys in particular, but what she felt caught in Mrs. Owen's gaze surprised her. Those same eyes, which both enamored and frightened the hormonal middle school boys, flooded Dylan with warmth. If this woman decided to defend her, no one would dare argue against her.

"How about we go into my office and talk?"

Dylan nodded.

They walked side by side down the quiet hallways. Only a few stragglers stopped in their tracks, allowing their minds time to form a story worth passing on to their classmates. Mrs. Owens's heels clicked against the floor. She held her head high. She answered to no one. Dylan snuck a glance at the woman only a few times on the hike to her office.

"Have a seat," the dean said, gesturing to the chair in front of her desk. She swung the door shut, and the world fell silent. Her office smelled of scented candles, despite school fire codes.

Probably no one dared tell her she couldn't light one if she so desired.

She walked around her desk and settled into the leather chair. Behind her was a wall of shelves decorated with diplomas and family pictures. Two young blond children smiled wildly in a family beach photo. Happiness glinted in their eyes as if they had just chased each other down the beach, plopped into their parents' laps, and allowed the wind to tousle their hair for the photo. Her husband had sandy brown hair and a strong jawline. They all wore khakis and white shirts. They were perfect.

Dylan wasn't aware she was staring at the photo until Mrs. Owens picked it up and pointed to the little girl.

"This one is Kate." She gestured to the younger of them, a boy. "This one is Alex." She set the picture back on the shelf. "It's a few years old now, but I love it. They both look so happy. No one would know they had just had major meltdowns. If I try hard enough, I can even pretend the day was perfect. Most days aren't though, are they?"

Dylan shook her head.

"Life can be tough sometimes. Life in middle school is almost always tough. You know, those years were my least favorite. I had braces." She laughed. "My teeth were so crooked I couldn't even chew my food right. It's amazing how off something can be, and with time, patience, and persistence things straighten themselves out."

"You remind me of myself."

Dylan stared at her in shock. Who was this woman? She looked back at the perfect picture. Dylan was nothing like this woman. Her family was nothing like the dean's family.

"It wouldn't be appropriate for me to share my whole journey with you. How I went from a depressed middle school girl who didn't fit in to going to college to fight for all those children who feel just like I did. The journey was long, and it contains some secrets I shared with the right people when needed. We all need the right people, don't we?"

Dylan nodded.

"I'm sorry about your friend. Marybeth seems like a sweet girl. I was thrilled to see the two of you hanging out." She paused, but Dylan stayed silent. "I'm sure you're very scared."

Dylan looked down at her clasped hands. Was the dean watching her, rooting for her like a guardian angel?

"I want you to know you can talk to me, but I also need to be honest. I am legally bound to report some certain details kids might share."

Dylan's gaze darted to hers. Had the dean seen the fear in her heart the words 'legally bound' created?

"Is there anything you want to discuss with me now?"

Dylan shook her head.

Moments passed as the dean gave her time to change her mind, but Dylan couldn't. Not with the law threatening to throw her into some juvenile school for delinquents or worse.

"Well, I'll let you get back to class, but remember, I'm here for you whenever you need me."

The dean stood, walked to the door, and opened it. Dylan stopped for a moment before passing through the doorway. She wanted to hug her, to get lost in the sweet, perfume smell of her embrace, but instead she mumbled, "Thank you," and hurried from the office.

A week passed before Marybeth's parents allowed Dylan to visit their daughter. Claire drove her to the hospital and walked her to the ICU. Marybeth's father sat in a chair in the hallway, his head resting in his hands.

Claire and Dylan stopped a few feet from him. Dylan's mother wrapped her arm around Dylan's shoulder and rested her hand there protectively. When Mr. O'Brien's gaze settled on Dylan, anger and hurt filled his eyes. Dylan's heart sank. She wanted to turn and run from his glare and the powerful tsunami of guilt building inside of her. What would he have said to her if her mom had not stood next to her? Her eyes burned with tears, imagining the onslaught of accusations he might spew at her.

Mr. O'Brien looked away from them and stood, pausing in what appeared to be an attempt to catch his balance. Then he gestured for them to follow him into the hospital room, where Marybeth lay unconscious.

When Dylan entered the room, a rush of memories swarmed her. Hayden, his tiny body, in the bed, the beeping of the monitors, the tubes attached to his still body. Hayden never left the hospital. The tubes, the doctors, the nurses, the medicines, none of those things saved her brother. Dylan's knees grew weak as the blood drained from her face and kept draining as if she were melting into the floor. She took a shaky, deep breath before focusing on Marybeth. Mrs. O'Brien's head rested on the side of the bed. One of her hands clasped the hand of Marybeth, who lay lifeless. Her beautiful red hair sprawled across her pillow, making her appear like an angry angel tangled in tubes. Waves of nausea again threatened to send Dylan running. Sensing

Dylan's tension, her mom wrapped her arm tighter around her.

Mrs. O'Brien lifted her head. Her empty gaze fell on Dylan. She stood and walked like a zombie to her husband's side. He wrapped his arm around her.

"We'll give you a few moments," he said. The weight of the tragedy was evident, and it had undoubtedly taken a toll on them.

Claire walked to the side of the bed and rubbed Marybeth's forearm. "Keep fighting, sweet girl. Don't give up." She wiped a tear from her cheek. "Dylan, do you want some time alone with her?"

Dylan nodded. After squeezing Dylan's arm, her mom drifted out of the room. Once the door closed, silence encircled her, begging to be filled. Dylan sat in the chair previously occupied by Mrs. O'Brien. She couldn't touch her friend, afraid that if she did, Marybeth's skin would feel foreign to her, as if they were nothing more than strangers to each other. This person in the hospital bed wasn't Marybeth. This wasn't the girl who'd giggled with her over silly things. The face in front of her was not the one that had lit up when she'd fed a calf for the first time, or the one that had whispered secrets from the pillow next to Dylan until they both fell asleep. This stranger had stolen her friend and was holding her captive.

"Marybeth," Dylan whispered. The words came hard at first, and then with urgency. "You have to wake up. I don't know what to do." Her voice cracked. "I'm so scared. We're all so scared. Please wake up."

The machines ticked. Dylan watched her friend's

heartrate. She was right there. Her heart still beat. Her chest rose and fell even if it was with assistance.

"Damnit, Marybeth. You have to wake up. I don't know what to do."

Dylan curled her legs to her chest, and she hid her face in her knees.

"If you wake up, we'll get revenge. We can go to the police together. They all blame me. I know it. Everyone thinks I influenced you. But together, we can tell them it wasn't my fault or the fault of anyone else in my house. It was David. He'll go to jail. Everything will go back to normal, just don't make me do this on my own. Please, wake up."

The sobs came from deep within like water rushing through a broken dam. They kept coming until a hand touched her back.

"Dylan, let's go home."

Her mom helped her stand and then held her tight in her arms. When they left, Mr. and Mrs. O'Brien never spoke to Dylan. In their eyes, Dylan was responsible for hurting Marybeth. Who else could it have been?

After that, notes were passed back and forth around the classroom, yet Dylan never laid hands on any of them. This final sign signified her brief time in the inner circle had ended. The way people's gazes diverted to her after reading the contents only added to her pain. She wanted to scream the truth, but the truth was too close to the lie they believed. So close that the line blurred even for Dylan. Marybeth would be alive if she had never befriended her. That part was true, but it was also true that she tried to stop Marybeth from taking the drugs. That's not what any of them would ever believe, even though there weren't drugs in Dylan's system, not the night of the sleepover or any night before or after.

CHAPTER 37

Jeremy Biggs
Present Day

ALLEN WAS SITTING IN a booth, reading the local paper, when Jeremy entered Little Italy. On Allen's table, an ice-cold soda glass created a puddle of condensation threatening to soak the paper and melt the words. Patrons at a few tables were still finishing a late lunch, but they were out of earshot.

"What's caught your interest?" Jeremy asked. Allen was not the type to read anything more than a paragraph.

Allen glanced up with creased brows.

"You see this?" He slid the paper toward Jeremy. "The feds arrested a farmer, Earl Tyler. Ever hear of him?"

"Can't say that I have." Jeremy's heart raced, but he didn't want Allen to sense the panic coursing through his veins.

"You know the lunch lady, Ms. Susan? That's his wife. Their son's Logan?"

"Yeah. I guess."

"They say he was hiding the drugs in the rolls of hay. Some informant turned him in for suspicious activity."

"Lupo told David there was an informant. I guess he was right." Jeremy slid in the booth and pulled the paper to him.

He studied the picture of the man in cuffs. "Maybe the feds will think they've caught all the guilty parties now. Maybe they'll back off."

"Is that the feeling you get from this? I'm not so sure." Allen's voice shook. All his cockiness had again disappeared. Jeremy studied the scrawny man-child and saw him for what he was. A phony. Always pretending. Allen was never as brave or street-smart as he led on. In fact, watching him squirm in the seat across from him, all Jeremy could see was weakness. And this was his partner in crime. Jeremy needed to get out of this town before it was too late.

Jeremy looked back down at the paper. "Can't be sure of anything in this business." Earl Tyler's sullen gaze stared back at Jeremy from the front page. Hadn't he seen him entering The Coffee Shop across the street some afternoons? He didn't seem like a drug dealer.

"I guess we're going to find out tonight." Allen said.

"Yeah, I guess so." Jeremy stared at Mr. Tyler's picture. Where had the farmer screwed up, and how could they do things differently? Would his own face be on the front of tomorrow's paper?

Allen took a breath and regained his composure. "Just because he got caught doesn't mean we will. Don't let it stress you."

"I think you're the one that's stressed."

Allen stood. "Whatever. I'm going to go start the dishes. Don't be all day."

As Allen walked away, Jeremy began reading:

Local Farmer, Earl Tyler, Arrested for Drug Trafficking

Earl Tyler of Derby Line, VT, was arrested yesterday after an anonymous tip led police to his farm. Canine units detected marijuana in the haybales, and after further investigation, officers discovered duffle bags full of marijuana hidden within several bales. Earl is now being held in the Derby Line County Jail pending a bail hearing. The investigation is still ongoing.

Jeremy eyes darted over the following paragraph. Words jumped out at him like arrows.

He set the paper down hoping the guilt within him would subside. He couldn't read about the horrific incident they referenced. He rested his face in his hands, hiding the tears that filled his eyes, then took a deep breath, and pushed away the memories. He gave thanks that at least the article didn't mention the Phillips's farm, but it was only a matter of time before the police were all over that place again. Jeremy flipped to the inside of the newspaper, where the article continued. He resumed reading.

The Hidden Killer: Fentanyl

Fentanyl is an opioid used to treat pain. When produced by a licensed manufacturer and used under a doctor's care, it is known to benefit people suffering pain due to cancer or other chronic pain issues. Fentanyl becomes dangerous when produced by outside sources and put into different drugs. Organizations that commit these practices do so to cut costs and get their customers addicted to whatever drug is laced with the substance. It only takes an amount the size of one or two grains of salt to kill a person. When unauthorized people lace drugs with Fentanyl, they do so without regulating the dosing. One portion of the drug may have little to no Fentanyl, while another may contain double the amount, which is why, within the same group of people, one person can be unaffected while another dies. According to DEA.gov, six out of every ten Fentanyl-laced drugs contain lethal amounts.

LSD is a drug taken by placing a tiny piece of paper on one's tongue. This dangerous drug can be bought online from other countries. China, for example, sells LSD on sheets, which may appear like stickers. The sheets are mass-produced and not regulated. The amount of LSD and possibly Fentanyl on each tiny bit of paper may vary greatly. Our country is in a constant battle with illegal drug producers and traffickers. As quickly as one substance is banned, slightly different variants are created. It is close to impossible to regulate and stop the flow of drugs coming into our country.

Fentanyl is also making its way into knockoff illicit drugs such as Xanax and Norco. The consumer cannot detect whether Fentanyl is in the drug because it has no taste or color. This drug does not discriminate between someone who is a straight A student and has never tried alcohol or drugs before and someone who is a hard-core user. Good kids will mess up, and all kids are worth fighting for. It's important to have conversations with your children. Let them know one time can be fatal. Parents and children should see the warning signs of an overdose. Such signs may include slow heartbeat, shallow breathing, clammy skin, nausea, vomiting, and finally, loss of consciousness. Contact 911 immediately. Drugs such as Narcan can save lives if administered in time.

If you or someone you know struggles with addiction, call the hotline at 1-800-662-4357. Together, there is hope.

Bile rose in Jeremy's throat. How had his life ended up here? How had he become this person? A couple of bad choices, and he was nothing more than a hoodlum with no way out. He needed to find the stashed money and run without looking back. He wasn't such a big player that anyone would hunt him down. He just needed a chance, just one break, and he would do all he could to become someone with a future worth fighting for.

CHAPTER 38

Dylan
Past

DYLAN WAS DOING HOMEWORK in her bedroom when her mom tapped on her door.

"Can I come in?" she asked through the small opening.

Dylan didn't answer. She didn't need to. The pencil slid from her fingers as she gazed upon her mother's somber expression. Dylan knew the news would be horrible, yet she still hoped it was just an update about slow heartrate, a slight loss of brain activity, or some other similar life-changing but not life-ending shift her mother had warned Dylan could be possible outcomes.

Her mother sat on the bed. Dylan, only a foot away at her desk, now turned to face her mom. Claire smoothed the wrinkles from the comforter, as though the rhythmic motion might ease the situation.

"I have some really bad news, honey."

A sob burned in Dylan's throat She wanted to scream so loud she'd never hear her mother's words.

"Marybeth passed away. Her mom and dad were with her."

Dylan rushed to her mom's side and sobbed into her chest

as Claire held onto her. She cried and cried, while her mother rocked her in her arms. Some time passed this way until her mom spoke again.

"Are you ready to hear more?"

Was she? No. So much of her didn't want to hear another word, but she had to know. Dylan nodded.

"Marybeth's brain waves stopped, and she was declared brain dead. Only the machines were keeping her alive. The O'Briens decided as a family to let her go."

"Why didn't they let me say goodbye?"

"Honey, you remember how much pain we were in when we lost Hayden? We're still struggling years later. This pain is so fresh for them. They just needed to be alone, as a family. You understand, don't you?"

"They blame me. They think I did it."

"Honey, to be honest, I don't know what they think. They're hurting. They need space."

"They hate me." Dylan sobbed again.

Claire's hand slid repeatedly over Dylan's long hair, from crown to ends, but Claire didn't speak for several minutes.

"Dylan, why do you think they hate you? Is there something you haven't shared with me?"

Dylan stopped crying. In fact, she stopped breathing, keeping her face hidden in her mother's shirt.

"I was her best friend. They must think I know something."

"But do you?"

Still wrapped in her mom's arms, she shook her head. "I don't do drugs, Mom. You tested me. I hate drugs and all the people who sell them."

"Do you know people who sell them?" Claire's words were

slow and controlled, as if she didn't want the answers she was seeking.

"No," Dylan sobbed again. "I don't know anything." She wanted to tell her the truth, but all the reasons she could not still held her back. The truth would prove everyone right. Marybeth died because Dylan was her friend. Marybeth walked into their dismal lives and died. Everyone would hate her. Marybeth's parents and everyone at school would believe Marybeth took the pills due to Dylan's influence, and Marybeth could not tell the true account. Ever.

The room fell into an awkward silence. Her mother's arms loosened from around her. "I'm here for you, Dylan. We're family. We'll figure it out."

"Marybeth's dead, Mom. There's nothing to figure out anymore." Her eyes couldn't meet her mom's. "I need to be alone."

"Okay." Claire stood and walked to the door, only looking back once. Sometimes the only treatment for pain was time, and as Dylan crawled under her sheets, she wondered if a lifetime would be enough.

For Dylan, sleep came more easily in the days than at night. Maybe it was her body's way of avoiding everyone and everything. But when the world turned dark and quiet, the demons wrestled in her brain. The only place she found solace was in the barn where she and Marybeth had made their best memories. Marybeth's ghost lingered in the shadows, haunting her. The fact that Marybeth could not answer any of Dylan's questions ravaged her mind. Did Marybeth forgive her for introducing her to David? Should Dylan go to the police and beg them to believe her? Should she run for her life?

She had fallen asleep on the bucket in the coop and woke with her hand resting on Lady Bella's back. Something had awoken her, but now the subtle sound seemed as though it was part of a dream rather than reality. It was still midnight black, with morning light far from dawning, but she'd brought her flashlight, Dylan stood and placed Lady Bella back on her nest. The chicken nestled into her spot without objection. As Dylan removed her hand, she noticed the looseness of the sideboard, which served as the six-inch base supporting the nesting boxes. Had it always been so loose? She had never noticed it being like that in the past.

Curious, she jostled the board, and it slid to the side easily. It had definitely not been that loose. Behind the nests was a large black crevice. Dylan grabbed her flashlight and shone it into the darkness. Something was back there. She scanned the area for spiders, and although a few webs lined the side, she told herself she could handle them. Marybeth would want her to be brave. She reached in and felt what she thought to be a plastic storage bag. Behind that one was at least one more. Carefully she pulled one out, and at the sight of stacks of bills, dropped the flashlight. From what she could see, the bills were hundreds and fifties.

David! She'd known he was no good. Her mind spun with ways to send him to jail with this evidence. But then, her father had built the boxes. Wouldn't he also know of the hidden space perfect for stashing illegally earned money, for it had to be illegally earned. There was no other explanation. A sad numbness overtook her when she considered her father, the man who once played baseball in the fields with his children and sat next to them on the church pew, could now be a desperate, corrupt criminal. Did their mother know? Was that why they barely spoke? Dylan stared at the cash through the clear bag. How far could she run with this much money? She would guess very far away, and she could keep running for a lifetime. Jessie's face formed in her mind. She couldn't leave her sister. She would do anything to protect her, anything, and if Dylan deserted her, Jessie would be alone in this dark world.

"Marybeth, if you're here, help me. What do I do?"

The barn remained quiet. Dylan tucked the money back behind the nests and adjusted the board so no one would suspect she had moved it. For now, she needed to stay quiet and hope some answers revealed themselves.

CHAPTER 39

Eli Simmons
Present Day

ELI STEPPED INTO HIS camper, set his grocery bag onto the counter, and unpacked the few contents—creamer, eggs, bread, peanut butter, and jelly. While he appreciated the invitation given to eat meals with the Phillips family, the awkwardness of sitting at a table of sullen strangers proved too much some days.

He poured himself a hot cup of coffee and sat at his small table. The window beside the table overlooked the pasture where the cows grazed today. How could someone be so angry that they could violently kill one of these graceful creatures? Even when one of them frustrated him with a sloppy tail to the face or by knocking the grain off the top of the wheelbarrow, he could never be angry enough to injure one of them. Perhaps it was the drugs Jessie had suspected David had been on that had made him so violent. Eli had never tried drugs so he couldn't say if that was possible.

Or had there been more to David's violent behavior? Jessie said Dylan hated David even before he'd killed the cow.

Eli should mind his business and not care. But there were too many questions left to be answered. Invisible hands had wrapped around him and strapped him in. Life brought him to these people, this farm, these problems. And until something unfolded, the invisible hold on him would not release its grip, of that he felt certain.

His gaze drifted to the headline on the front page of the paper: **Local Farmer, Earl Tyler, Arrested for Drug Trafficking.** He skimmed the article, focusing on the final paragraph. *Law enforcement officials have been out in full force following tips on drug trafficking and an increase in drug-related crimes, including the death of a local middle school student last April. Months later, police have yet to trace where the student purchased the Fentanyl-laced pills. The female student who attended the local middle school overdosed on Fentanyl in the basement of her home during a sleepover. No one in attendance admits to knowing from whom she obtained the drug, and no one else at the party is accused of using drugs.*

The elevated number of overdoses in the state have forced local law enforcement, DEA, and Border Patrol to work together to find the sources responsible for the influx of drugs into the community.

A sinking feeling overwhelmed Eli. What had he gotten himself into? He thought about Conner and how he often hid himself in his shed, a shed he kept locked. He remembered the conversation with Mr. Sullivan, the breeder. And of course, there was the fact that a corpse was decaying in the fields around him. How could Conner not be involved? All the evidence screamed he was in way over his head with the wrong people. And what about the teenager who'd died from Fentanyl? Who was she? Had the girls known her?

He glanced back out his window. A large older cow stood close to the camper, staring back at him. She chewed her cud nonchalantly as she watched him with her large brown eyes. What had she seen as she stood trapped in her stanchion? What had she heard within the walls of the barn? This creature might have all the answers he sought, yet she could tell him nothing. After a moment, she turned and sauntered away.

When Eli walked across the pasture and prepared to cross the road for the evening milking, an old Chevy passed him that evening. He locked gazes with a young man driving the car. The driver was going slower than expected on the country road. Despite its fifty-five-mile-per-hour speed limit, cars often sped by at speeds exceeding seventy. Eli had seen this car before and recognized the man's face. The memory tickled the back of his mind until it surfaced. The driver was the same one he'd seen leaving The Watering Hole, helping his drunk friend the night Eli went to spy on Claire. Why would he be interested in the Phillips property?

Sometimes, when the media ran an article about the drug trafficking problem, they would mention the jawbone found on the Phillips's property. Eli had noticed in the weeks he had worked for Conner that traffic picked up when the farm was mentioned. Curiosity drew people to the unknown. As they passed the cornfields, they probably imagined that the rest of the body was hidden between the stalks of corn. People became a part of the story just by using their imaginations, and that's what folks, especially in small towns, craved. They wanted to be a part of something bigger, even if bigger meant dangerous.

But something about the young man piqued Eli's interest. The man had scanned the farm as if looking for something or someone. Not a ghost, but something more plausible in the realm of this world. If David had ties to organized crime, then maybe he was not alone, and Eli suspected this man knew something.

Once the car passed Eli, it sped up until it was out of his sight. At least his camper was not visible from the road. Not only did the Phillips family lack viewing access, but so did the curious strangers who studied the property as they drove by.

When he entered the barn, Jessie was waiting by the back door next to the chicken coop. She glanced over her shoulder and gave him a half-smile that warmed him. A bond was forming between them, still fragile, but at least there was one. He depended on that small bit of trust to get him some of the needed answers.

"How was school?"

"It was amazing. Me and all my friends made plans for the weekend, and I aced my science test."

"Would that be sarcasm?"

"Yes. I'll be milking cows this weekend, and although I didn't get my grade yet, I'm pretty sure I failed the test."

"I would say I could help, but school wasn't my strong suit."

"I would bust on you about the traveling camper thing and your loser life, but I'm starting to think it sounds pretty good right now."

"It's not for everyone, and it's not a cop-out. Not for me. But I have a feeling it's not the right life for you. You'll find your people. Middle schoolers are like lumps of clay. God is still forming them into who they are meant to be. They're just blobs of potential, struggling to find themselves. You have something deeper than most of them. It may feel like a burden right now, but it will be a blessing one day. I guarantee it."

Jessie stared at him for a moment. "You say weird stuff." But the contemplative look in her eye as she turned away told Eli she had heard him.

"Hey, can I ask you something?"

"You can ask. I'm not sure I'll answer."

"I was reading the paper today."

"Yikes."

"Yikes? Why do you say that? Did you read the article?"

"I don't need to. I eavesdrop. It's the news but juicier," Jessie said with a smile.

"True."

"It is true. You should try it."

"Maybe I will." Eli hesitated before continuing. "The article mentioned a middle school girl overdosing several months back. Did you know her?"

Jessie's breath caught for the quickest of moments. With glistening eyes, she stared out at the cattle ambling to the door. "Yeah. We all knew her. Marybeth was..." Jessie stopped. "She was like an angel."

Eli expected she might have known her, but not like this. "I'm so sorry. What a tragedy."

"Marybeth was Dylan's best friend. She was her only friend. They hung out all the time. Right in there, actually."

Jessie pointed to the coop. "Dad bought them the chickens for a science project."

"Wow. I don't know what to say." Eli wanted to wrap his arms around her and somehow hug them both. How could these girls have suffered so much? Even Eli, a man with deep faith, understood how sometimes holding onto the rock could seem impossible.

"There's more." A tear rolled down Jessie's cheek, and she quickly wiped it away. "Dylan was with her when it happened."

"What?" Even though Dylan was difficult, this fact shocked him. She was too young to be involved in drugs.

"Dylan didn't take any drugs. All the kids who'd been at the sleepover that night had to be tested. The cops tried to figure out where the drugs came from, but they never did."

"Dylan doesn't know?" How could that be? Dylan had to be hiding something, which was eating away at her.

"No."

"That seems hard to believe since she and Marybeth were so close."

Jessie laughed. "That seems impossible to believe." She swung open the door, and the cows pushed forward. The conversation was over.

CHAPTER 40

Jeremy Biggs
Present Day

DURING HIS BREAK, JEREMY rode out to the Phillips's property hoping to identify hiding spots David might have used for the money, but his drive-by had not gone unnoticed. He had locked eyes with a man standing by the side of the road who studied him with knowing eyes. Who was he? A hired man, perhaps? He could only hope that whoever it was had forgotten about the moment as soon as Jeremy's car was out of sight, but something told him otherwise.

The moment unsettled him, and as Jeremy and Allen returned under the full moon, Jeremy could not get the image of the man out of his mind.

They had been given instructions on where to find the duffel bags in the back of the cornfield at ten o'clock. The drugs would be hidden under a board leaning against a large rock. Jeremy didn't expect Allen to meet Lupo, but he suspected Lupo would be nearby, watching from the tree line, just as he always was with David.

Inside Allen's jacket was a wad of cash he would leave under the board for Lupo. If everything went as planned, the exchange would be easy, and they would both make a good profit from the deal. More money than they would make in a month washing dishes.

Jeremy drove down the dirt tractor path with his lights off, once again letting the moonlight guide them. He shut off the car, and the two sat silently.

"Well, are you going?"

"Yeah." Allen placed his hand on the door handle. "You think that Lupo guy killed your friend?"

"I've told you everything I know. You decide for yourself."

Allen nodded. "If I'm not back in thirty minutes, you can leave. Contact Carlo."

Jeremy laughed. "We're on our own out here. He isn't sending help but might appreciate the heads-up to protect himself."

Allen stared into the darkness and then opened the door. He shut it carefully so as not to make any noise and disappeared into the night.

Jeremy sat in the dark, watching for movement. His hair stood on his neck whenever the wind blew through the cornstalks. He sensed David's ghost out there, trying to tell him something, but damned if he knew what it was.

Ten minutes passed, and Allen had not returned. After fifteen minutes, Jeremy saw the silhouette of a man walking toward him. His breath caught in his throat. The figure became lost in the backdrop of the cornstalks so much that he couldn't judge the size of the person closing in on him. As he got closer, Jeremy could tell he was carrying something large on his shoulder. When he was five feet from the car, Jeremy breathed a sigh of relief, and

Allen opened the back door, tossed in two backpacks, and climbed in the front.

"Let's get out of here."

Jeremy started the vehicle and began backing down the path. "Did you see anyone?"

"Yes." Allen's voice was even and controlled.

"Seriously." Jeremy slowed.

"Keep going. I want to get the hell out of here."

"What did he say?"

"Nothing. Lupo was standing near the tree line. When I approached, he walked over to me and stared me right in the eyes."

"Like he did with David." "Yeah. Like Lupo did with David right before he went missing."

"What the hell?" Jeremy's chest tightened with fear. "Did he do anything? Did he count the money?"

"No, he just watched me, but I'm sure he counted it as soon as I walked away. If the cash wasn't all there, I wouldn't be having this conversation with you."

Jeremy's hands shook on the steering wheel as he backed out onto the country road and headed toward town.

"I don't like how he stared me down," Allen said.

"He was just trying to intimidate you. Don't let it get to you."

"Well, it did."

"Let's just get the drugs to Carlo and call it a night. I've had about all I can take today."

They rode in near silence down the pitch-black country roads. Carlo owned a camp outside of town where he ran his business away from his family. Carlo's family home was one of the best in town, a large white house with pillars that, in Jeremy's opinion, looked out of place amongst the surrounding homes.

Jeremy parked the car a few houses down from Carlo's, leaving the engine running.

"Do you know the dealers in town that Carlo hands this stuff off to?"

"David and I dealt with one of them. David knew him better than me. He was shady."

"He's a drug dealer. Would you expect anything else?"

"I suppose not. Carlo has several contacts. Some around here, some from other towns. Who knows how far these drugs travel?" Jeremy opened the door. "You stay here. Call my cell if you see anything suspicious."

"Are you getting paranoid?"

"You're in trouble if you're not," Jeremy said before shutting the door.

When he returned to the car, he handed Allen a wad of money, which his friend quickly counted.

"Not bad for a couple of hours' worth of work," Allen said, smiling.

"No. Not bad at all," Jeremy responded, but after everything with Marybeth, the thrill of the profit had dissipated. He couldn't keep doing this.

Two days later, Jeremy finished his morning shift and grabbed a paper and a discounted employee lunch, which he occasionally splurged on. He unfolded the paper and lifted the forkful of pasta to his mouth. The sketch of a wanted person stared back at him. The sketch was too large not to catch his attention. The man was wanted for questioning in cases of fentanyl overdose. The population of Derby Line ranged from somewhere between six and seven hundred people. Those numbers made it nearly impossible to go unnoticed or unseen, yet this man was a stranger to him. But was he really?

Jeremy recalled David's description of Lupo: thin face, dark wavy hair, goatee. The description matched the picture. Searching for clarification, Jeremy's gaze darted across the page. According to the article, an anonymous source helped the sketch artist finalize the drawing. Authorities believed the man to be a Canadian citizen guilty of meeting people along the borders of Canada to smuggle drugs. Jeremy's heart raced. If the cops closed in on Lupo, they closed in on all of them. The authorities also wanted to question the sketched man about the disappearance of David Miller.

And then Jeremy saw it. *The man, who goes by the nickname Lupo, is most likely armed and dangerous.*

He needed to call Allen, but not from the restaurant. There were too many ears, specifically Amber's. He grabbed his jacket and headed to the door.

"Hold up. Where're you heading off to so quickly?" Amber sauntered over to the table he had just vacated. The paper lay open to the picture. She picked it up and looked from it to Jeremy. "Is this what has you all in a frenzy?" She smirked and turned the picture to face him.

"I just have some errands to do."

Amber glanced back at his uneaten food. "Sure, you do." The sneer grew on her lips. "I think you're lying." She stepped closer to him, her gaze freezing him in place. She stopped inches from him and looked up into his eyes. When she spoke, the words were a breeze on his face, dancing flirtatiously around their target. "I think someone is being a naughty boy."

"You don't know what you're talking about." He wanted to turn and walk out the door, but his body refused to respond.

"You better be careful, pretty boy. Haven't you already had your share of trouble with the police?"

Jeremy swallowed hard.

Her lips were inches from his. "If I recall, you've been arrested twice already? Doesn't look like someone has learned his lesson."

She smiled up at him, her gaze never leaving his.

"Don't worry. Your secrets are most likely safe with me." She winked, lingered one long moment, and then turned back to the kitchen, tossing her towel over her shoulder as she sashayed away.

Jeremy darted through the door and raced around the corner before bending with his hands on his knees and gasping for air. He found his car, fought with the key as his hands trembled, and finally settled into the driver's side. He scanned the area. No one was around. He leaned back on the headrest and breathed in and out until his racing heart rate slowed to a normal pace; then, he picked up his phone and dialed Allen's number.

"They're going to think you ratted him out," Jeremy told him after summarizing the article. "You just saw him, and now they have a sketch of his face."

Allen was silent on the other end. Jeremy didn't know

what his friend was thinking, but he was sure of one thing: He needed to find the money David had hidden, and he needed to find it quickly.

CHAPTER 41

Eli Simmons
Present Day

DAYS AFTER EARL TYLER was arrested, a sketch of a
man suspected of trafficking drugs across the border
showed up in the paper. Even Eli, an ordinary citizen, found
the connection obvious. Earl must have been helping the
officers to lessen his charges. The officials were closing in
on the culprits who lingered about the town and across the
border, but for some reason, Eli, a strait-laced man of faith,
did not know exactly whom he was rooting for anymore.
The Phillips family had grown on him, even Conner, with
his abrasive tone and cold-hearted attitude. But if the family
patriarch was involved, he had to pay the price. Could
Conner make a plea bargain like Earl had, or was it too
late? Maybe Earl had told the investigators everything they
needed to know, and now it was only a matter of time.

The news of Earl's arrest deepened the tension on the
farm. Conner was drinking more, and for the first time, it
wasn't only the smell of alcohol giving his addiction away.
Conner's hands shook when he adjusted the milkers.
Occasionally, Eli witnessed him place a hand on something
for balance. When lunchtime came, Eli followed him inside

to the quiet kitchen where Claire had tuna sandwiches with toasted bread waiting for them. The paper sat on the table, which was not general practice. Claire was speaking a warning without even being present. There was something Conner needed to see.

Conner pulled his chair up to the table with a screech, jolting Eli and making him catch his breath. His boss stared at the folded paper for several moments before unfolding it. The headline was all Eli could make out from reading upside down—*Man Found Floating in the Tomifobia River Matches Sketch.* Conner stared at the paper. By the steadiness of his eyes, Eli could tell his boss wasn't reading the article. He then closed the paper and tossed it on the floor by his chair.

"This town is going to hell and taking some people with it."

"Did I see someone drowned?"

Conner studied Eli through his untrimmed eyebrows before refocusing on his lunch.

"They didn't say he drowned." Staring at his plate, Conner took a bite of his sandwich. The edge in his boss's voice had told Eli to end the conversation, and they ate the rest of their lunch in uncomfortable silence.

Eli needed to know more. The best place to find out about town gossip was the local coffee shop, named just that. Usually, he stayed away from such places, but nothing about the recent events was normal.

Several tables at the premises were filled with patrons. Eli ordered a black coffee and grabbed one of the remaining papers from the rack. He paid with barely a word between him and the employee and found a seat in a booth next to two young women. Eli scanned the article and learned the body was believed to be that of the man from the sketch. Lupo, the nickname he went by, was suspected of trafficking drugs across the border before he turned up floating in the river. He'd also been wanted for questioning regarding David Miller's death. Eli stared at the reprinted sketch. Though nothing more than pencil markings, the eyes sent a chill up his spine. Had this man killed the man who had once milked the same cows Eli did now? The idea made him feel close to death. Not a peaceful rest but an unsettling darkness. The officials believed Lupo had ties to organized crime. There were only so many reasons someone in organized crime would kill off one of their own. One, the person had become a traitor, or two, a liability. Which scenario fits Lupo?

Eli finished reading the article and pushed the paper to the side. Everyone who drifted in and out of The Coffee Shop was a stranger to him, but even strangers could offer something in their conversations. Eli couldn't hear many of the people's words, and the two young women beside him kept their voices low but not low enough. They both wore jeans, oversized sweatshirts, and sneakers. Eli guessed them to be in their early to mid-twenties.

"This is what happens when you live in a place where the Canadian border splits the town's buildings apart," the girl facing him said to her friend. "I used to think it was cool that the border went right through the Opera House."

"It is still cool if they can only catch the people smuggling the drugs."

Eli had found the proximity to Canada intriguing, but

for others, the location tempted them to forget the legalities of a border.

Eli had seen Border Patrol walking along the back fields several times but had never suspected that members of organized crime families could have also been lurking about in the tree line. The paper said Lupo had been strangled and then thrown into the water. Who had he upset enough to get himself killed? Or was it not that at all? Perhaps Lupo had been killed because of something he knew.

The woman wearing the green sweatshirt with CCV printed across the front took a drink of her coffee and wiped the whipped cream from her upper lip. "It's so creepy that a man was floating in our Tomifobia River. Even if he was part of the Canadian mafia, it's still creepy."

"I know. Isn't the mafia a New York City thing?"

"Right? Aren't they supposed to be hanging out in Italian restaurants and doing drive-by shootings or something? What are they doing in Derby?" the one in the green sweatshirt asked.

"Apparently, helping the farmers make some extra cash by turning a blind eye to things."

"Can you believe Earl Tyler was involved? I was friends with his son, Logan, before he started dating that girl from Little Italy. I can't imagine him running the farm," green sweatshirt added. "And poor Ms. Susan. I heard she had to quit work at the cafeteria to help on the farm."

"Was Logan dating the girl with all the tattoos?"

"Yes, her. She is always right on the edge of where trouble is happening yet never gets in trouble herself."

"It's a shame he's dating the likes of her."

"I think it ended. I heard she's moved on to someone else. I think the guy works at the restaurant with her." She sipped her coffee and looked out the window as if in thought. "I know Earl was wrong to get involved, but I still feel for him. He was a good man. I've always liked running into him here. He always remembered my name and asked about my family. I can't believe he was arrested for stashing drugs in his hay bales. He must have been desperate for money."

"Do you think he was the unidentified source who helped make the sketch? Maybe he did it to cut a deal."

"It would make sense. But if Earl was involved, it makes you wonder who else is working with the mafia. Maybe they're wandering our streets. This town is so small, I recognize everyone except..."

Her voice trailed off, and Eli glanced up to catch the woman looking over her friend's shoulder at him. Then she whispered something too softly for Eli to hear. The women grabbed their drinks within a few moments and headed down the sidewalk. The curly-haired woman glanced back once and caught his gaze through the window before quickly turning back around, grabbing her friend's arm, and picking up the pace as they disappeared around the corner.

Should he have said something? Introduced himself as the new hired man on the Phillips's farm? No. Nothing he could say would ease their suspicion of him. All he could do was wait for the clouds to part, allowing some light to fall into the mysterious crevices of his present situation.

During the following week the police came to the farm several times, pressuring Conner to harvest the corn. He'd insisted it wasn't ready. With the death of Lupo, the townsfolk were unsettled, knowing organized crime had their hands in local businesses, family affairs, and the welfare of their children. People wanted answers, and they were growing more convinced those answers, whether they made sense or not, lay in finding the remains of David Miller.

How could the death of a mobster have anything to do with the Phillips family? Yet, somehow, Eli knew that it did. Sometimes, he wished he could see the Phillips house from his camper, allowing him to watch them when they were unaware, to see who left and how long they were gone. The day before Lupo was found dead, Eli had been with Conner until after the evening milking, but he had showered and been in bed by nine-thirty, as usual. Anything could have happened after that time.

Eli tried to remember if he'd heard a truck leave their driveway, but he couldn't. He had fallen into a deep sleep so quickly he wouldn't have heard anything unless someone had slammed into the camper's exterior. The idea sent a chill through his bones.

Maybe Claire had been at one of her study sessions. Maybe Conner became angry when he saw her with the male nursing student who had caught her attention the night Eli saw her in the bar. Eli breathed in deeply and let the breath slowly ease out of his lungs. His imagination had taken over. Eli had never seen Conner become violent. Angry, controlling, sinister—yes, all of that. But not violent.

Before heading to the barn for the evening milking, Eli cleared his head of the negative thoughts that had begun to spin webs in his mind. On the way across the street, he saw a car parked on the side of the road. Twice now, Eli had seen the exact vehicle with the heavy-set woman sitting in it, looking at the cornfield. Everything about her screamed hardship, from the rust eating away at her gray sedan to the crushed-in bumper. Eli stopped at the barn door and watched her swipe at her tear-streaked face. What was her story, and why did she stare at the cornfields?

Conner walked up beside him. They watched the woman for a bit without saying a word. Finally, he placed a hand on Eli's shoulder.

"Sometimes we need to be reminded that someone is suffering just as much or more than we are."

Eli looked at Conner, surprised by the tenderness in his voice.

"You know her?"

"It's David's mother. I've seen her several times. She's enduring the worst kind of pain. One I don't wish on anyone. I guess in her mind, she's visiting his gravesite."

Silence settled between them. Eli wasn't sure if he should speak his following words, but the time seemed to call for it.

"I heard about your son. I'm very sorry."

Conner's hand slid from his shoulder. Eli didn't dare look at him.

"It was my fault." A sad chuckle escaped Conner. "I've never admitted that out loud. I guess I felt I didn't need to. Everyone who mattered already believed that to be the truth. It was my fault," he said again. "Mine and God's."

"How do you figure?"

"About me or God?"

"Both, I guess."

"Do you know how rare it is to get a flesh-eating bacterium? Only about two hundred people a year get it. Of all the millions worldwide, only two hundred a year are infected. Do you know how many of those two hundred people die in a year? One to five. And my Hayden had to be one of them. That's on God. I own the part when I told my wife our son would be fine. I dismissed her hysteria, and then our Hayden died. It was only a blink of time in our lives. A little decision one day, and the next day, I finally agreed he should be seen, but it was too late. Now, God and I talk less than my wife and I do, if possible."

"If you don't mind me saying, I think they are both waiting for you to start the conversation. One wants you to yell and scream about how angry you are at Him, and one wants you to bear the pain with her. It might be hard, but I believe they are waiting for you. Once the words start coming, you'll wonder why you've never spoken the words aloud. Just like now. I've had to have a few tough conversations with the man upstairs myself over the years."

"And look how He answered you. You're drifting around in a beat-up camper with no family to call your own."

Eli smiled. "I think you have it wrong. I'm always standing on a rock that doesn't budge, and I never feel like I don't belong to a family. I have a heavenly father. Took me a bit to accept that. I wanted what the people around me had. I thought something was wrong with me because I had been rejected by my earthly mother and father, not to mention endless foster families. Life broke me until God healed me. There's a lot of brokenness in your family. I see it in you, your wife, and the girls. He can heal you when you're ready."

This time, Eli placed his hand on Conner's shoulder. "You can join me at Sunday's service if you choose. The first step is the hardest, but once you take a few, you'll start running toward redemption like it's the only thing you've ever craved."

Eli tapped his boss's shoulder and walked away, leaving him alone to stare at the weeping mother.

As Eli neared the milk house, Conner approached the parked car. When he was nearly ten feet from reaching it, the woman driver sped out of the ditch and down the country road, leaving Conner standing in the dust watching her race away. She wouldn't know what his purpose was in nearing her car. Was this man the one who murdered her son? Was he coming to threaten her? Was he coming to scream at her for being parked on his property? Knowing the conversation that he had shared with Conner, Eli doubted either of these assumptions was correct. But as Conner stood alone, watching the car speed down the road, Eli feared what his boss was thinking. He had taken a step forward and made to feel foolish.

Eli looked to the heavens in question. Sometimes, despite his faith, he still wondered about God's timing.

CHAPTER 42

Conner Phillips
Present Day

CONNER LOCKED THE SHED door with a shaky hand, blocking access to everything hidden within its walls. His stomach burned from the alcohol he had swallowed straight from the bottle. There were too many empty bottles hidden under his worktable to count. Somehow, he would need to get rid of them before the day his family inevitably found them.

The farm was quiet around him. Claire had gone to the school because the counselor had called with concerns. His wife hadn't asked him to join her, and he hadn't offered. Conner didn't need some stranger telling him how to raise his children. As he thought this, guilt washed over him; deep down, he knew that he needed to have someone guide him through the challenges of parenting. Conner had failed in his duties as a father and had no idea how to handle the difficulties parenting presented. Yet, he would never listen to anyone else's advice. For him, listening felt like an admission of defeat, which was too difficult to bear.

Eli had either gone to town or was hiding in his camper. And while he enjoyed Eli's presence in a strange and unexplainable way, he was happy to be alone. Eli would notice his effort to walk straight and speak without slurring. He wanted to suffer alone, and that feeling grew stronger each day. The alcohol and the contents of the shed served to help him savor the pain he'd taught himself to believe he deserved and had somehow learned to be addicted to. Each sip put pressure on the bruise, causing just the right amount of discomfort, so he mistook it for pleasure. Eli's kindness and concern for their family started illuminating a new path out of their situation but reaching for that branch felt frightening. Sometimes, it seemed easier to remain in the muck than to risk falling from great heights back into it once more.

Conner's head swam from the whiskey as he walked unsteadily to the cornfield's edge and stared down the row. "Where are you, David Miller?" He took one step and then another until he disappeared into the forest of stalks. He closed his eyes and listened. The breeze passed through the rows, making the sticky leaves crinkle around him. He placed his hand on a corn cob. The bottom was full, but the kernels were still only nubs as he reached the tip. When he pushed his nail into the kernels, a clear liquid emerged. The corn wasn't ready. It was as simple as that. If it was ready, the pressure would have caused a milky fluid to squirt from the kernel. He had some time. But for what? How could he change what had already been done?

Chances were that David's body would be found on his property and any hope the dog had traipsed off across the border and discovered David's jawbone there would be destroyed. Conner's family would look guilty. After Earl Tyler was arrested for smuggling drugs, the local farmers became suspects. Earl's arrest made the townspeople believe farmers were desperate men unable to pay their bills, struggling to put food on their tables, and willing to do anything to make ends meet.

In addition to the gossip about their family, the townspeople probably saw Claire in the bars with all her young friends. If folks had any observation skills whatsoever, they would suspect her marriage was in trouble. Hell, he was surprised she hadn't left him years ago. Sometimes, after a few drinks, Conner considered reaching across the bed to wrap his arms around his wife, but then he envisioned her icy reaction. Instead, he stayed on his side, facing the wall, and she did the same on hers.

But it wasn't just his marriage that was crumbling. What is a farmer without his farm? Without his land? Without his family? Farming was all Conner had done other than some small high school jobs. He didn't have a resume full of experience. He was aging out of jobs requiring physical conditioning.

He'd heard of farmers going bankrupt and then trying to pass physicals to become correctional officers. Could he pass the test? And what if he did? He'd be working at Northern State Correctional Facility. It could be worse. A cousin from New York had to work in Sing Sing hours away from his upstate town, waiting to win a bid to get back to a prison closer to home. Northern State Correctional Facility was only a twenty-minute drive. Conner cringed at the thought of being locked in a building with hardened criminals. The idea terrified him, but he wasn't allowed to be terrified. He was the man, the head of the household. He couldn't show any of those emotions. He had to be strong.

But he wasn't strong. He wasn't courageous. He'd proved those facts to himself when they'd lost Hayden. When he lost his son, he turned to the only source he trusted to temporarily numb the pain. Even now, he could smell the whiskey seeping from his skin after yesterday's drinking binge. He couldn't lose this farm, but he had no clue how to keep it. Even more than the farm, how could he hold onto a family that had been shredded apart through the years?

Where was happiness in this terrifying and depressing world? Conner dropped to his knees as if in prayer, but he hadn't prayed in so long he didn't know how to begin. Instead, he gazed up into the bright sky through teary eyes and waving cornstalks. He didn't speak. He didn't pray. He only looked in the direction of the heavens, hoping someone up there would see him and reach out a hand. He felt ready to take hold of the slightest bit of hope for the first time in years, but he was too weak to reach out.

He closed his eyes, and a tear rolled down his cheek. He didn't wipe the wetness away. Inside his chest, a sob collected into a ball. Physical pain filled his chest, and for a moment, he feared his heart was breaking in two.

"Help me," he cried into his hands. And with the words, the dam released into guttural cries. "Help me."

A cloud drifted in front of the sun, darkening the sky. Conner lifted his face, and large raindrops fell against his skin, washing away the tears. Too tired to lift his body, he let the rain soak his clothes and moisten the ground around him. How was this help? Why did his plea lead to being pounded by rain? For some reason, despite the response making no sense, he heard one thing loud and clear: The conversation between the God he used to know and himself had begun again.

CHAPTER 43

Claire Phillips
Present Day

CLAIRE SAT STIFFLY IN the chair facing the desk as Mrs. Owens shut the door. Heat rose from Claire's chest and neck. Dylan may have caused the meeting to be called, but Claire felt on trial.

Mrs. Owens walked around the desk and took the seat facing her. A strained smile showed straight white teeth. The woman looked perfect—untouched by life. Glowing family pictures mocked Claire as she squirmed in her seat.

"Thank you for coming, Mrs. Phillips. I've been eager to meet you."

"You have?" The heat rising from her neck and chest intensified.

"Certainly." The dean rested her folded hands on the desk and exhaled. The fresh scent of mouthwash flooded the air. "Your family has been through a great deal, and I would be lying if I told you your girls seem unphased by all of it. It's quite the opposite."

Claire nodded and swallowed her words. Whatever she could say would somehow be wrong.

"Did Dylan mention I spoke with her the other day—just to touch base?"

"No, she didn't."

"The teachers have expressed concerns."

"They have?"

"Yes. All of them have."

Claire nodded again.

"How is she doing at home?"

"Dylan's very quiet. You know middle schoolers." Claire released a strained chuckle. "You can't get inside their heads."

The dean's gaze penetrated her. "Do you mind me asking how she reacts when you try to talk with her?"

Claire tensed in defense. What the dean was politely asking was whether Claire had tried talking to her.

"When Marybeth died, Dylan mostly cried on my shoulder. She didn't say very much."

Half of a year had passed since she and her daughter had shared that sort of intimate moment, but Claire couldn't admit that to this woman.

Moments ticked by, and then the dean pulled a piece of paper from a drawer. She laid it on the desk in front of Claire.

"Dylan drew this in art class." Claire watched the dean's manicured hand drift back to her lap before focusing on the drawing. Her attention settled on the beautiful and heart-wrenching image, as if she were being given a glimpse into her daughter's soul. Who was this girl who could create so much emotion with what appeared to be colored pencils? With expert detail, Dylan had etched out their driveway, their house, the barn, and the cornfields. With strokes and shadows, she'd depicted the dark world they were all enslaved in. Claire reached for the picture and pulled it closer. Beneath an immense cloud, Claire could see the bone fragments scattered amongst the stalks. The head of Sarge peered through the leaves. On the ground surrounding the bones lay bottles shaped like Conner's whiskey bottles. When she pulled the paper even closer, she saw a hoe like the one David had used to kill the cow. The tool was hidden in the design in a way that reminded her of the old childhood magazine she had enjoyed for hours, searching for hidden objects. Any other onlooker could easily have missed it.

Claire's heartbeat slammed against her chest in a steady rhythm. She'd been so consumed with the cornfield she hadn't noticed the camper off to the side of the farm. Lines of sunbeams struggled through the clouds and illuminated the camper's metal wall. Tears filled her eyes. Eli had brought warmth into their lives in ways she could not describe. This was proof that Dylan felt it too, a small spark of light shining in the corner of their world.

The dean may have called Claire to the school to warn her of the ominous scene portrayed in the drawing, but she was already too aware of the darkness. The only part of the picture she cared to focus on was the sunbeams. A smile tugged at her lips as she wiped away a tear.

"Excuse me, Mrs. Phillips, but are we looking at the same picture?"

"Yes," she choked.

"And what do you see in this picture?"

Claire looked from the drawing into the concerned eyes of the dean.

"Hope."

When Claire returned to the farm, she marched across the road and through the pasture to the camper parked among the grazing cattle. She didn't know what she would say, she only knew she needed to speak to the man who had come from—where? Where was Eli from? She knew so little about him.

She stepped up to the camper and gave three quick knocks on the metal door. After a moment, she heard footsteps inside. When Eli opened the door, his eyes widened at the sight of Claire standing in front of him.

"Mrs. Phillips, is everything okay?"

"Please call me Claire, and yes, everything is okay. I just wanted to talk to you."

"You're welcome to come in."

Claire walked up the creaky steps and entered the camper. Eli remained quiet as she scanned the small room, studying it as if it could reveal all his secrets.

"You like to keep things simple," Claire noted.

"It works for me."

Claire glanced around again. "I'm sure it doesn't take all day to clean, either."

"No," he laughed. "It doesn't. Can I get you some coffee?"

She started to say no but changed her mind. "That would actually be nice."

"Have a seat." He pointed to one of the benches by the table. "I'll have it ready in a moment."

Claire slid into the seat and glanced out the window. Two cows grazed on the grass, unbothered by their new neighbor.

"Do you mind the cows roaming around your home?"

"Quite the contrary. They entertain me and keep me company."

The single-serve coffee machine spat out its final drops. Eli handed her the mug, and she wrapped her chilled hands around it, enjoying the warmth it provided. She smiled out the window. "It's peaceful out here. It's right across the road from us, and yet it feels like another world."

As Eli brewed his own cup, a comfortable silence passed between them until he slid onto the bench across the table from her.

"Conner said he used to take you and the girls to his hunting camp. The memory sounds very peaceful."

"He spoke to you about that?" She studied Eli in awe.

"I'm not saying we've shared many memorable conversations, but there have been a few."

She gazed back out the window. "Those were good days. The kids would fish with Conner, and I would read my book and half-listen to their conversations, believing there would be many more to come. I wish I could go back and savor those moments more. That old saying, 'You don't know what you have until it's gone,' is truer than I care to admit."

"And what about today?"

"What about it?"

"What would you miss tomorrow if you woke up without it?"

Claire stared at Eli as if he had spoken a foreign language, and for reasons unknown, she'd understood it.

"I haven't thought..." Her voice cracked.

"It's hard to not focus on what we've lost, but if that's all we see, our blessings fade into the shadows."

A tear rolled down her cheek. "I would miss my girls."

"And Conner?"

She looked down at her hands, which grasped her coffee mug. "To be truthful, I don't know."

"Would he miss you?"

She laughed. "I've never considered whether he would. But I'm not sure. I guess I've become a shadow to him, too. I've been more focused on his shortcomings than worrying about my own."

"Sometimes the best way to get out of your head is to get in someone else's. Why do you think Conner doesn't like you going to nursing school?"

"The money."

"I know he's stressed about that, but there's something deeper than money bothering him. You know that don't you?"

Claire took a sip of her drink, fighting back a cry that threatened to escape. "He's scared of losing me." The moment the words left her mouth, she felt the weight of their truth. A deep sense of tenderness for her husband enveloped her. His anger and distance had created a barrier, making it hard for her to see his love. She understood that while he cared for her, expressing his true emotions was a struggle for him.

"And should he be?"

Claire shrugged, but Eli had been in the bar. He had witnessed her wondering eyes. Although she did not feel judged, she did feel exposed. A wave of shame washed over her. Conner and her inability to communicate had pushed them apart. How did they allow this to happen to their marriage?

"I'm just so tired and alone. I don't have any more fight in me."

"Then stop fighting, Claire, and start healing."

CHAPTER 44

Jeremy Biggs
Present Day

JEREMY DROVE DOWN THE road to the Phillips farm, leaving Allen behind again. Their relationship, albeit better than before, was not what he would consider a friendship. Allen hid behind a tough façade, but his fear slipped through the shell every now and then. That part of him tempted Jeremy to get to know him more, give him a chance. But when Allen's eyes had lit up at the mention of the hidden money, red flags had flown in all directions. Why had he even told him about the money? What was to stop Allen from looking for it himself?

Jeremy drove by the farm and noticed the same man he had seen on the last drive-by walking through the pasture across the road from the barn. He glimpsed a camper hidden behind the cornstalks as he slowed his car. The hired hand was living on-site, which could complicate things, but perhaps it wouldn't be as difficult as it seemed. Jeremy just needed to find a place to park where he wouldn't be visible.

The next obstacle was the dogs that roamed the farm. Jeremy had met them all when he had brought David lunch, but that didn't mean they wouldn't bark at him if they saw him creeping into the barn at night.

He tried to scan everything, including the doors, the windows, the shadowy areas that might not be lit up at night by the large floodlight attached to the front of the barn, but if he went any slower, he would catch someone's attention. Hopefully, they were used to people slowing down to gawk at the farm since David's jawbone had been discovered.

Jeremy drove up to the neighbor's driveway. He had an idea. Quickly, before the neighbor noticed him in his driveway, he adjusted his phone in the holder and started the video. Then he drove back down the country road toward the farm, allowing his phone to remember all the small details his mind would not be able to as well. He slowed to fifty miles per hour, hoping the footage wouldn't be blurred.

No one was outside, and there was no sign of the hired man in the field. He must have gone inside the old camper.

Once past the property, Jeremy reached for his phone to end the video and nearly hit an oncoming car. He swerved, almost going off the rough edge of the road, and corrected himself before any damage was done. Once his heart stopped racing, the image of the car came back to him. He knew that vehicle. He and David had taken it on many joy rides through the years. The driver would be an overweight woman in her forties, looking for something the world took from her, knowing she would never get it back.

Thoughts of David haunted Jeremy's mind later as he lay staring at the moldy ceiling in his room. Why hadn't David shared the location of the money? Jeremy recalled a conversation with his friend when he'd joined him for lunch in the barn one day.

"My mom's been snooping in my room. I'm moving the cash. Thought you should know."

"Where are you putting it?"

"I've got some ideas."

"And they are?" Jeremy asked, his impatience growing.

"Listen, man," David had said, "I'll tell you when I choose the spot."

"Why not hide it here in the barn?"

"I don't think so."

Jeremy recalled David's gaze shifting, which often happened when he didn't want Jeremy to read his thoughts.

"Why not?"

"I don't know how long this job will last." Again, David refused to make eye contact.

Jeremy studied his friend as he took another bite of his bologna sandwich followed by a swig of soda. "You in trouble with them?"

With his mouth still half-full, David said, "Not yet, but you know how jobs go with me. It won't be long until I'm cut loose."

"I can put the money at my house. My old man never steps foot in my room."

"No. If one of us gets caught, the police will search both of our houses, right? I'll tell you the new spot soon enough. I'm still thinking."

"I hope that's all there is to it."

David gave Jeremy a friendly pat on the back. "Have I ever led you astray?"

"My life is astray."

David laughed. "Look at the danger I've put myself in to protect you. It's at my house. If they find it there, I'm the one in trouble. Not you. See what I do for us?"

"What's to say you don't take the cash and just up and go like you have in the past?"

"I have never up and gone with a penny of your money. I only took myself and what was in my wallet."

"We've never had this much money before."

"No, we have not, my friend." David took another huge bite of sandwich. "I'll have the hiding place soon. Don't you fret."

Time passed, and Jeremy continued to receive the same reply. Jeremy had wanted to set eyes on the money again, but when he mentioned going to David's house, he was always redirected.

"Trust me, my friend," Jeremy heard over and over. When Jeremy dug through David's room after the funeral, he wasn't surprised to find the money had been moved. As much as he wanted to believe his friend was getting around to telling him the new hiding place, Jeremy knew better. David was never anyone's friend.

Jeremy grabbed his phone and pulled up the video of the farm again. He had been on the property countless times, and David had given tours of the area during multiple lunches. Beside the barn, stood a small shed. David had told him his creepy boss always kept the door locked. The money couldn't be in there.

What about the large barn? It consisted of the haymow, the milk house, and the area where they milked the cows. David had walked Jeremy through the haymow, an ever-changing pile of bales. At this time of year, the haymow would be filled to the ceiling in preparation for winter. The haymow would have been nearly empty when David disappeared, awaiting the summer haying season. Jeremy doubted David would have hidden the money in a place where it would eventually be buried under thousands of hay bales.

The milk house was small, and the only cupboard contained the cleaning chemicals that were used daily.

The big space where they milked the cows was made of cement and had no good spots to hide stuff except for a cupboard. But that cupboard got opened way too often for medicines and supplies, so it wasn't a great place to stash the money.

A small hallway led to the smaller barn, where the family penned the calves and kept the chickens. Several pens contained calves of various ages. Again, this was not a place to hide money.

Near the pens was a battered door that had hidden an empty coop at the time of the conversation. It wasn't until Dylan and Marybeth started their science project that the chicken coop had any relevance to the farm, and even then, David had paid the room little attention.

Remembering the chickens made thoughts of Marybeth creep into Jeremy's mind. He had only met her once. He could still recall how the setting sun shone through her red hair, giving her a halo effect as she stood beside his car. His stomach turned every time he envisioned her, overflowing with happiness and trust. Her death wasn't his fault. Not really. But he would forever feel guilty for his part. He listened to David and brought the drugs to the farm. Her death was even more reason for him to find the money and run far away from this town and everyone in it.

He tried to envision the girls laughing and holding the chickens, but he couldn't. He couldn't imagine them in the coop because it was the one area of the barn David had never let him see. Jeremy jolted up and tossed his phone to the side. He didn't need to watch the video one more time. The money was in the chicken coop.

CHAPTER 45

Dylan Phillips
Past

D*YLAN'S PARENTS LET HER sleep in the following day. When it came time for her to do her chores, no one came to her door. She didn't know if Jessie covered for her or if her mother did. She didn't care. She only was happy they allowed her time to be lost in nothingness. The next day, being a Friday, they let her stay in bed again. Two days out of school wouldn't destroy her future.*

Her mother placed food by the door: peanut butter and jelly and a bowl of fruit cocktail from a can. When Dylan's stomach screamed loudly enough that she couldn't sleep, she forced herself to pick up the spoon, place the syrupy fruit into her mouth, and swallow. Then she would curl back up into a ball and let sleep take her from the dark, miserable world once again.

On Monday, she went to school wearing a black hoodie she'd pulled from the hamper, jeans, and an old pair of Converse sneakers her mother had bought from a lawn sale. Normally, Dylan would have worried someone would recognize them as their old, discarded pair, but not this day. This day, she cared about nothing. The teachers didn't even ask her to remove the hoodie from her head. She heard nothing anyone said.

She walked through the halls like a zombie and would form almost no memory of the day, as if she didn't even live it.

Monday after school, she trudged into the quiet house. Jessie walked slightly behind her, no doubt willing to offer support if only Dylan cared to turn around and notice her, but she did not. Her mother was at class, and her father was somewhere in the barn or the fields. She didn't know which and didn't care. She was unaware of so much, except for one thing: Her home had become nothing more than a house full of people cohabitating but not connecting. The happiness had been stripped away, and as much as she missed her friend, she wished she had never met Marybeth. Her family's collective pain had become a calloused layer of skin over the wounds Hayden's death had created.

Marybeth had taken away that protective layer and opened the injury once again. Had Marybeth lived, had David not killed her, maybe she would have been the family's first step to healing. Expose the wounds to the light of day, so the elements could do their magic, but that was not the fortune they'd experienced. Marybeth had exposed their deepest hurt, and life had thrown a dagger in it.

When four o'clock came around, Dylan slid her boots on and headed to the barn to scrape down the cows and prepare for the afternoon milking while David grained the cows. With eyes like knives, she watched him pass between the cows while scooping out the grain. She wanted him dead more than she had wanted anything in her life, but she wasn't a killer. Nevertheless, David needed to be punished, and that she could do.

She set the hoe against the wall and waited for him to

turn back down the manger and head back her way. Maybe she should have felt frightened, but she didn't. An immense strength overtook her, making her feel untouchable.

He scooped out the last bit of grain, turned, and headed her way, pulling the wheelbarrow behind him. He saw her waiting for him. For only one second did he pause, and then his face turned to stone as well. Determined, but not frightened. This didn't faze her. He didn't know what he was dealing with. She was no longer a scared fourteen-year-old girl.

When he was a foot from her, he set down the wheelbarrow and stared her in the eye. He placed his hands on his hips. "What?" His voice dripped with annoyance.

"I'm going inside right now. I'm telling my father you gave us the drug. You killed Marybeth. You're going to prison, and I hope you rot in there."

She didn't break the intensity of their locked gaze. Instead, she searched David's face for the fear she hoped would soften his set jawline. He bent down, putting his face inches from hers, and let out a forced laugh. "Do you know who you are dealing with? Do you know my connections? Apparently not. If you speak one word, bad things will happen." His voice was a whisper laced with venom. A smirk spread across his face. "They won't happen to you. That would be too nice. But your little sister?" He tsked. "She won't see the bad stuff coming. You can't put us all in prison. You don't win when you mess with my people, little girl." He stood to full height. "Now get out of my way."

Her heart racing, Dylan stepped to the side. She watched him disappear into the hayloft to refill the wheelbarrow, and then she bolted toward the house. Fear, anger, and despair made her stomach turn. When she reached the tractor parked in the driveway, she doubled over, heaving onto the gravel the little bits of food she had been able to take down.

"Are you okay?"

Jessie stood over her. Wiping her mouth with her hand, Dylan glanced from her sister back to the barn door. Had Jessie been in the barn? What had she heard?

"Why are you here?" Dylan snapped. "Where were you?"

"I was with the chickens."

Dylan stared at her sister's innocent face and knew that David had her cornered. Dylan would never put Jessie in harm's way. Even if she had to see David every day for the rest of her life.

CHAPTER 46

Eli Simmons
Present Day

A s Eli walked across the field toward the barn, the cornstalks rustled in the morning breeze. Conner stood by the door, focused on something in his hands. As Eli approached, his boss held up a plump ear of corn.

"I guess it's time to find out what's out there." The husk had been peeled back, revealing yellow corn formed all the way to the tip of the cob. "See when I push here?" With a shaky hand, Conner pushed his thumbnail into the top kernels, and a milky substance emerged. Was the drink or anxiety causing his shakiness? Conner's gaze drifted back to the cornfields. "Have you ever harvested corn?"

"On a few of the farms."

"You'll be helping me. After we finish the morning milking, I'll show you what you need to know. I want to get the cops off my back as soon as possible. I'm borrowing another corn harvester. You'll pull mine so you don't break someone else's." Conner stared out at the field of waving stalks. "It's time we put this whole thing behind us."

Conner headed to the barn, and Eli followed. What did it say about Conner that he wasn't afraid of the police finding the body? Or maybe the guilt was getting to be too much.

After lunch, Eli stepped out of the camper. Cold air blasted against his back and washed an eerie warning over him. As he approached the barn, two police cruisers slowed and turned into the driveway. Behind them was a news van. He watched as four officers, two of them he had seen before, stepped from the vehicles. When he turned his gaze to the barn, Conner stood by the door, seemingly unfazed by the visitors.

Eli approached Conner. "Are you ready for this?"

"I've prepared myself, but I'm not prepared for what this will do to my family. I would do anything to protect them from this, but I can't. It's one thing I keep failing at."

Eli watched his boss's profile as two of the investigators approached. Conner didn't look prepared. He looked like he could crumble.

The officer nodded toward Conner. "Which one of you two will be driving?"

"Both. I have two tractors."

"An officer will ride on each one."

"Suit yourselves. I don't have any desire to dig up bones anyway. I want things to get back to normal as fast as possible."

"Finishing this search does not mean your farm will be anything like normal for some time."

Conner squinted in the bright sun, making his features sinister looking.

"I think we all suspect you'll find the missing parts of David Miller. No one wants them off this property more than me." Conner kept eye contact with the officer as he spoke. A cold breeze blew between the men, and the maple trees let go of a few dying leaves that drifted to the ground.

"The tractors are parked on the other side of the barn."

"Lead the way."

Camera crews recorded as the investigators followed Conner and Eli to the tractors. Claire was home but stayed tucked inside, and the girls were safely away from everything at school—at least for a few more hours.

Conner gave Eli a sideways look and pointed to one of the tractors. "You take that one. Start in the field across the street from the neighbor's house. I'll start in the field between our houses. Those would appear to be the most obvious choices."

"On it. Which one of you is riding with me?" Eli asked the cops. Despite the situation and the questions he had, a protectiveness washed over Eli. He reminded himself the investigators were only doing their job, but he wanted them to go away, to leave them all alone.

"I'll go with you," the red-haired officer with the straggly beard answered.

"I hope you brought gloves. You'll have to hold on. It will be mighty cold sitting on the metal tire hub."

The officer reached into his pockets and retrieved a black leather pair. "You don't have to explain riding tractors to me. I was born and raised in this town."

"Well, let's get started."

Eli climbed into his seat first, and the officer adjusted himself on the metal seat to the left side of him. The tractor came to life, and Eli backed it up to the Dion F41 Pull-Type Forage Harvester. He jumped off, hooked up the machine, and climbed back into his seat. Eli drove his tractor across the road to the cornfield near his camper while Conner began with the field between the barn and Tim Burrows's property. "Here we go," Eli mumbled, more to himself than the officer. He turned on the combine and ever so slowly began ripping through the stalks that covered the possible crime scene. Yes, the tractor would disturb the ground, but without harvesting, there was no hope of locating the body.

Hours passed, and half the field resembled a buzz cut. Investigators with dogs followed in the path, hoping the combine would uncover a clue, but the day passed uneventfully. Darkness filled the sky, and afternoon milking could not be put off any longer. Conner and Eli drove their tractors back to the barn and shut off the engines.

"Same time tomorrow," Conner said without emotion.

Conner sauntered off to the barn, and Eli followed behind. When Eli glanced over his shoulder, the investigators were heading back to the fields, determined to find their evidence. But despite their efforts, the answers would remain buried for another day.

CHAPTER 47

Dylan Philipps
Present Day

DYLAN LAY IN BED, awake and staring at the ceiling. The day's activities, including all the police, dogs, and news trucks, had given her insomnia, and after hours of tossing and turning, she gave up on sleep.

Earlier, Eli and her father had begun harvesting the cornfields, and she and Jessie had been put in charge of the milking duties until the sun set and the men could join them.

Jessie had paced between the cows and the doorway, spying on the activity, until she noticed the reporters were also spying on her. They had been given strict orders to avoid the children, but that order apparently did not include pictures.

"Do you think they'll find him?" Jessie asked. Her expression was creased with worry.

"I don't know." It's the only answer Dylan could think of that felt safe and true. And it was true. Dylan didn't know if they would find what was left of David or even if she wanted them to. But this all had to end. Somehow, it had to end.

After giving up on sleep, Dylan crept down the creaking staircase and tiptoed into the kitchen. She slid open the junk drawer and felt around in the dark until, by near miracle, she found a working flashlight. Carefully, she opened the squeaky screen door and held the handle until it closed, avoiding the typical slam.

The world was quiet and peaceful now compared to the afternoon of chaos. The moon peeked out from behind a cloud as she made her way to the barn. One of the barn dogs raced up to her, but she was able to settle him before he began barking. After some attention, he crept off to finish his slumber in some hidden part of the haymow.

She slipped through the chicken coop door. Her hens, the three original and the babies that now looked full grown, slept in the cubbies or piles of hay. The rooster was nestled in the bedding on the floor by himself. "Sorry for waking you," she whispered as she picked up Lady Bella, who had become her favorite. Only a moment passed for them both to be settled in her spot. Dylan let her hand drift over the hen's soft feathers as she closed her eyes and tried to think of nothing except for the soft feel of one of the only things she could call her own.

As she drifted into a place between awake and sleep, one of the dogs gave a slight bark. Dylan sat up straight and listened. Every part of her was on high alert. Then she heard a man's voice, calming the dog. Could it be Eli? Why would he be in the barn in the middle of the night?

The chicken coop door started to creak open, and her breathing stopped. A man's leg entered first, and then he paused, turned, and whispered to the dog some more. "It's okay, buddy. Go back to sleep."

And apparently, the dog listened.

He entered, keeping his back to her. She couldn't see his

face but knew it wasn't Eli. The man closed the door and then turned toward her.

"Holy shit," he gasped.

Dylan stared at him wide-eyed, her hand frozen on the chicken's back.

"What are you doing here?" he asked.

She tried to form words, but her tongue was like lead in her mouth.

"I know I must have scared you. But I'm not here to hurt you or anyone. I'm just looking for something."

He must be looking for the money. There was so much of it, enough that someone desperate enough might kill for it, despite what he claimed. Should she scream before it was too late? Scream, her brain told her, but her mouth wouldn't form sounds.

"You're Dylan, right?"

She nodded.

"Do you remember me?"

Her fear had subsided only enough that her brain could start working again.

"Yes." Anger welled inside her, but she was too afraid to let it show. "You're David's friend."

"Yes. I am. Or rather, I used to be."

"Then you can't be here for any good reason. You must be as evil as him."

"In some ways, I am."

Dylan's heart pounded, her breath heavy.

"And I'm also not. Listen. David left something on this farm, and I need it. It will change my life."

"Money?"

"You've seen it?" Excitement filled his voice.

"No." She hoped the lie came out quickly enough. "But everyone thinks money will change their lives."

"Sometimes it can. Listen, I know you probably hated David. Everyone did. But I'm not him. I just need a break, kid."

"Your drugs killed my friend. Did David tell you that?"

Jeremy sighed and knelt into a clean pile of hay, making him eye level with Dylan. "I'm so sorry. I told David not to give them to you. Do you remember? I tried to stop him, not because I knew they were bad, but because you're so young. You shouldn't be taking drugs."

"Don't parent me."

"I would never. Listen, we're not dealers. We bought the pills from someone. If she hadn't taken them, we would have."

Dylan's throat tightened to hold back her cry. "So, if we hadn't taken them, Marybeth would be alive, and David would be dead?"

"Or I would be dead. Not that you would care about either of our lives, but we didn't know. That's the God's honest truth. I wake up at night thinking about it. I know you hate David for it, but the two of you did exactly what we did. You spun the wheel taking recreational drugs, and for some unfortunate, unexplainable reason, your friend ended up dead. And yes, the world would have been better with her in it and one of us gone. I don't know why it happened like it did, but I am sorry about your friend."

"I don't know about any money, but what would you do with it anyway?"

"I need to get out of this town, go somewhere where

people don't know me. I need to get an apartment and clothes that make me look respectable enough to get a legit job with no side gigs. Once I get a bit saved, I want to take classes. I want to be better. I truly do, kid."

Dylan slowly and deliberately rubbed the back of her chicken from head to tail.

"How much money is there?"

"Are you asking for a cut? I can give you some if you help me find it. That would be great. I can't keep creeping around here, or I'll get another... Anyway, I'll pay you."

"If I find it, why would I give you any of it? You were friends with David. You're a part of the reason my friend is dead. I can keep the money for myself."

Jeremy fell silent. "Yes. You can. I'm going to tell you that it's illegally earned. It's tainted. If your family keeps it, and people get suspicious of where the money came from, they might think your dad is smuggling drugs. The money is right here on his property."

"Now you sound just like David. Threatening me to stay quiet."

"Did David threaten you?"

"He said he would hurt my sister."

Dylan swore his eyes glistened with tears. "I'm so sorry." He shook his head. "He really said that?"

"He told me he knew people."

Jeremy let out a deep breath. "David lied to you. He wasn't even liked by the bad people he worked for. I don't think anyone would have hurt your sister. David never told me he'd threatened you. He was scared when your friend died. He did say you'd better keep your mouth shut or you'd end up regretting it. I told him not to talk crazy, but he didn't say he'd spoken with you. I guess I should have known."

A tear rolled down Dylan's cheek. She wasn't sure how to feel about that news.

"I promise you, I'm not threatening you. If you keep the cash, you keep it. I would never hurt you or your family. I would never tell a soul. If I did, I would only be ratting myself out. I'm stating that as fact, not a threat."

Dylan sat silent, petting her chicken.

"I'm sorry. I am truly sorry about your friend and David's threat. I don't know how to make it up to you or her parents. It's impossible to make it better. All I can do is promise that I will improve myself."

Jeremy reached out his hand. Dylan looked at it with tear-stricken eyes. "In case you don't remember, my name is Jeremy. You have no reason to trust me, but I'm pleading with you to give me a chance."

Dylan didn't take his hand, and he let it fall to his side. He found a piece of concrete that had crumbled in the corner of the floor. "I don't have paper." He walked to the corner of the coop where it faced the back wall, a place only Dylan would ever look. He scratched out something and tossed the concrete piece back onto the floor. "I'm leaving my number. Please consider looking for the cash, and remember, if the police find it here, it doesn't look good, so you might want to look soon. I see they started harvesting. Once they officially find the body on the property, they will be searching everything and everywhere. Getting rid of the money will be good for everyone."

CHAPTER 48

Eli Simmons
Present Day

Eli lay in bed tossing and turning, hoping the sounds of the owls and occasional coyote would lull him to sleep. Instead, the world outside was silent. Too silent. He stared at the ceiling with the heightened awareness of an animal waiting for a storm. The sound of a car approaching broke the silence. Nothing was peculiar about a vehicle traveling down the road at all hours of the night, but when the engine slowed as it approached the barn, his heart began to race. He thought about the car he had seen earlier and the young man who had seemed to be searching the property for something. It seemed no one in town was on the Phillips's side. What bad intention would a person have creeping around the farm at night? Vandalism? Planting evidence? A million possibilities raced through his mind. He had to look out for this family.

Eli crawled out of bed, threw on warm clothes, and crept into the moonlit night to investigate. The car had disappeared, but he was confident he'd heard it stop. Maybe it was parked on the tractor path in the uncut part of the cornfield?

And then he saw him. A man entered the barn where they'd parked the manure spreader. Eli could only make out the shape of a person, which could have been female, but Eli instinctively knew it was not.

Perhaps the man creeping around the barn was connected to David and everything happening with the drug deals. Was the intruder looking for drugs? Money? Eli considered going into the barn, but he didn't own a weapon and dreaded the possibility of using one. Should Eli wake Conner?

All these ideas spun in his mind as he stared at the barn from the cover of a large maple. His heart raced. Of all the moments on the farm, this one unsettled him the most. Since he didn't think the cattle were in danger, he decided to watch from afar and gather as much information as possible. He would report his findings to Conner in the morning unless something seemed imperative tonight. This delay would most likely be met with frustration, but it was Eli's call to make, and he was sticking to it.

Through the barn windows, he watched a beam of light from a flashlight reach the smaller barn where the calves and chickens were housed. And then the light disappeared. Eli needed to get closer. There was a window in the back of the building near the coop, and he made his way to it as quietly as possible. His breath was heavy from fear and exertion as he hid beneath the sill. Voices, male and female, came from inside the coop. Carefully, he stood, peeking ever so slightly into the barn before dropping back down. The coop door was cracked open, but he couldn't see anyone. Who was in there with the intruder? His ears strained, trying to make out the words, but it was impossible. Several minutes passed before the beam of light traveled back down the walkway and toward the larger barn where the trespasser had entered.

When Eli heard the coop door shut, he dared to glance back through the filthy window. Dylan walked toward the little barn exit wearing the same green, puffy jacket she often wore to do chores. What had this young girl gotten herself into? How did she know this strange man who would sneak around their property? Eli snuck around the barn and watched her cross the yard to the house. She was wiping away tears that no one besides him and the stranger would ever know were falling.

CHAPTER 49

Dylan Phillips
Present Day

WHEN DYLAN AND JESSIE'S bus pulled in front of their farm the next afternoon, reporters and police cars lined the road. Some kids pressed their faces against the windows to take in the scene, while others stared at Dylan and Jessie and shouted disparaging comments.

"Someone's going to jail today."

"See you on the news, freaks."

Dylan glanced at Jessie as she grabbed her backpack off the seat. The color had drained from her sister's face.

"Ignore them," Dylan whispered. "Just get off the bus."

They raced as best they could down the aisle, and Dylan didn't breathe until their feet hit the gravel driveway. As the doors closed, a boy yelled, "Have fun in prison."

The bus slid away, revealing the scene across the road. Uniformed officers were traipsing around the backfield. Reporters cased the property on the heels of the investigators. Cameras turned on her and Jessie, and she could already see their underaged blurred faces broadcasted throughout the homes of their town, maybe even the country. How big was this story?

It might be too late if she didn't devise a plan tonight. Should she take the money and run with Jessie? The money hiding in the coop could be her getaway money. Should she go to the police and hope they believe and understand her side of the story?

She studied Jessie while doing their chores, wondering if her younger sister would leave with her if she asked. What if she said no? Was Jessie strong enough to make it in this world without her? Would she be better off without her older sister? Jessie was her best friend and, in many ways, had even been a better friend than Marybeth. Dylan and Jessie had been through so much together. How could she leave her little sister to fend off life alone? But how could she drag her into the unknown?

When the chores were finished, Eli and their dad were nowhere to be seen. But when Dylan prepared for bed, she glanced out the bathroom window and noticed the light was on in the shed. The windows had blinds to prevent anyone from looking in. But she could see her father's silhouette pace back and forth.

When she and Jessie headed toward the stairs for bed, their mother called to them. They froze in their tracks, not knowing what to expect. Claire walked over to them and wrapped them both in her arms. Dylan's body tightened in resistance, but as the hug continued, her muscles relaxed, and she fought back tears. Dylan buried her face in one of her mom's shoulders as Jessie buried hers in the other.

"I know you both must be scared, but it will be okay."

Dylan wanted to scream, "How do you know that? It's

not going to be okay. It will never be okay again." But had she spoken, the tears would have followed.

"Get some sleep, girls. I love you both so much."

These words were too much for Jessie, and the dam broke, giving way to giant sobs. Claire rocked them in her arms until Dylan broke the moment by saying she needed to go to bed. All night, she tossed and turned, remembering the conversation with Jeremy and what he'd promised the money would mean to his future, but what about hers? When Dylan considered running with the money, she was overwhelmed with sadness for herself and her sister. And, even though her relationship with her parents lacked what it once had, she loved and needed them more than she wanted to admit.

She must have fallen asleep at some point because the rooster's call woke her. She threw on her clothes for school. Jessie's alarm sounded in her room. Her sister would repeatedly hit the snooze button before crawling out from her warm blankets. Dylan had time. She opened the screen door and held the handle as it slowly closed, making the act almost inaudible.

She didn't want to enter the barn before school, but if she moved fast enough, she might outrun the smells that wanted to stick to her clothes. The chickens were clucking quietly, like a soft purr. She opened the coop door and walked in. The chickens were nestled into the cubbies, keeping the eggs warm while the rooster pecked away at the hay on the floor.

Dylan reached under the warm belly of each chicken and collected five eggs. But that wasn't what Dylan was there for. She looked over her shoulder. The barn stood empty except for the animals. She set her basket down, went to the side of the coop, and reached into the deep hole. The rooster crowed. "Be quiet," she hissed. Her fingers found the plastic bag still full of cash. It was still there. Her heart calmed. The barn door drifted open, and Eli coughed as he entered. Quickly, she replaced the board and stepped out of the pen, holding her basket of eggs. Eli looked at her wide-eyed, not expecting anyone to be in the barn so early.

"I had a craving for eggs." Dylan lowered her gaze and brushed past him.

"Is that why you were out here in the middle of the night?"

Her jaw dropped, and she struggled to regain composure. "What?" How much did he know? Had he heard everything? The barn spun around her, making her feel as if she could fall over.

"Dylan, you know what I'm talking about. You were out here in the middle of the night with some man. I haven't told your father yet. I wanted to talk to you first."

She stared at Eli speechless. She searched her mind for a reason, but there was no good excuse. If her father confronted her, she would end up telling him everything.

"Who was he? Let's start there."

"I don't..."

"You do know. I gave you a day, hoping you would tell your father about someone being in the barn at night, but you didn't. I think he would have mentioned that to me. If you didn't tell your father, then I'm afraid that you might be in danger."

"I'm not."

"Who was he?"

"He was David's friend."

"Why doesn't that make me feel better?"

"I'm not sure it should."

"Why were you meeting him in the barn in the middle of the night?"

"I promise you, I wasn't. I came out to the barn because I couldn't sleep. Sometimes it calms me to be with my chickens. The guy just walked in the coop while I was there."

"Why? What was he looking for?"

The barn was freezing, yet Dylan began to sweat beneath her jacket. "I don't know."

"Yes, Dylan, you do." Eli sighed and placed a hand on his hip. Dylan took a deep breath, and her protective wall began to crumble. Not because she wanted it to give way but because she was losing the war. "You are a child, Dylan, dealing with adult problems. You can't handle them alone, and you shouldn't try to. Serious crimes have happened on this farm. The police are searching for bones on your property. Men are trafficking drugs in the fields. These are not problems you have the capabilities to solve. Neither do I. Don't do this alone."

"He was looking for money." Dylan said the words so fast that she couldn't rethink sharing them.

"Drug money?"

"I don't know where else David would have gotten cash. It wasn't his payments for working on the farm. Dad paid in checks."

"Do you know where the money is hidden?"

Dylan stared at the ground.

"I get it. You don't trust me. You don't have to tell me

where it is, but I need you to start being open with me and trusting me. You need someone, Dylan."

Dylan headed toward the door and then stopped. "Please don't tell my parents. I'll consider talking to you only if you promise me that."

"I promise you that I won't talk to them without telling you first, and I will only do so if I feel it is completely necessary."

Dylan left the barn petrified that her secrets lay so close to the surface, but even more than that, a feeling of relief washed over her. She wasn't alone anymore.

CHAPTER 50

Eli Simmons
Present Day

THE GIRLS WERE ALREADY at school when Eli climbed up on the tractor with the same investigator as the day before. Other officers stood around with tracker dogs, ready to sniff out whatever the harvesting uncovered. Since the death of Lupo, Eli was more hopeful that David wasn't in the cornfield at all. The chances that he'd been killed on the other side of the border seemed more plausible.

Eli's tractor chugged to life, cutting through the tense air. He glanced across the driveway and met Conner's gaze just as his tractor roared to life. Although Eli couldn't quite read the expression on his boss's face, he could sense the weight of unspoken feelings behind it.

Eli headed across the road and into the cornfield, thankful that the tractor and turbine noise made conversation nearly impossible. He focused on the world around him, seeking comfort from the reality before him. The leaves of the maples surrounding the fields were bursting with color, yet they hadn't reached their peak. A bird flew overhead, unaware of the horrors of men. Eli imagined soaring with the creature through the crisp air far above the cornfield.

Hours passed. Occasionally, the investigator stood in the cramped spot near the tire hub that served as his seat. The cold, hard metal, and the bumps they encountered had to make for a miserable ride. Other investigators walked behind them with the dogs sniffing the ground. They were reaching the backfield; only half an hour more and the field would be clear. Across the road, Conner was nearing completion as well. Hope swelled in Eli. Maybe his earlier hopes would soon be confirmed. David's killer had lured him to a concealed spot across the border, killed him, and hidden his corpse well enough that only a dog that had haplessly wondered too far from home could detect the scent of the body. And now that David's killer had met a similar fate, the Phillips family would be able to put this nightmare behind them.

His thoughts drifted to his conversation with Claire when she'd visited his camper. Had she spoken to Conner? Had she considered trying to save her marriage? These were questions he had no right to ask. He could only patiently wait and see if the answers revealed themselves.

Eli was so lost in thought that when the investigator yelled, "Hold up," he jumped. "Stop the tractor," the man shouted again. Eli shut down the machine as the investigator hopped off and headed over to where one of the canines barked wildly. Eli climbed down as well and started to follow.

He stopped in his tracks, but even from where he stood, Eli could see bones protruding from the ground. Any doubt that they were human bones was distinguished due to the piece of denim material hanging from what appeared to be a leg bone. And unless the field had become a dumping ground for whoever had placed them here, which was doubtful, these bones belonged to David. The bones were in the back part of the field on the opposite side of the road from the Canadian border.

He gazed across the field where he stood, looking at the road and the distant area along the border. How could David's remains have ended up all the way over here if Lupo had killed him during a drug exchange near the border? The color drained from his face as he searched his mind for a plausible scenario that didn't involve the Phillips family. There was none.

CHAPTER 51

Eli Simmons
Present Day

THE FAMILY SAT AROUND the dining table Saturday afternoon, their voices hushed, enveloped in a thick silence. No one wanted to talk about the bones yet discussing anything else seemed out of place. Even the aroma of chocolate chip cookies baking in the oven seemed off limits.

Eli scanned the faces of those around him, reflecting on the myriad conversations he had shared with each family member. Jessie possessed the least information but had become willing to share what little she knew. Meanwhile, Dylan clung to the belief that by shielding Jessie from the harsh realities of their situation, she was protecting her, unaware that this tactic only deepened Jessie's sense of isolation. Claire fought to regain the love and commitment she once had for her family. With determination, she prepared comfort food—boxed macaroni and cheese— that had become a staple in their home. Eli observed her efforts, sensing her desire to rekindle the motherly warmth that once radiated from her. Conner, weighed down by an invisible sorrow, carried the burdens of grief for his son and his daughters while wrestling with the nagging feeling of disappointment he believed his wife harbored toward him. Despite the shadows looming over them, Eli held fast to the belief that hope could shine through even the darkest of times, though he couldn't shake the unsettling thought that his faith was being tested.

Claire stood to clear the plates. "Can I get anyone anything else? I made cookies."

Jessie's face lit up at the offer. She smiled at her sister, who forced a smile back. Eli caught Dylan's gaze, and she quickly looked away, hiding behind her bangs.

"I'll take a cookie," Eli said. "Smells like chocolate chips."

Claire's smile almost met her eyes. "They're a family favorite."

"I'll take one, too," Conner said, sitting back in his chair. The last bit of resistance gave way, and Claire's smile beamed.

"Me, too," Jessie said with excitement.

"How about you?" Claire asked.

"Yes, please," Dylan answered.

Claire pulled the warm plate from the oven and placed it on the table between them. Their coos of compliments were drowned out by approaching sirens. The family stepped outside, drawn to the lights like bugs to a zapper. Claire, clearly unsure of where the next hour would lead them, wrapped her arms around the girls' shoulders. But the fact was, the police were coming for someone.

Detectives headed toward Conner and handed him a paper. "We have a warrant to search your property."

Conner took the paper and glanced down at it. His skin had gone ashen at the sound of the sirens, and the color had yet to return.

"We need you to let us into the shed unless, of course, you prefer we break the lock."

Conner reached in his pocket and pulled out a small key. He walked slowly to the shed, and with a shaky hand, he unlocked the padlock. He didn't open the door before stepping away. Conner's gaze remained focused on the ground even though Claire's searched for contact. When she didn't get any, she pulled her girls closer and gave one nervous glance toward Eli.

The officers, like dogs on a hunt, practically salivated for downed prey. Handcuffs jingled at their sides, waiting to imprison Conner once the predicted money and drugs were revealed. Or possibly, they assumed incriminating papers hid beneath a floorboard. Either way, a body was cause enough to assume guilt.

Eli was driven by a deep desire for truth and understanding. His heart raced with concern for a man who felt like a kindred spirit after he had started to peel back the layers. Could poverty and heartache have pushed Conner to the brink of desperation, leading him to make such a tragic choice?

The creak of the door hinge cut through the chilled air. Claire squeezed her girls tighter. Both girls uncharacteristically leaned into their mother. For them, the walls of the shed were as thick as the walls built around the man they knew and loved. Fear tightened Claire's fingers around her daughters' arms. Eli looked away. He wanted more for all of them.

The officers exited the shed holding bags of what they considered to be evidence of a crime: a rope, empty bottles of alcohol, a Bible, and a piece of paper. The officer read it silently and then looked up at Conner. "What's going on, Mr. Phillips, that is so bad you would want to leave a goodbye letter to your family?"

Claire gasped softly.

"The letter is private." Conner reached for it, but the officer pulled it closer to him.

"Nothing is private anymore, Mr. Phillips."

The officers eyed Conner as they discussed their course of action. Voices called out over walkie talkies as the investigators continued their search of the barn and house. When it was obvious the search would go on for some time, Eli invited the family back to his camper. At first, they said nothing, and then Claire declared the idea was perfect.

Conner let the officers know where they could be found, and together they walked across the pasture to the Eli's home now fully visible without the corn hiding it from view.

They walked up the shaky steps one at a time and entered the tiny camper. Eli invited them to sit at the table as he stood against the counter near the sink. Dylan wouldn't make eye contact. She carried secrets that were too cumbersome for such a young girl. But one fear each one of them must be struggling with is knowing the investigators would believe Conner was involved in David's death. They would take the letter as evidence against him.

After an awkward silence, Conner said, "I'm sorry, Claire. I'm sorry, girls."

"Why were you leaving us?" Jessie asked.

Eli thought of the rope. Did Jessie understand what the goodbye letter really meant?

"I'm not going anywhere, Jessie. I promise. I was upset when I wrote those words." Jessie wiped a tear from her cheek. "I promise you, I'm not going anywhere."

Eli placed some tissues in the middle of the table, and one by one, each of them took one to dry their tears. Their wimpers eased, and the kitchen quieted.

"Now what?" Conner asked.

"If you don't mind, I'd like to say a small prayer over your family."

The girls glanced from Conner to Eli until Conner nodded. "I guess if there was ever a time for prayer, this is it."

"Heavenly Father, you promise that You hear us when we call out to you, even when we are in the darkest places. We are in a dark place. Protect the Phillips family and heal them from their pain and their afflictions. Forgive them for their transgressions and offer them a way out so they can begin their journey back to You. In Jesus's name, we pray. Amen."

When Eli looked up, Conner's hands were folded in prayer, and his eyes were sealed tightly, encouraging the family to follow suit.

"Now, on a lighter note, I hear you all like a good game of Blackjack."

Conner laughed. "Yes. We do, and these girls have yet to beat me."

"But I have," Claire said with a smile. "And I feel pretty lucky today."

Eli grabbed a deck of cards, a cup of change, and an extra chair. Outside, the world was being ripped apart, but inside the camper, a family was beginning to heal.

CHAPTER 52

Conner Phillips
Present Day

After returning from the camper, Conner crawled under the covers before his wife had prepared for bed. He didn't want her to see him, to watch as his tears hit the pillow. But when she entered the room, she must have seen his heaving shoulders. The bed shifted as she crawled in next to him, and then her arms wrapped around him. Her cheek rested against his back.

"I'm so sorry. For everything," he said. "It's my fault we lost our son. It's my fault we could lose the farm any day. And it's my fault you hang out in bars trying to find happiness."

Conner began sobbing, and she held him tighter until the shaking calmed. Then she forced him to face her.

"It's both of our faults, and it's neither of our faults. How did we know when we got married that we would suffer such horrible pain? How do you prepare for it? You can't. No one can. Part of how we reacted wasn't choice. It was a reflex to pain. We moved away from what we thought was causing it. You didn't know Hayden would die from his wound, and neither did I. I questioned myself when I wanted to take him to the hospital. You didn't tie us to chairs to stop us from going.

I listened because a part of me believed, just like you did, that he would be fine. I could have taken him, but I didn't."

Conner touched his wife's face with the back of his hand like he did long ago when they were still so very much in love. "Why? Why did God let that happen?"

"I've thought about that a million times through the years. And then I thought about the millions of people who have lived and died throughout history. We believed in God when it was someone else's wife, or husband, or child. We believed in God even though we know history and all the tragic events that have led to other people's deaths. And then tragedy hit our home, and for some reason, we stopped believing. I began thinking of the countless ways we could die. How many breaths each of us is allotted. Each one is a gift, but somehow, in the same breath that we give thanks for our lives, we forget that our lives can't be taken for granted. We know that we have a finite number of years, and we all expire when our time is up. One by one, way by way, our time ends. It shouldn't make us doubt God when we see life turn to death. And yet, we do, because it hurts so much when we lose someone we love."

"Did you lose faith?" Conner asked.

"Not faith so much as hope. I wanted to recover. I wanted to make our family stronger. But I gave up on us. I gave up on you."

Conner studied his wife. "I haven't looked at you in so long." He traced her cheek with his thumb, and the wall around his heart crumbled. He had left his wife long before she started hanging out in the bars. He pushed her away from him and then blamed her for leaving.

A tear rolled down her face. "I know."

"You're so beautiful. How did I ever stop looking at you?"

Claire gently cupped his cheek in her hand, and they lost themselves in each other's eyes, sharing a moment of deep understanding and connection.

"I was ashamed to look at you, Claire. I didn't want to see how I looked in your eyes. I was scared of the anger and disappointment I would see."

"You would have only seen sadness. If I was angry, it was only because I didn't know what else to do with my feelings. I wasn't in control of them for a while."

"You were angry then?"

"With everything. With the world. And that's okay. It's expected. But now we need to stop being angry."

"How?"

"This is a start." Claire curled up in her husband's arms. His chin rested on the top of her head. "Conner, would you have really taken your life?"

His chest rose in and out in heavy breaths. He considered lying, but the time for that was over. The truth, as hard as that might be, would save them. "Yes. I'm afraid, Claire, that if I would have lost you, lost the farm, lost the girls, then I would have. Sometimes, the pain was so much that I wanted it to hurry up and happen. I couldn't picture another option, so I did things to push you all away to give me a better excuse."

Claire wiped a tear from her cheek.

"I'm sorry. I wish I could tell you that all wasn't true, but it is. All I could see was darkness. David ends up dead because of a bunch of warped drug dealers. Marybeth dies. It was like there was this little bit of hope that got stomped out. Over and over again, life, it just hurts…"

"I don't have the answers. I know we can't fix the world. It all seems so overwhelming. Drugs are being smuggled into our town. Kids are dying. Bones are found on our property, for God's sake. Sometimes I want to crawl into a hole myself. But we can't. It's time to fight for our small corner of the world, and if we can add a little light into our family, well, who knows. Maybe someday we'll even be ready to help someone else. We just have some healing to do first."

Conner tightened his grip on his wife. "Yes, we do, Claire. Yes, we do."

A sound at the door silenced them before their girls rushed into the room. He wrapped them in his arms, and a new overpowering feeling filled him. He would fight for his family with every drop of energy in his body. They would never feel alone again.

CHAPTER 53

Jessie Phillips
Present Day

HER FATHER PROMISED HE wasn't going to leave them, but Jessie needed more understanding of why the rope, the empty whiskey bottles, the Bible, and the goodbye note were discovered in her father's shed. Did they think she was too young and naive to know what that all added up to? Her father was contemplating suicide, and no matter what the police thought that meant, Jessie only cared about the one fact: She could have lost the only father she had ever had, and despite his faults, she loved him.

But beyond that, beyond the fact that the police had scoured every inch of their property, finding nothing incriminating enough to make an arrest, Jessie had enjoyed the best afternoon that she'd had in a very long time. Once the cards came out, and the games began, no one mentioned the police or bones. They only focused on the game and each other. She cared nothing about winning or losing despite her smack talk. Even Dylan laughed and threw in her jabs. The small camper had transported them back to the mountains of the Adirondacks and into a rustic old hunting camp where they'd stayed up late drinking soda and eating junk food until their eyes refused to stay open.

Jessie smiled up at the ceiling as she lay in bed reliving the afternoon. She was still awake when her parents came in, kissed her forehead, and bid her goodnight. She listened as they crossed the hallway and entered Dylan's room as well. Jessie pulled the comforter up to her chin and embraced the warmth surrounding her.

Soft voices pulled her back to consciousness as she drifted off to sleep. Down the hallway, she could hear her parents crying. Jessie and Dylan both opened their bedroom doors at the same time. They looked at each other and reached an unspoken agreement to tiptoe down the hallway to eavesdrop on their parents. Just hours before, laughter and joy rang through the camper; what had changed? The girls pressed their ears against the door, so they could decipher their words.

Muffled words escaped. "It's all my fault, Claire."

"No, Conner, it's not. I never blamed you. I swear."

Had her dad been talking about Hayden? Dylan held a finger to her lips, a warning to stay quiet Jessie didn't need. Was their whole life in shambles because of Hayden? Nausea washed over Jessie. It had been a long time since the memory of how it all happened hit her so harshly. Hayden had died because of her, not her father. She and Dylan had climbed up on the beam that ran across the haymow. Very little hay covered the floor since spring was in full bloom, and the winter supply had already been used. The cows fed on fresh grass growing in the pastures, and haying season had yet to begin again.

That day, Jessie had dared her older sister to jump first, since Dylan, a short while before, had dared Jessie to climb to the top of the silo which had led to her mother giving her a small whipping with the flyswatter. For fifteen minutes, they both contemplated the outcome of the decision. If Dylan jumped perfectly, she would hit the small pile which should be enough to break her fall, or so Jessie thought. Dylan decided it was a bad idea with the hay that low, but Jessie remembered how much fun they had had in the past when the hay was slightly higher. She wanted to do it; she just didn't want to go first.

And then she got a brilliant idea. Hayden could go first, and according to her thinking, since he was smaller, he wouldn't fall as hard. Dylan agreed. Together they went to find Hayden. He was building roads with his Matchbox cars in the dirt driveway. Their dad was fixing the tractor, paying little attention to his son whom he felt was completely happy and safe. They waved to Hayden to come into the barn, and they led him into the haymow. After many assurances that they had been jumping off the beam all afternoon and having a blast, Hayden climbed up on the beam.

"I'm scared," he whimpered.

"It's so much fun. We'll do it right after you," Jessie promised.

Hayden took a deep breath and pushed himself off the beam and into the haystack. And as promised, they followed suit. They jumped several times before their father appeared in the doorway wondering what the hell they were thinking and telling them to get off the beam immediately. He also warned them not to tell their mother about the incident, which was great with all of them because the confession would have led to another bout with the flyswatter.

Hayden's scratch seemed like nothing at first, but as the infection grew, questions were asked, and the story of how he got injured came out. Claire was too concerned about Hayden's leg to find the flyswatter the girls had hidden in the basement. In fact, how the scratch had happened became lost in history. All anyone seemed to remember was that Claire had wanted to take him to see the doctor, but Conner thought he would be fine. Jessie, through the years, had learned to push the memory to the back of her mind where it seldom threatened to destroy her, and Dylan never brought it up, perhaps feeling some of the blame as well.

But now, on the other side of the door, a man she'd never seen shed a tear sobbed over his guilt.

"We have to tell him," Jessie whispered.

"Don't you think he knows? Hayden wouldn't have gone up on the beam on his own."

"They don't know it was my idea."

Jessie put her hand on the doorknob. "Jessie, wait," she whispered, but too loudly.

The voices on the other side went silent.

"Girls?" their mom asked.

"Can we come in?" The need to release the truth overwhelmed her. She could no longer contain it within the small walls of her preteen body.

"Yes, girls," her mother said softly. "Come in."

"Dad, it's not your fault. I told Hayden to jump off the beam. I did it. It's my fault he got sick. Please don't kill yourself, Dad. We love you." She ran and jumped in the bed while her parents' arms wrapped around her. Dylan walked timidly to the bedside.

"I promise all of you, I won't leave you. No matter what happens, we are together. We are a family, and we will get through this together."

Jessie sobbed with an overwhelming feeling of sadness and relief.

"I should have told you. You wouldn't have been so angry with each other if you knew."

"Oh honey, this isn't your fault. Your dad and I need to learn to hurt without hurting each other. We all need to do that, I guess."

"I'll do anything to make it right. I'll do my chores without complaining. I'll clean my room. I'll be nicer."

Claire rubbed her daughter's back as her tears drenched her nightgown. Dylan sat on the edge of the bed; her eyes glistened with tears.

"I love you, Dad. Please don't hurt yourself." Jessie whimpered.

Conner choked out his reply. "You never have to worry about that. Ever again." He opened his free arm, welcoming Dylan into the family embrace. She crawled up the bed and settled in beside him. "From now on, we will do better. We will all do better."

CHAPTER 54

Dylan Phillips
Present Day

The following weeks were a whirlwind of inter-rogations focusing on the Phillips family. Forensic analysis showed that David's bones had wounds consistent with being run through a piece of machinery. After investigating the farm and its equipment, the blades on the manure spreader matched the type of damage the bones had withstood. The family watched the machinery get hauled away and thanked the good Lord that another farmer was willing to loan them his, despite the rumors running rampant around the town.

Conner's arrest followed the correlation between the bone fragments and the blades. The court appointed their family a lawyer, Mr. Roberts, since they could not afford one. The lawyer had a terrible record of losing more cases than he won, but despite this fact, the family experienced a calm that they had not experienced in years.

Conner spent hours being interrogated. He agreed to a polygraph and passed without a doubt. After days without a breakthrough, Mr. Roberts, the man who couldn't win a case, had Conner back home to his family. One loose end kept the doubt in everyone's mind—the man floating in the river and David's possible involvement with the mafia.

The dean had agreed to let Dylan and Jessie be homeschooled until things got sorted out. This took the pressure of their classmates' judgmental taunts off the girls' already full emotional plates. Dylan sat on her bed doing her homework when her father, looking ashen, entered her room. Moments passed before he spoke. Dylan's pulse pounded in her ears as she waited for him to speak.

Conner placed his hand over Dylan's. "Honey, I don't want you to be scared..."

Dylan felt the blood drain from her face.

"The investigators want to speak to you, because you were the one driving the manure spreader that day."

Speechless, Dylan stared at her father. The room spun around her. She couldn't talk to the police. Not again. Memories of Marybeth and the morning she found her friend dead beside her stabbed at her heart. Did her father see the sweat beading on her forehead?

"Don't be afraid. Your mother or I will be in the room with you. They'll ask a few questions, and you'll be right back home with us." Her father squeezed her hand. "Are you okay?"

She nodded.

"You sure?"

"Yeah. It's just a bit..."

"I know. But it will be over quickly. You have nothing to be afraid of."

"Are they trying to put you back in jail?"

"The investigators only want to make sure they've done

all they can to find out what happened to David. It's their job."

Sweat dripped down her back as her father rambled on about it only being part of the protocol and she had nothing to worry about. The investigators were going to speak to Jessie and Claire, too. It was just routine. Her thoughts drifted to the money hiding in the coop. How had the police overlooked it? It was now or never if she wanted to run, but when her dad walked into her room an hour later to drive the family to the station, Dylan went with them.

Jessie and her father went into a room with some investigators, while Dylan and her mother waited. A long thirty minutes passed before Jessie and her father walked out. Jessie caught Dylan's gaze. Her skin was ashen, and guilt riddled her expression. Dylan knew that the only guilt she would feel was for saying anything that might be used to hurt one of them.

The investigators motioned for Dylan and Claire to follow them into the room Jessie had just exited. Dylan sat in a cold, hard chair next to her mom, waiting for the investigator to begin. She squeezed her hands together until her knuckles turned white. Only when she looked up at her mother did she become aware of how obviously nervous she was.

Claire's gaze left Dylan's hands and met her eyes. "It will be okay." But the words didn't soothe Dylan.

The six-foot tall investigator hovered above her and cleared his throat. "Can I get you something to drink?"

"No, thank you." Her voice cracked. She put her hands under her legs to stop them from shaking.

"Suit yourself." He took a seat, and the female officer settled in beside him. She smiled warmly at Dylan. She wouldn't be fooled. She was familiar with the good cop, bad cop routine.

"Dylan, I'm Officer Bennett, and this is Officer Campbell. We're going to ask you a few questions if that's okay."

Dylan nodded.

Officer Bennett led the conversation, while Officer Campbell took notes and continued to smile reassuringly at her.

"According to your father, you were the one who woke up for morning chores the morning that David went missing." Bennett leaned in, folding his hands on the table in front of her.

Dylan stayed silent.

"Is that true?"

"Yes, sir."

"Also, according to your father, you were the one to run the manure spreader the day that David went missing. Is that true?"

"Yes, sir."

"Did you see David that morning?"

"No, sir."

"He was dropped off at your farm." Bennett raised an eyebrow when he spoke.

"But I never saw him. It's hard to remember. At the time it all happened, it was just a normal day to me. I wasn't paying attention to every detail. Maybe he got there before I got to the barn."

"Maybe. What makes you say that?"

"Because I never saw him. Sometimes, I oversleep a little bit, and David would get there before me. I can't remember if I was running late that day. I only know I never saw him."

"Did you think that was strange?"

"No."

"Jessie said that your dad had a fight with him the night before."

Dylan's eyes widened before she could prevent the reaction. *Why had Jessie said that?*

"Is that true?"

She nodded.

"Can you tell me what the fight was about?"

A tear rolled down Dylan's cheek.

"Did the fight upset you?"

Dylan nodded.

"Take your time. It doesn't mean your dad is in trouble because he was angry with David. We're just trying to understand what happened that morning."

"David killed our cow." Dylan blurted out the words.

"He did what?"

"He was really angry because this heifer didn't want to get in her stanchion. He was chasing it in and out of mangers."

"Where were you?"

"I was standing in one of the mangers feeding the cows."

"And then what happened?"

"David..." She choked on a sob, and her mother took her hand.

"It's okay. Take your time." The woman officer handed her a tissue.

"David took a hoe and hit her on her head."

Dylan cried into the tissue. The officers remained quiet for a moment.

"She fell down right in front of me. She was dead right away."

"I'm sorry. That must have been terrible to see."

Dylan nodded and wiped her eyes.

"What did you do after that happened?"

"I ran inside to get my father."

"He must have been very angry."

Dylan nodded. "He told David he owed him for the cow."

"Was your dad yelling?"

"Yes, and they were shouting cuss words at each other."

"How did it end?"

Dylan blushed. "David made a gesture like this." She made the gesture of jerking off. "And then he stormed out of the barn. He walked down the road, and we figured his friend picked him up."

"He didn't finish work that night?"

"No. We thought he'd quit. That's why I wasn't surprised when he didn't show up the next morning."

"Did you know he texted your dad an apology?"

"No."

"Your dad told him to come to work the next day, and they would talk."

Dylan was silent. She didn't know any of that.

"Your dad never mentioned that to you?"

"That's not something he would share with me."

"Really? Why not?"

"He never discussed those kinds of work things. He was very private."

Officer Bennett let out a sigh.

"When did your dad come out to the barn?"

"About an hour after me. Saturdays were his day to sleep in a little bit."

"Did he seem surprised when David wasn't there?"

"He never said a word about it. We just did the chores."

"How was his mood?"

"He was a bit grumpy. I figured he was still mad about the cow."

"Do you often run the manure spreader?"

"No. Usually my dad or the hired man does that, but I know how. I do it some Sundays when the hired man doesn't work."

"You didn't notice anything strange?"

"No."

"Did the machinery seem to be having any trouble?"

"The manure spreader always has trouble. It chugs and catches. My dad is always fixing it. I can't remember if it did it that morning, but I wouldn't have thought anything of it. It's just what it does sometimes."

The officer leaned back in his chair and folded his hands on his belly. He studied her face as she struggled to find the correct expression for the situation.

"Dylan," he said in a way that told her to look up. "This isn't the first time I've talked to you, is it?"

The blood drained from Dylan's face. "No, sir."

"I'm sorry about your friend."

Could he tell she wasn't breathing?

"We never did find out where she got those drugs, did we?"

Dylan shook her head slightly.

"Strangest thing."

His gaze pierced into her soul, but she didn't flinch. Something inside her told her doing so would be deadly.

CHAPTER 55

Conner Phillips
Present Day

DINNER WAS AWKWARDLY QUIET again. The peace that had settled over them had faded like moments of euphoria tended to do. One moment, the mood was as real as the grass under one's feet, and the next, the moment was more like a beautiful sunset that's untouchable and never intended to withstand time.

Conner lifted a forkful of mashed potatoes to his lips, wishing someone would break the silence. The interrogations had drained everyone's energy. As he loaded his fork with meatloaf, he watched his daughters scrape their plates, pushing the food around without eating much.

"I'm sorry I told them about the fight." Jessie's voice cracked and she pushed her chair back, ready to bolt.

"Sit down, Jessie." Conner's voice was firm but not intimidating.

She pulled her chair back in and sniffled back a sob. Claire reached for Jessie's hand and held it tightly.

"Honey, they already knew about the fight because of the text I sent to David," Conner said.

"Why didn't they say that?"

"They were probably just trying to get you to tell more, and that's okay. This is a time to be open and honest. You can and should tell them everything."

Claire rubbed the top of Jessie's hand, consoling their daughter.

"But I told them how mad you were. I shouldn't have done that."

"Jessie, look at me." Conner put his fork down, while Jessie clearly struggled to make her gaze meet his. "I was mad. That doesn't mean I killed him. A jury would understand my anger over him killing the cow. The investigators can't one hundred percent prove that it was our spreader that killed David. They didn't find anything on the blades. Months of use would have wiped it clean even if there had once been something. There are no cameras in the barn. And Dylan has already told them I wasn't even in the barn that morning."

"Won't they think she's covering for you?"

"You can't send someone to jail because someone thinks you did something. The investigators have to prove it, and they can't."

"How do you know?"

"My prints are all over the machinery because I touch it every day, so finding prints means nothing. Your mom also told them that I was in bed beside her that morning. That means there are two people vouching for me. It made complete sense that we believed David didn't show up for work. When I texted him to come to work after he apologized, he never responded that he would. He never responded at all, and the investigators can see that. And the fact that he apologized helps prove we were going to work things out. If he showed up, it probably meant he was willing to at least work off what he owed me."

Jessie wiped her nose on her sleeve, and Claire handed her a napkin to discourage the behavior.

"But how did he end up in the manure spreader?" Jessie asked.

"Damned if I know. You'd have to be pretty strong to wrestle a grown man over the side of that thing. I'm assuming he was already dead or unconscious before he was thrown in, otherwise he would have crawled out. Whoever lifted him would have been lifting dead weight. I suspect David had ties to some bad people. The police just haven't proved those ties led to his death. Once they make stronger connections, everyone will see I had nothing to do with the murder, and life will start over for us."

Jessie nodded.

"Jessie," her father's voice was soft, "do you actually think I would have killed David?"

She shook her head.

"Are you sure?"

"It's just..." Jessie began to sob.

Conner leaned back in his chair and let out a heavy sigh while rubbing his forehead. Claire pulled her chair beside Jessie and took her in her arms. And Dylan watched them in silence.

"What kind of father have I been?" Tears glistened in his eyes. "My own daughter thinks I'm a murderer."

"I don't," Jessie sobbed.

"You question me, and that is enough. Jessie, I promise

you with all that I am, even if that isn't very much right now, I had nothing to do with David's death."

A tear of relief ran down Claire's cheek.

"I hope that someday, you will one hundred percent believe me."

"I do. I do now, Dad. I'm sorry."

Conner rose, placed one hand on Jessie's back and one on Claire's. "Someday, this will all be a thing of the past. We will get through this. I promise." Conner stood, grabbed his coat, and headed to the door.

When Conner stepped off the back porch, he heard a car engine shutting down. A middle-aged woman stepped out of an old, silver minivan. It took a moment to recognize her, because she'd looked young and vibrant the last time that he'd seen her. The woman now standing in his driveway appeared worn and haggard.

"Susan?" Why was this old friend showing up now? The last time he had spent quality time with her and her husband, Earl Tyler, was before Hayden died. She and Earl had come over for cards and pizza as they often did. Dylan, Jessie, and Hayden had watched movies in the other room with their son, Logan. So much had changed since then.

"Conner." Susan's voice was soft and uncertain. "It's been a long time."

"Yes, it has."

Conner didn't get into town much or have social occasions, but he did read the papers. He knew that after Earl's recent arrest on drug charges, he had made bail by leveraging his family's home. The evidence against him was significant, and things were not looking very good for him.

"Let me get Claire. She would love to see you, I'm sure." In truth, he didn't have the right words and didn't want to be left alone with Susan.

"I'll only be a minute." She shifted on her feet. "I'm assuming you know about my misfortunes, just as I know about yours."

"I do. For what it's worth, I'm sorry for what you're going through. "

"I can't believe Earl was so stupid. I would have let him sell off the farm before I agreed to sell drugs. You must know that."

"I do. I also know that no one's buying farms. Earl, like most of us, is probably facing bankruptcy. It's hard to start over when you lose everything and have no credit for a loan. I'm guessing he got desperate."

"That he did." Susan looked down at her shoes as she kicked at the gravel. "Listen, Conner, I don't know how involved you were, but I, for one, am not against you. I don't condone any of it, but I understand being desperate."

"Susan, I wasn't selling drugs, and I have no clue what happened to David Miller. The police will eventually have to let this all go."

"I'm glad you weren't involved, but David was. That's what I'm here to tell you. I'm going to go to the police and tell them what I know, but it will involve my son. That's why I've held back. But your family needs to put this behind you."

"What are you talking about, Susan?" His curiosity outweighed any anger.

"Logan dated this girl, Amber. We didn't care much for her. She was always asking too many questions. Her questions were irritating, but I thought they were harmless. After all, I never thought my husband would be involved in anything illegal. But somehow, she knew."

"What makes you think that?"

"Right after they arrested Earl, she broke it off with Logan. I had too many things on my mind to care about their relationship ending. After a few days, I noticed how quiet Logan had become. I figured it was normal because of his father's arrest, but during dinner, I asked my son how he was doing, and he wouldn't look me in the eye. That's when I knew there was more bothering him than his dad being in jail. It took a bit of coaxing, but Logan finally broke down and told me that he thought it was all his fault."

"Why would it have been Logan's fault?"

"Amber shared things with Logan about the people who worked at Little Italy." Susan looked down at the ground, and when she met Conner's gaze again, her eyes had filled with tears. "She made my son trust her, and eventually he told her that he found drugs in the hay." A tear rolled down Susan's cheek. She wiped it away. "We believe Amber went to the police about Earl."

"I'm sorry, Susan. I'm sorry that Earl had become that desperate for money, and I'm sorry that Logan ended up in the middle of it." Conner shifted from one foot to the other, not knowing how to comfort his old friend. He glanced back at the house, hoping Claire would come outside, but the house stood silent.

Susan pulled a tissue from her pocket and wiped her nose. "I'm sure you're still wondering why I'm telling you all this."

"Yes. I am."

"What Amber told Logan about Little Italy was also about your farm."

"What? How?"

"According to Amber, Carlo, the owner, is part of a drug ring. She said that the dishwasher, Jeremy, is also involved."

"Did you say Jeremy?"

"Yes. Jeremy. David's friend. The one who supposedly dropped him off here the morning he went missing. At least that's what I heard on the news."

He should be furious at this fragile woman standing before him who chose to wait until now to speak up, but instead, his heart raced with excitement as his mind struggled to put all the pieces together.

"Holy shit."

"Amber said that David would meet Lupo. Remember the man found in the river?"

"Yeah."

"He would meet Lupo in the back of your fields and bring the drugs to Jeremy's car. Jeremy would then bring them to Carlo, who dispersed the drugs to dealers."

"They were using my farm to traffic drugs?" Anger filled Conner's words. He'd suspected a million things in the past months, drug trafficking among them, but to hear proof of the crime agitated him.

"Yes, they used your farm."

"Well, then the authorities must know that, too. If Amber went to the police about your husband, then she would have told them this as well. Why didn't they bring this up to me?"

"Logan doesn't think she mentioned your property."

"That makes no sense. If she is an informant for the

police, then wouldn't she tell the police about Jeremy and David?"

"I don't think she was working with the police. She was helping Carlo and making sure David and Jeremy were not straying. Carlo was trying to take out anyone that was cutting into his paycheck—my husband and Lupo.

"How was that?"

"Amber said things were falling apart between Carlo and Lupo. She heard Carlo on the phone with him arguing over his cut of the drug money. Carlo wanted Lupo out of the picture. Lupo, we suspect, was also working with my husband. When Lupo went through my Earl, Carlo wasn't getting his share. He wanted that avenue shut down and for Jeremy and David to be the only source of trafficking. Lupo made more if he sold to my husband. He figured if he got David out of the picture, then it would at least slow down sales going to Carlo. He never saw Jeremy and may not have even known about him."

"Susan, this means that Lupo could very well have killed David and put him in the manure spreader. It's the only possible scenario that does make sense."

"I agree. The investigators only need an ounce of doubt that it wasn't you. I'd say this is more than an ounce."

"Are you and Logan willing to go to the police and tell them all this?" His hands shook with excitement, and this time when he looked over his shoulder for Claire, it wasn't to get away from their old friend.

"That's why I'm here. I wanted to tell you that we will be speaking with the authorities today."

Conner embraced Susan and released a breath that felt

as though he'd held it for months. Behind them, the screen door banged shut.

"Is everything okay?" Claire called.

"Yes, Claire." Conner pulled from the embrace and smiled at Susan. Her lips struggled to return the expression. "I believe that everything will be more than okay."

Two days later, the paper announced that the death of David Miller was believed to be the result of drug trafficking and organized crime. The article went on to report that the events were believed to have taken place on the Phillips's farm unbeknownst to the family. The gossip lasted only days, before the conversation in The Coffee Shop settled on more mundane topics.

In celebration, the Phillips family pulled their lawn chairs up to the fire pit. Claire brought out graham crackers, marshmallows, and chocolate bars. They each slid their sticks through the marshmallows and watched as the sugary surface browned. Occasionally someone's treat would burst into flames, leading to amused scrambling to extinguish the flames before losing the marshmallow into the fire. They stayed next to the burning fire until their appetites were satiated, the flames turned to embers, and the laughter settled into silence. And then, each one of them, alone in their thoughts, drifted to their beds, where all but one slept peacefully.

Across the road, Eli studied his map and planned his next adventure.

CHAPTER 56

Dylan Phillips
Present Day

DYLAN ROLLED OVER IN bed after a restless night's sleep. The case was closed, but nothing felt settled. Outside, a car slowed and came to a stop. She could tell the vehicle had not driven up her gravel driveway by the sound of the tires against the paved surface. She knew without looking who it was.

She climbed out of bed, bringing her blanket with her. The room was bitterly cold, as winter had settled in, and their wood stove struggled to heat the second floor. A large woman, carrying a small bouquet of flowers, hobbled across the field. Bethany Miller had parked on the road by the cornfield many times since her son's bones had been discovered on the property, but she had never spoken to anyone or gotten out of the car before now.

Dylan's heart raced. She couldn't avoid the woman forever or the haunting feeling inside of her would remain with her. She scrambled to find warm clothes and slid out the door. Her mother was in the back room doing laundry and unaware that Dylan slipped outside. Her father, Eli, and Jessie were in the barn beginning chores. The large barn door was closed now due to the frigid temperatures.

Bethany sat on a blanket in the field across the road, her back toward the house, and was unable to see Dylan approaching. When Dylan got close, she froze in place, not knowing how to begin. Like an animal can sense a hunter, Bethany straightened when Dylan stood behind her.

"I would like to be alone." She sounded sad and cold.

"I wanted to talk to you, to tell you I'm sorry you're sad."

Bethany laughed. "You think that I'm sad about losing my son."

The words caught Dylan off guard. "Yes," she stuttered, "That's why you're here, right?"

The woman was quiet for so long Dylan almost ran back to the barn.

"Did you like my son?"

Dylan didn't respond.

"It's okay to be honest with me."

"No, ma'am. I didn't."

"Not many people did. But I did. He was my son." She picked at a loose string on the blanket. "But I also didn't like him. I loved the boy I gave birth to, and the one I dreamed of him becoming, but David was difficult. No matter how hard I tried, I still failed him. That's the thing I feel really sad about. He was my chance to be worth something, to create something beautiful, and I didn't know how to parent him. I didn't know how to make him good."

"He made his own choices."

"Yes. We all do, but I needed to be a better mom."

"I don't know you, but I don't think it's all because of your parenting. We all have to own our mistakes."

Dylan knelt next to her. The ground was still cold and hard despite the blanket.

"David killed my friend." A tear ran down Dylan's cheek, but Bethany didn't see it. She continued to pick at the loose thread. "He gave her those pills. He made us feel dumb and unliked. Marybeth wanted to fit in, so she took the pill. She wanted the other girls to like her and not think she was boring."

David's mom's face grew pale.

"She was my best friend, my only friend, and he killed her." Dylan sobbed into her hands until a heavy arm wrapped around her and pulled her into her large bosom.

"Why didn't you tell anyone?"

"He said he would hurt my sister. He said he knew people."

The only sound she could hear was her heartbeat in her ears mixed in sync with David's mom's heartbeat.

After some time, Bethany asked, "Do you know what happened to David?"

With her was head still pressed against Bethany's large chest, Dylan nodded. David's mom squeezed her tighter.

"You don't have to tell me more, and I don't want you to tell anyone else what my son has done. The damage stops here. Nothing will bring him back, and I don't want his death to cause anyone else pain. I knew my son's life would end violently or while wasting away in prison. I'm just so sorry he hurt so many people in the process."

Bethany's arm fell from Dylan as she rocked and cried. There was nothing more to say. Dylan stood and ran through the field, trying not to trip on the cut cornstalks, as her lungs burned from the frozen air. David's mom heaved anguished cries toward the heavens. Dylan knew Bethany would never come back to visit the site again. As for Dylan, she had one last mission on her mind: She needed to save Jeremy.

CHAPTER 57

Jeremy Biggs
Present Day

JEREMY SCRUBBED HIS LAST pan and placed it on the rack. His body ached from leaning over the sink. Between work and the cops hovering around him, he was exhausted. The only good thing was that Carlo was not having him go on any runs. In fact, Carlo was staying so low-key, Jeremy had barely seen him in the last few days. Instead, a young Italian guy had been opening and closing the restaurant in his absence. Carlo hadn't left town yet, but Jeremy thought he would as soon as he found a way to escape his business without losing money.

The bell on the door sounded. "What now," Jeremy mumbled. The place was about to close for the two hours before the dinner shift, a new practice that allowed Carlo more freedom to do whatever he was frantically doing. When Jeremy peered into the dining area, his heart stopped. Dylan, looking lost, stood by the door. He tossed the towel onto the counter and butted in front of Amber who was already on the way to greet her. "I've got this."

Amber huffed and went back to counting the cash in her drawer. "We're closing," she called out, refusing to give in completely to Jeremy's interference.

Dylan didn't respond to Amber. She focused on Jeremy through her long bangs as he approached her.

"What are you doing here?" He peered out the window, looking for a car. An old farm truck was parked outside.

"I'm picking up our order."

Jeremy glanced back at the to-go rack and saw a solitary bag sitting on the rack.

"Amber, she's here for that to-go?"

She huffed and put the money drawer back in place. "Well, come get it."

Dylan eased up to the counter, occasionally looking over her shoulder at Jeremy who stood still, watching her every move. Dylan paid, the cash register closed, and in a sarcastic tone, Amber wished her a good day. "You better hurry. I think your daddy's gonna leave you."

Dylan picked up the bag of food and slowly headed toward the door. Amber finally got bored and went to the back.

"I'll be in the chicken coop tonight at two o'clock. I have to wait that long to make sure everyone is asleep. Come see me before I change my mind." As Jeremy stared wide-eyed, Dylan raced out the door and into the truck.

Jeremy pretended to go to bed early but stared at his dark ceiling until the bedside clock read one-fifteen. Then he tiptoed past his father, passed out on the couch, and walked out into the night. Before starting the truck, Jeremy scraped off the frost already forming. He needed to be ready to leave the second he started the engine.

His pulse pounded in his temples. In the next hour, his

life would change forever. Either he would realize a young girl had set him up, or that girl would give him a chance to become someone else.

The night was dark and silent. The moon was nowhere to be seen, and the deer had already hunkered down in the fields. When he approached the farm, he searched for a place to park. The cornfields would no longer serve as a barrier. All he could do was park a half-mile down the road and walk through the fields, hoping not to be seen by neighbors or suspicious Border Patrol agents. He entered the barn from the back as he'd done before and made his way to the coop. He could hear the quiet clucking as if someone had already awakened the hens from their sleep.

"Dylan," he said before pushing the door open. If it wasn't her, then maybe, just maybe, he could outrun whoever waited on the other side.

"Come in," Dylan whispered.

The door creaked open. Dylan sat on a pail, holding one of the chickens. A flashlight lay on the ground, eerily illuminating the two of them.

"Why did you tell me to come?"

Dylan tucked her bangs behind her ear, revealing the face of a girl on the verge of becoming a young woman.

"I thought about what you said."

"And..." Jeremy's heart raced. No one had ever trusted him or thought him capable of being more than a hoodlum. Why would Dylan?

"I have no reason to trust you, but I don't want the money. It's not mine. I don't want to give it to the police and raise more suspicion. The case against my dad has been dropped, and I want it to stay that way. And I don't need the cash to run away anymore."

"Is that what you were going to do with it?"

"I thought about it."

"Why did you want to run?"

"Don't all teenagers want to run away at some point in their lives?"

"I guess so." He didn't press her, even though he believed there to be much more to her story.

"The money is behind the chicken boxes." She nodded in the direction. Jeremy eyed her suspiciously as he stepped toward the loose board. "Put your hand in the hole and take whatever is back there."

Jeremy swallowed hard, pushed the board to the side and slid his hand into the dark hole behind the boxes. Very quickly, his fingers felt a plastic bag. He pulled it out and reached in again. There was another. His third reach came up empty. He held up the bags, not believing what he was seeing. It was far more money than David had confessed to having.

He looked at Dylan. Was he in the clear? Could it be that easy? He tried to read her expression, but it was flat and revealed nothing.

"The choice is yours now. No excuses."

Jeremy smiled. "Thank you."

"I hope you weren't lying. I hope you end up good." The young woman he had glimpsed disappeared, and the child she truly was sat before him.

"I wasn't lying. Someday, I hope you hear I did something great."

"Maybe I don't need to. Maybe if you live a life that no one ever has to write about in the newspaper, then that's good."

Jeremy laughed and squeezed the money close to him. "No excuses." Jeremy studied the bags of money. One question nagged him. "Are you ever going to tell Marybeth's parents."

Dylan stared back at him. "Don't you think they already know? Especially now. I could tell them I tried to stop her from taking them, but they won't believe me. They are going to blame me forever. I can't change that."

Jeremy nodded. Dylan was probably right.

"You should go now."

"Yeah, I should. And Dylan, I hope someday you have a life you never want to run away from. You deserve that."

CHAPTER 58

Goodbyes
Present Day

WHAT DYLAN DIDN'T UNDERSTAND, what she couldn't fathom at all, was why Eli needed to leave. He tried to explain that it had always been his intention. Every home he ever became a part of had a chapter that included him for whatever reason, and when that chapter ended, something inside him told him it was time for him to move on and become a part of someone else's story.

Both girls joined him to complete chores, giving their parents a night to go on a date. The girls ordered pizza and watched as their parents came down the stairs, smiles lighting their faces.

"Isn't your mom beautiful?" Conner said as he held her hand above her and spun her in a circle before catching her in his arms. When he smacked her softly on the backside, the girls giggled. Their father wore khaki pants and a long sleeve T-shirt that still had the tag sticking out. Claire caught sight of it as he passed, and she grabbed the pair of kitchen scissors and snipped it off.

That night, the girls didn't know that only a year would pass before bankruptcy became necessary or that Conner would pass the physical to become a correctional officer. They didn't know their mother would get her RN degree and begin a long career as a beloved nurse. Conner would rent the land back from the bank when no one bought the farm. The barn would slowly fall apart, and the pastures would become overgrown with weeds, but their home would be stronger than ever before. When the day came to retire, Conner had a pension and health insurance, something he would have never had if the farm had not failed. Claire made enough to get their daughters through college while Conner paid the monthly bills. How could they have guessed that behind the dark clouds, opportunities were forming and that all the changes waiting for them, as scary as they were, would be blessings?

What the girls did know on this final night, as they finished their chores and then carried the pizza across the field to Eli's camper, was that they were once again happy.

Eli pulled out the cards, and the three played Blackjack until they heard their parents' car pull back into the driveway. Claire called for them across the field.

"Coming," Jessie yelled out the camper door. She turned back to Eli and threw her arms around him. "Will you come back to visit?"

"Only time will tell, but I think we should say our goodbyes for now."

He squeezed Jessie and then wrapped Dylan in his arms. They all walked down the camper steps, and he watched as they raced back to the farmhouse. Before too much distance came between them, Dylan stopped and turned to face Eli. Although the distance muffled her voice, Eli could read the gratitude in Dylan's expression. She waved one last time before running to catch up with Jessie. Eli stood under the stars, listening to the owls hoot, and the coyotes howl. Although he couldn't see them wandering through the night landscape, he knew the world brimmed with amazing life. And despite the darkness, the sun always shone around the corner in its due time.

EPILOGUE

Dylan Phillips

I DON'T OFTEN THINK of the days of David anymore. As a young woman, I visited Marybeth's gravesite and said a final goodbye. It felt good and right, and I was ready to leave the past in the cemetery. I stayed away from the farm until my children begged hard enough that I could no longer resist them.

I had come to terms with almost all of it, except for the morning when David went missing. The memory had been buried under so many layers of the story that I felt redeemed and forgiven. But now, as I stood where it all happened, I realized I had yet to forgive myself.

I never meant for it to happen, and if I could take it back, I would. I mean that, or at least I believe I do. But the truth is, I hated David that day. I hated the way he glared at me. I hated how, when I walked by him, he whispered, "How's Jessie? Is she sleeping soundly?"

My stomach had lurched, and I dry heaved into the gutter due to the nerves and anger brewing inside of me. David laughed. "Oh, you have no idea how scary I can be."

He sauntered up and down the barn like he was untouchable, and he was. I carried secrets too big for a young teenage girl. The secrets were too big for anyone. He had killed my friend by giving her harmful drugs, and I couldn't tell a soul without endangering my sister.

We carried the milkers down to the first cows and adjusted them onto each one. David reached into his pocket and pulled out a bag of multi-colored pills. He popped one into his mouth. I'll never know what the drug was or the effect it had on his mind except to say his behavior became erratic. He was dancing around in some tribal way with his tongue hanging out and looking crazy. I wanted to run into the house and get my father. He didn't need to know the backstory. David's behavior would be enough to get him fired, especially after killing the cow.

The memory hit me again. David's face had been full of rage as the hoe smashed down on the cow's head. The image of her falling would haunt me for years, yet David had tossed the hoe to the side and stepped over the poor animal like she was garbage. I'd finally breathed again and run as fast as possible to find my father. David was crazy that day, just as he seemed crazy the day he went missing to the rest of the world.

As David danced around, I tried to ignore his behavior by focusing on my chores instead. The area under the cows was covered with manure, and I was the only one who would bother to clean it. I grabbed the hoe and began scraping, and then I felt his breath on my neck. I swung around and pushed him as hard as I could, making him fall to the ground. His gaze shifted from crazy to malicious. In an instant, he was on his feet, coming toward me. "I'm going to kill you, you little shit." He hissed his words, and for a moment, I froze.

And then, as he was almost to me, I swung the hoe, hitting him with the pointed edge in his temple. He dropped to the ground as the cow had the day before. The milking machines pulsed around me as I stood frozen, staring at his still body. With shaky hands, I bent next to him and felt for a pulse. There was nothing. His chest did not rise and fall as it should.

A force overtook me. I was me and yet not me as I shoved his body across the floor and into the gutter cleaner. The spreader was half-full. I raced for the switch and started the belt. The chains ran around the gutter, lifting the manure up the ramp and into the spreader. David's arms and legs flopped over the edges, and I scrambled to keep his body from tipping over the sides. If that happened, I would not be able to lift him back in. The belt struggled under his weight, so I grabbed the hoe to push him along, taking some of the work off the moving parts. Long minutes passed before he toppled over the edge and landed in a sloppy thud in the machinery.

I don't know how long I stood there, staring at the manure dropping into the spreader and covering any part of him that had not sunk. When I finally turned around, two milkers lay on the floor, and the others clung to empty sacks. I placed them on the next cows and hung up the ones David had been using. I would tell my father I had attempted to run them all, but it was too much. At most, I would be scolded for the attempt as it wasn't healthy for the cows.

When my father came to the barn, he was grumpier than usual. Instead of asking about David, he took over his side of the barn. I was way ahead of him, so avoiding eye contact was easy. When I finished, I offered to run the manure spreader, and he mumbled a 'whatever.' I didn't lie when I told the police the machine was known for catching and chugging, but I failed to say to them that, on that Saturday, my heart stopped each time it did. I didn't tell them that I stared forward, petrified that I would see unthinkable sights if I looked back. And I didn't tell them I took the hoe with me and turned the ground to cover any evidence before returning to the barn and throwing the hoe far up onto the fragile loft.

As I stood where David had fallen, the barn closed in around me. My younger self had gone up against an evil she didn't understand and never would. Her actions had been self-defense, and no court could say otherwise.

Chrissy and Thomas skipped up and down the barn, laughing as children should, while I battled the ghost of David for the last time. I wrapped my arms around myself as if hugging my younger self. *You had to protect yourself.* I closed my eyes and saw David running at me with his wild expression. I could almost feel the hoe in my hands one more time. I watched as the tool found his temple, and his body fell to the ground. Had I even been aiming? No. I acted on impulse.

I stared at the spot and saw only the concrete floor. David was gone.

After Eli left our farm, we went on to make new memories—good memories. But the times that had happened before had been tainted by the horrors that David brought to my life. My childhood had remained visible but only through a dark filter. The laughter was stifled, the colors less vibrant, the bonds less significant. No more.

I walked out of the decrepit building and into the bright

sunshine, knowing it would be the last moment I spent with the guilt. As the dark memories drifted away like a thunderous cloud, other memories danced in the wake. I shut my eyes and felt the cornstalks against my face as I chased Jessie and Hayden through the stalks. I tasted thick bologna sandwiches we ate on a blanket in the yard. I gazed at my mother's smiling face as she carried warm chocolate chip cookies to our picnic. I heard my father's contagious laugh as he chased a giggling boy around the bases in the mowed hayfield.

And I remembered the man who had changed everything. Eli exuded a warmth that felt otherworldly yet was always within our reach, if only we dared to accept it. Life had extinguished the flame that once burned inside us, but Eli fearlessly walked through hell to share his light, knowing that even a small flame can illuminate the darkness. We'd only needed to be reminded.

The End

AUTHOR'S NOTE

WRITERS ARE TOLD TO write about what we know. Our knowledge becomes the paint palette we use to create vibrant and believable storylines. In my past novels, I have pulled from memories, feelings, lessons, trials, and tribulations and expanded on them until they became unrecognizable. Some of my novels have demanded extensive research and strayed far from my life's color wheel. But this story is special because it is the closest one to my heart and to my past.

I grew up in Potsdam, NY on a dairy farm owned by John and Gail Sheehan, my parents. Our property stretched out over 460 acres that became a play yard for me and my six siblings, born in the following order—Cindy, Judy, Lisa, Tracy, Kim(my), Johnny, Mindy. Our house was built in the 1870s, or so the date sketched in the cement wall of a cistern in the basement tells us. When writing the story, I envisioned our farm because it made it easier. We had a neighbor, but the neighbor in the story is fictional. I envisioned the proximity between the two houses when writing certain scenes. A field, sometimes used as a cornfield, separated our two houses that shared an interesting past. Long before my time, a part of our house was rolled down the field on logs pulled by horses and used for a room in theirs. Why they didn't just build that room with the rest of the house rather than rolling it down the field is a mystery to me.

My father passed away in 2018 after years of battling emphysema and a shorter battle with lung cancer. He was a hard-working man who seldom had a day off. Many years, my mother worked beside him in the barn, and at other times, she managed the household chores and the demands of raising seven children. This was not an easy job, and we were not always the easiest of children.

After my father's passing, some of my siblings wanted me to write a story that would include my dad's remarkable story that happened in his final months, along with memories of growing up on our farm. Very quickly, I realized that our lives were not interesting enough to fill enough pages to form a novel, so I turned the story into a fictional piece including the mafia and a murder or two. Yet, it was important for my family that my dad's end-of-life miracle be recorded in some way.

When Grandma Sheehan, my grandmother on my dad's side, was on her deathbed, she told my mother that she had another child, which my mother did not believe. She had known him to be the only child all their lives together. After checking with some older relatives, she was able to get small bits of information out of them. My grandmother had indeed given birth to a baby boy before she married my grandfather. She gave this boy up for adoption immediately and no one spoke of the birth again. For years, my father had no interest in learning more about his half-brother, and the topic was dropped.

A year before my dad passed, he was hospitalized and on a ventilator. The doctors said that without the ventilator he would most likely not survive, and we had to decide if we were ready to say goodbye. My sisters prayed healing prayers over him every day. And then, the day before Christmas, he was taken off the vent and woke up. He became known as the Christmas miracle. I wondered why and how because, after all, everyone prays for miracles when their loved ones get sick. Why did we get blessed with more time?

Nearly a year passed, and his quality of life was okay. In November of 2017, he agreed to use Ancestry.com. Almost immediately, my sister received an email from a woman named Jessica who asked her if she knew of a Pauline Sheehan, my grandmother. Jessica had tried three times to use a different company, but each time the order was backordered. She then turned to Ancestry.com, allowing the connection between my father's and Jessica's father's DNA to be discovered. We learned his name was Richard, and he had always wanted to find my father but did not want to hurt his adoptive mother by looking for her. He decided to wait until she passed. She lived to see 102.

In the following months, my dad was able to meet his half-brother two times and Facetime with him several times. The last in person visit, my father was on morphine. No one can be sure if he was aware of Richard's presence, but Richard was able to say goodbye to the brother he had always wanted to meet. He told my father to have a fishing pole waiting for him in heaven. Richard passed years later. I like to picture the two of them sitting by a quiet pond, a beer in one hand and a pole in the other.

Writing the story, despite it being fiction, allowed my

family to walk down memory lane, dredging up memories long forgotten. One interesting part of this journey is that as close as we were growing up (despite the sibling fights), our memories differed. Sometimes of the same event, and sometimes one person remembered times the rest of us did not. Memories are funny that way. But one idea remains clear. Our family and the days on our farm remain a core part of each of us. So even when some not so pleasant memories came to mind, they didn't shadow the big picture. After all, if a person is lucky enough, their journey through life will include both beauty and bumps. It's what makes us interesting and sympathetic people.

I will forever be grateful for the years of growing up on the farm and for all the humbling and character-building aspects gained from that way of life. We found happiness in each other and creating our own fun. As children, we built forts in the woods, caught crawfish in the streams, ate strawberries growing in the cow pastures, and jumped off haymow beams. We learned to fish and eat fish toast cooked over a fire (quite possibly my dad's invention). We raced three wheelers (without helmets) through the fields, played baseball in the fields when the many chores were complete. We showered in the milk house because it seemed like a fun thing to do sometimes. We made snowmen in the winter, and in the fall, my dad raked leaf piles so we could jump in them and scatter the leaves everywhere. This may not have been his actual intent, but he didn't seem to mind. We raced bikes down the country roads, set up tents in the fields, held a million puppies and kittens, and helped hundreds of calves come into the world and learn to drink from a pail.

I climbed to the top of the silo, an adventure that ended with my mom's favorite go-to punishment—the flyswatter—after a sibling (Lisa) tattled. Our basement was filled with flyswatters, well hidden from the not-so-terrifying hands of my overwhelmed mother. Generally, by the time my mother found her weapon, she had forgotten why she was angry. My brother, on the other hand, had graduated to the wooden spoon. Fortunately for him, he had discovered that if he reached the dining room table, he was safe. The punishment became a cat and mouse game that the rest of us watched, sometimes cheering for my mom, and other times, hoping my brother escaped his beating. The beating never happened to my knowledge. My brother's antics always made my mother laugh, and the desire to beat the devil out of him subsided.

We never took a vacation because we lacked both time and money. When we did get away for a night, it was to a run-down hunting camp in the Adirondacks, where we learned to play Blackjack under the lantern light and where we slept on mattresses that I'm quite sure we shared with mice.

I can tell of a million awesome parts of my childhood—starry nights in the country, driving tractors, speeding past our neighbor's Saint Bernard named Sarge on our bikes, and laughing over the silliest things. I tried to weave some of them into the fabric of the story, but many of those warm memories did not help the fictional tale where darker events took over.

When it comes to the darker elements, some of them also came from twisted accounts of real events, but I assure all readers, if it would have landed me in jail, I would not have included it in the story, which means no one was killed by anyone nor did the idea ever cross our minds. And as much as an author should do their research to make sure their story line is credible, putting someone through the manure spreader would have been frowned upon, so therefore the research was not completed. If I were to guess, the type of manure spreader we owned would not have been powerful enough to have done the damage it does to David Miller. We mostly dealt with the crazy parts of our lives by developing a strong and distorted sense of humor. Not to mention, I am quite a rule-follower by nature, so besides partaking in teenage activities before the ripe old age of twenty-one, I haven't broken any laws. I'm boring—not even a speeding ticket to date.

The story of Hayden's accident comes from a combination of two memories. One was when a stick went through my sister's leg while she was driving a tractor near the bushes, and the other was of us jumping off the beams in the haymow into impossibly small piles of hay. To test the action's survivability rate, my older sister and I told our younger sister we had been doing it all day and had her jump first. Once she proved it was possible, we joined in the fun. I thought of that story every time my children did something that made me wonder about the creature that had grown inside of me. The same sibling was emotionally scarred for years due to being tied up in the back field and left there for some time. I'm sure the flyswatter came into play that day as well. Children's brains truly are not completely formed for the years they spend under our roofs.

As for hired men, sometimes life is stranger than fiction. Throughout our time on the farm, all my siblings have had unpleasant experiences with one or more of them. There was the man who threw a pitchfork that punctured a foot, the ex-con who walked around with certain body parts exposed, and the one who carried a bag of pills he ingested daily. He would open the bag and say, "I think I'll take a yellow one today." The statement would be met with teenage eyerolls. It was this hired man that tied our only stool around his waist, not allowing anyone else the relief of sitting. And like true teenagers, we did throw the stool into the haymow where the floorboards threatened to cave in with the slightest footstep. The stool is most likely still there today, but the fictional, infamous hoe was never there. We did also have decent hired men, but both the good and bad ones drifted on to other opportunities quickly.

The scene where the cow was hit in the head and killed did happen in front of me. That hired man walked off in the same manner David Miller walked off when told he owed money for the young cow. My one sister remembers that he hit the animal with a hammer and not a hoe. Either way, the memory remains horrific. Note, my dad did not fire him even for that since hired men were hard to come by, but we never saw him again or the money he owed us.

There was a man who turned up in the Raquette River, and who could have had ties to the mafia, but this could also be a part of my faulty memory. In fact, beyond this one iffy memory, I never heard of a Canadian mafia while living in Potsdam, although I now know one did or does exist.

We were poor, my parents' relationship struggled, everything broke, my mom cried when she paid bills. Chores had to be done despite broken bones and illnesses. Cows needed to be milked in the morning and in the evening, seven days a week, every day of the year. At any given time, we would have one hired man working for us, and that person would never work on Sundays, and even if he did, running a farm could not be done by one person, so therefore, we did not get vacations, ever.

My family ended up going bankrupt while I was in college. My father passed the physical and became a correctional officer. He needed to work in Sing Sing until he was able to transfer to a local prison. My mother became a nurse's aide. We did have a vet that left us gum, but my favorite memory of him was when my dad had to tell him that we were going bankrupt and would not be able to pay our bills. Dr. Bartlett told him to hold his head high, and that he had nothing to be ashamed of. I know his words helped my father tremendously.

One fictionalized part of the story is the number of drugs in the town. To my knowledge, drugs were not a serious issue in my school back in the 80's, although I'm sure there were some experimental moments. Marybeth did not exist, nor did anyone that resembled her. The story did not take place in Potsdam because I liked Derby Line's proximity to the border and how it made the drug smuggling aspect work easier. Derby Line may be a very quaint town with little to no drugs or crime, and I mean no disrespect to its citizens. One day, I want to visit Derby Line, but all my research came from scrolling my computer. As for the other characters, although every school has its cliques and bullies, and other stereotypical groupings, my hometown was a nice town to grow up in, and the students were much kinder than the students in this book.

Conner's mancave is symbolic of the walls I never broke through with my father. When I left for college at eighteen, it would mark almost the end of my living under my parents' roof. I went home for a couple of summers, but as I moved farther and farther away from my hometown, the visits became less frequent due to life's demands. In many ways, my siblings got to know my father far better than I ever did, which is unfortunate to say the least.

I learned some things while collecting memories from family members. One such thing being that before I was born, my father was adamant that the family attend church and donate weekly. By the time the memory portion of my brain had formed, we were too busy for church, and only my mother taught us about religion and faith. My dad's faith was a mystery to me, but I believe it remained in his heart.

Of all my novels, this one hit closest to home and explains best why my characters often struggle to find peace and understanding in one way or another. Life is an amazing mix of beauty and pain. The real story includes both and understanding that the hardships are as important as the beauty is when we truly find peace on our lives. The two elements both have purpose in our story, and the purpose is not to destroy us, but to give our lives depth. As I look back at the whole picture, I understand the need for all the ingredients tossed into my beginnings and know that seeds planted in manure tend to grow strong and beautiful.

ACKNOWLEDGEMENTS

THIS STORY OWES MUCH to the support of my family, friends, and professionals I have met along the way. My first readers—Judy Deon, Lisa Cascanette, Edward Mickolus, Pam Bell, Stacey Horan, Christine Schmitt, and John Taylor—provided valuable feedback by identifying confusing parts, gaps, and errors. After incorporating their suggestions and making necessary corrections, I sent the story to my editor, Catherine Keane, who offered excellent advice and pointed out additional mistakes. Once I meticulously addressed those issues, my daughter Emily Tripp and husband Steve Tripp reviewed the manuscript again and provided further suggestions and corrections. I am incredibly grateful to all of them. Without their generous assistance in reading and refining the drafts, I would not have been able to achieve the same level of quality in my story. Their willingness to see the potential beyond the mistakes has been invaluable.

I also want to thank my formatter, H.D. Thomson, for formatting many of my novels and Mike O'Malley for creating the cover.

People often ask where the idea for a story comes from, and while I addressed this in my author's note, I want to expand on it as I prepare to publish this story. In the past month, I have been diagnosed with stage IV adenocarcinoma in my right lung. This diagnosis came as a surprise since I have never smoked. I have learned that this type of cancer is on the rise among non-smoking women and is often detected late, as they do not expect their symptoms to be related to lung cancer. My symptoms included shortness of breath, a burning sensation, and a feeling like there was a knot in my back or air trapped inside; that sensation ultimately turned out to be a tumor.

I'm uncertain about what the future holds for me, but I have had ample time for reflection throughout this process. As a writer, I have always wanted to stay true to my beliefs and not contribute unnecessary sadness to the world. In that sense, I considered myself a Christian writer, but I realized that to be a true Christian writer, I needed to follow specific guidelines that my storylines may have strayed from. In many ways, I have grown with each story I wrote, and within each one, I have hidden a part of myself and my spiritual journey between the lines.

Parting Gifts was my first novel, and its central theme revolves around forgiveness. My first significant romantic relationship involved both verbal and physical abuse—not to the degree of some of the more horrific cases. However, it still taught me that even a few negative experiences from someone you trust could lead you to feel unlovable and unwanted. In the novel, I explore the journey of forgiving not only the person who caused me pain but also myself. I often felt embarrassed for putting myself in that situation and for repeatedly returning to it. While the story, like all my novels, differs significantly from my life, it's remarkable how, as a writer, you can find healing by touching on the surface of your reality through fictional narratives.

Still Life deals with a woman who has an affair after her marriage runs into a challenging situation. I am pleased to say that I have been faithfully married to a wonderful man for thirty years, and that is not the personal issue I had to address here. If I asked my readers what the moral of the story is, they might mention several ideas, but somehow, the one that I most thought about while writing the novel is not as apparent as I would have thought. There is a point when an old man tells Samantha a Bible verse, "I will give you a new heart and put a new spirit within you; I will take the heart of stone out of your flesh and give you a heart of flesh." Sometimes we all live inside our heads so much that we become frozen in our problems and circumstances. The main character learns to see herself and her faults and then begins to grow spiritually. She stops living a self-serving, self-centered existence.

Something Like a Dream and *Awaken* represented the next steps in my faith journey. I learned to trust in where God is leading me, to believe that He communicates in unexpected ways, and to have faith that even when the world seems to be crumbling around me, something new and beautiful is forming.

When Ed Mickolus asked me to co-write *White Noise Whispers*, and after we saw that it was developing into a serial killer/war book, I told him I needed to find a way to hold true to my values while writing about horrific ideas. I tried to write as little gore as possible, only including details that would help define the character and his mental illness. I again went back to the forgiveness theme and tried to get the reader not to be okay with the killer's deeds, but to see into his wounded mind.

The Lies We Bury, as I have said, is special to me because it is most like my life. When I look back at my life, I am so thankful for all the experiences and the people that were a part of my journey. Eli didn't exist, yet he did. In the story, I did not want Eli to be Jesus, but someone that clearly allowed Jesus to shine through him. It's easy when we can see, touch, and hear a person, when we can ask a question and hear the answer in words we understand. What's trickier is when we must patiently wait for an answer sometimes given to us in the quietest part of our day. But I do know that we all do have our Eli, and that Eli is Jesus. He walks beside us, quietly waiting for us to turn away from the darkness that sometimes engulfs us. He encourages us to be someone else's Eli, to be His hands and ears on Earth. He is ready to listen, patiently waiting for us to start a conversation.